I0610350

The Galician Woman

The Andalusian Trilogy, Volume 1

William Mesusan

Published by William Mesusan, 2021.

The garden of the world has no limits

except in your mind

--Rumi

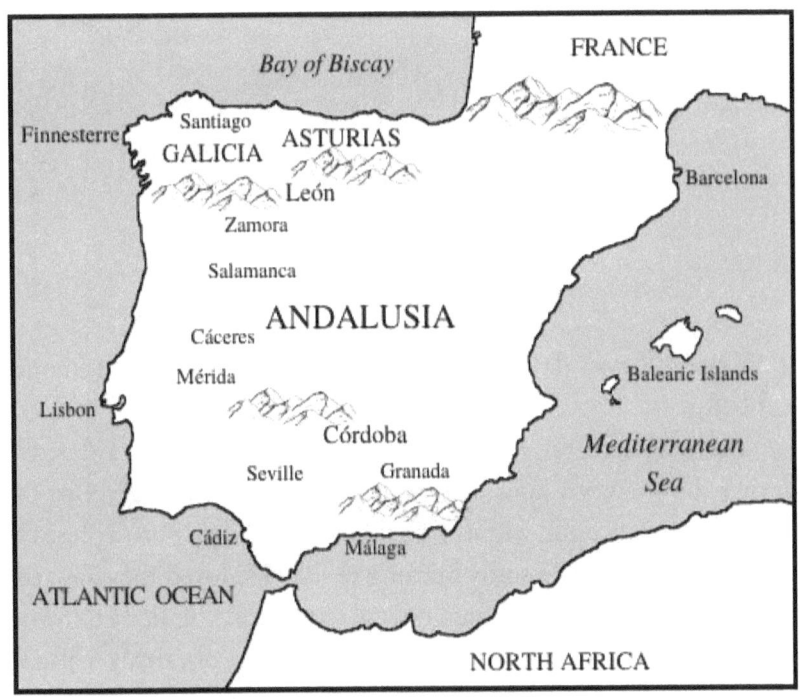

Tenth Century Islamic Spain

Chapter 1

Solomon Levy's day began like most, but it would end like none before it.

The poet had no way of knowing this as he worked quietly, during the predawn hours, dipping his quill into a small bowl of pomegranate juice and withdrawing it to place the tip onto a piece of paper illuminated by a softly burning candle. He loved the ruby red color of the juice and the liquid flow of letters dancing along to form words upon a page, words describing the wonders of earthly, sensual life, a realm his people hadn't portrayed for almost two thousand years.

His efforts weren't appreciated by those in Córdoba's Arabized Jewish community who were content to live within the status quo. They wanted to confine Hebrew to the synagogue. Solomon found support and friendship among a committed group of revolutionary Jewish poets who explored ways to describe a wider universe with their language. They tired of seeing their Muslim counterparts excel because their dynamic Arabic prose celebrated the world of their times, accepting the paradox that religion and science can peacefully co-exist. These Muslims walked, but not by faith alone. They also walked with their eyes and minds wide open.

Pale light began to shine through an open window as Solomon continued to write. The poet remembered the exhilaration he felt while walking one starry, moonlit night in the ancient city of Granada. He hoped to convey his impressions of the city's Jewish

Quarter, a place he'd visited for the first time earlier that year while engaged in a search for a rare manuscript. He recalled, with a certain fondness, the disheveled bookseller who helped him succeed in his quest. Those bloodshot eyes and bread crumbs nestling in a scraggly grey beard. How the old man lovingly touched each volume he shared with Solomon, caressing the book covers like lovers.

Quill to pomegranate juice to paper; the poet made notes for later revision.

Solomon loved the magical feeling of an engaged heart and hand. Smiling to himself, he felt an internal warmth infuse his entire being, a slow burn fueling his efforts to fashion poetry from his personal experience of the world. Solomon ran his hand through curly black hair as he contemplated the words just written. He understood that his limited time meant ceasing his avocation when daylight came in order to work at his principal occupation as a translator of scientific texts from Arabic into Latin. Writing poetry may have been his deepest desire, translating afforded him a good living.

Solomon had one more hour to work on his poetry, perhaps slightly longer. He took up his quill and wrote. And, he wrote and wrote in a trance-like state, but his reverie was interrupted by the proverbial knock at the door, only this was a deafening din, a series of hard raps employed to awaken even the soundest of sleepers from a deep and satisfying slumber. The poet sighed and put down the quill. He went to the door, opened it, and found himself staring at two Arabs. He didn't recognize either of them.

"The Foreign Minister requires your presence," said the shorter messenger.

The taller man handed him a folded dispatch bearing a waxed seal. Solomon studied the bold red "S." He tried to make some sense of the unexpected summons. Cousin Hasdai, he said to himself.

"I'll be right back," Solomon told them.

"Hurry," commanded the shorter Arab.

Solomon closed the door behind himself. He didn't want these men to see or hear what he was about to do as he walked over to his writing table and pounded his fist down hard.

Pomegranate juice spilled out across the table, but the poet didn't even notice it. It mattered not because he felt too angry to care. "Damn," he uttered to himself. "Not again, Hasdai."

Solomon threw on something warmer, a blue tunic over his cotton chemise and white pants cut long and snug at the ankle. He blew out the candle, and locked his front door. He soon found himself hustled through Córdoba's narrow, deserted streets. The chill in the air, along with the fast pace set by his escorts, awakened his senses. He felt a light breeze blowing through his hair as the two men whisked him out of the city through the Almodovar Gate, the main entrance to the Juderia neighborhood that Solomon called home. A nervous old driver, with a mule and two wheeled cart, sat waiting to rush him eight miles away to Muslim Caliph Abd al-Raman III's palatial city, Madinat al Zahra.

"Your driver knows the way," revealed the taller Arab. "We have to leave you now."

There came no further word of explanation so Solomon climbed up into the cart. The old driver shook the reins and the powerful mule trotted off, carrying the two men down the road. Solomon didn't have a clue why he'd been beckoned to Andalusia's corridors of power, but he suspected that his older cousin, Hasdai ibn Shaprut, had a new assignment awaiting him. It hadn't been that long since the kingdom's highest ranking Jew, serving as Foreign Minister and personal Physician to the reigning Muslim ruler, had pressed the aspiring poet into service as his private investigator.

They entered al-Zahra as the sun rose above the horizon to bathe the world in soft morning light. After the uneventful journey, the poet arrived at the Foreign Ministry's offices. The driver waited obediently outside.

What's the problem this time, Solomon wondered as he reached his destination at the end of a long, marble-tiled hallway and found a guard stationed in front of the arch-shaped doorway. Posting a sentry at the portal seemed unusual and Solomon noticed the sentinel at the door observing him with more than a casual interest.

He took a closer look at the guard. He's a *Tangerine*, Solomon said to himself using an Arabic slang term for black-skinned mercenaries imported into Andalusia through Tangier, a resilient port city sitting atop the northwest tip of the African continent.

The translator remembered the face securing the entrance to the Foreign Minister's office. He'd seen him deployed as one of the Caliph's personal guards during official state functions and other important social gatherings. Solomon was good at facial recognition, but terrible with names. He searched his mind, came up blank, and decided it wasn't important. The guard appeared nervous, his right hand resting atop the steel handle of a long, backward curved sword hanging in a sheath by his side, a cold chisel with a thirty-inch long cutting edge. Standing stiffly in his proud military bearing, the imposing, broad-shouldered mercenary remained guarded himself, offering the visitor little more than a curt nod.

"I'm here at the behest of the Foreign Minister," Solomon explained.

At first, no flicker of recognition registered on the sentry's ebony countenance. Observation and memory finally evoked recall. The sentinel had placed him so the royal guard relaxed his grip. A tight-lipped smile creased the blue shadows of his enigmatic black face and his hand left the scimitar's handle as he stepped aside to push open an elaborately carved door. Solomon entered the Foreign Minister's chambers and the heavy door closed behind him.

SOLOMON ENTERED A ROOM designed with a thirty-foot high ceiling and massive walls carved from translucent marble blocks. It's grandeur and openness offered an impressive sense of space. We're meant to feel dwarfed in the presence of the Caliph's hand-picked advisors, mused Solomon.

He failed to understand the seriousness of the situation, but this soon changed as Solomon found Hasdai sitting in the center of the well-appointed room slumped over and brooding behind an oak-carved desk. Solomon sensed a tension in the air and knew something was terribly wrong when Hasdai waved him forward without looking up to greet him. Cousin Hasdai, dispensing with formalities—no talk of family, translations, or poetry—quickly revealed the reason behind the portentous summons.

"The Caliphate might be under attack."

"What happened?"

Hasdai motioned for Solomon to sit down and the poet complied.

"The Caliph's nephew Umar was found murdered in his bed. His brother discovered him with a dagger stuck in his heart," explained Hasdai. "We think the last person to see him alive was a woman. She appears to have vanished."

It took a few seconds for Solomon to absorb the news. The severity of the crime had taken him by surprise and confirmed his earlier suspicions. This meeting had all the earmarks of a new assignment, one he might not be able to refuse though he would surely make an attempt. Solomon shrugged his shoulders and adopted a pose of nonchalance, but his quizzical expression met with an immediate response.

"I want you to find her, Solomon."

Time for a countermove, thought the poet.

"I've just regained my momentum," replied Solomon as he squirmed in his chair. "I'm feeling inspired."

"I'm sorry. I normally wouldn't ask, but this is a matter of the highest urgency."

That's what you said last time, thought the poet. Why me again? Why now?

"Are you sure I'm the right person for this mission, Hasdai?"

"You found the lost manuscript."

"*That* was a book," Solomon replied. "This missing woman is a living person."

"*That* doesn't matter. You have a proclivity for finding missing things."

Solomon knew better than to argue against the assessment of the Foreign Minister of the most powerful kingdom in Europe, especially when he found himself the recipient of his relative's probing eyes and raised brows.

"You seem reluctant," chided Hasdai. "I was hoping I could count on you."

There came a pause. A long, unsettling pause. The poet thought hard about whether he should share his true feelings, his deep reluctance to be recruited for yet another mission. In Solomon's world, the Foreign Minister had always been cousin Hasdai, eloquent son of his mother's brother, Isaac, the son of Ezra, from the sons of the Jerusalem exile. Although he wielded considerable political influence, his older relative didn't mind calling upon familial loyalties when he needed to exert a more subtle form of pressure. He'd utilized this type of persuasion once before when soliciting the translator's cooperation in matters of political intrigue.

"A cycle of inspiration doesn't often last, and I've already experienced one major interruption," he reminded Hasdai as frustration crept into his voice.

Hasdai gazed at Solomon for a moment, his face expressionless until a smile creased the edges of his mouth. He understood how much it meant to Solomon to write his poetry, and he remained a supportive, generous patron of the Andalusian poets. But he also knew how important it was for his people, for all of the peoples of the kingdom, to maintain the integrity of the Umayyad Caliphate.

"The survival of the Caliphate may be at stake which means our people's future is in jeopardy."

Although Solomon didn't appreciate this intrusion into his creative life, he believed that Hasdai was sympathetic to his plight; and, despite his well-founded trepidation at getting involved in a murder investigation, one that might last for weeks, Solomon also desired the continued good fortune of Jews in Andalusia.

"What do we know about the woman?" he asked.

"She from Galicia . . . she's a *quyib* . . . you know, a songstress. She lives with a roommate, another entertainer, in the old Christian quarter of Córdoba. Bishop Racemundo knows the women and says the roommate is a Mozarab. "

"Not much to go on," Solomon replied, sitting with hands in pockets and one foot nervously tapping the floor. "Is this Galician woman an agent of the Reconquest?"

"We're not sure. This entertainer is only one among many suspects. We have to discover the meaning of this event," continued Hasdai. "If it's personal, the family will absorb the loss. If it's political . . . well, the Umayyad Caliphate is fragile."

Solomon wasn't convinced.

"After two decades?" he wondered aloud.

"We still have enemies. Both internal and beyond our borders. The Fatimid Caliphate would like nothing more than to destroy us and you already know that Christians in the north are obsessed with the idea of Reconquest. The old Muwallid families are always seeking revenge and the Caliph's own family isn't above suspicion."

While he sat listening, Solomon detected the sweet aroma of ripe oranges. He guessed they came from the Caliph's private garden; only the best was good enough for the ruler's inner circle. He felt a spasm in his stomach and realized he was hungry, but he knew he'd have to wait to remedy this deficiency.

"Your people need for you to act on their behalf. Your poetry has to wait."

Hasdai is the Nasi, thought Solomon. As spiritual leader of all Sephardic Jews living in Andalusia, his cousin exercised a dual claim upon his services. Not easy to wiggle out of an assignment if Hasdai deemed it necessary.

Solomon cringed as he felt control over his destiny slipping away.

Chapter 2

Hasdai tapped his fingers nervously on the desk's hard surface. This drew Solomon's attention because his cousin was usually a model of composure. He began to feel uncomfortable in Hasdai's presence. His eyes wandered along the desktop until he spied the bowl of oranges sitting in one corner. He knew an offer wouldn't be forthcoming, and he decided not to ask for one of the fruits out of fear of seeming presumptuous. He took a closer look at his cousin who appeared much the same as the last time they'd gotten together with his luminous eyes and broad shoulders. Only now the square jawline was hidden by a sandy-colored beard and his eyes couldn't hide a sense of sadness.

"Andalusia is the light of Europe and we cannot and will not allow it to be extinguished. Our people's destiny is linked to the success of the Umayyad Caliphate," continued Hasdai. "They've given us a free rein to develop our own culture while contributing to the common good. Umar's murder could be the catalyst that changes this rare opportunity."

"You're right again, as usual," the poet grumbled.

Solomon felt wet perspiration soaking through his clothing, compounding his mental discomfort. He also experienced an element of emotional disquiet. In his resistant heart he realized that Hasdai spoke the truth. In Andalusia, almost every Jew looked up to Hasdai Shaprut and for good reason. The man had earned that respect. The extraordinary Hasdai Shaprut, personal physician to

Caliph Rahman III, displayed a brilliance and versatility far beyond his thirty-four years; and, like many of the hundreds of physicians practicing medicine in the twin cities of Córdoba and al-Zahra, Hasdai enacted a multitude of roles: advisor, diplomat, scholar, spiritual leader, benefactor and patron.

Hasdai had initially gained his reputation as a physician specializing in antidotes to poisons, a valuable asset in a political environment where intrigue and assassination were a common occurrence. Poison emerged as the most popular mode of revenge in mid-10th century Andalusia and its antidotes fueled Hasdai's meteoric rise to prominence. Summoned to the palace to treat the Caliph during a debilitating attack, the physician used his knowledge of herbal medicine to affect a cure. He might just as easily have poisoned the Caliph while acting as an agent for one of the ruler's numerous enemies. He earned the young sovereign's trust and respect for his integrity and soon found himself appointed Chief Customs Official, a lucrative and sought-after position.

This was only the beginning. The Caliph later sent Hasdai to León on a diplomatic mission to procure the freedom of a high-ranking Muslim nobleman captured at the battle of Simancas. Hasdai spent seven months in the Christian capital where he also recovered a personal copy of Rahman III's Quran, perhaps the most illustrious prisoner taken during the conflict. The Jewish envoy also embarked upon a mission to Barcelona that same year. This time he was entrusted with the task of forging a treaty with the Counts of Catalonia and those of southern France, a trade agreement ensuring that commercial exchange with Andalusia would continue uninterrupted.

A wise ruler and a loyal servant who pledged loyalty and peace; and, Hasdai possessed enough clarity of vision not to abuse his influence but to use it for the benefit of his ruler. Rahman III, being free of jealousy and possessed of great wisdom, rewarded Hasdai fittingly. It came in the form of a promotion to Foreign Minister. It wasn't long before the charismatic Hasdai Shaprut emerged as leader of the Jews in Andalusia. The poet knew how hard he'd worked and how much he'd sacrificed to help his people given Hasdai's long absences from family gatherings, Solomon sat quietly, his eyes trained on his cousin.

Hasdai pushed back his chair and stood and then walked over to an arch-shaped window, set into a recessed wall, on the far side of the room. Along the way he passed an impressive bookcase built from ornately carved woods, a massive piece of furniture rising from the floor with shelves arranged halfway up the wall towards the high ceiling.

Solomon joined his cousin at the window and the two men stood staring out into the distance. The poet turned to gaze at his cousin and found him looking pensive, almost withdrawn. What is he thinking, Solomon wondered as Hasdai looked down along the terraces of the Caliph's visionary, splendorous city of Madinat al-Zahra. Eight miles distant, beyond a broad, fertile plain, the old capital of Córdoba retained its regal majesty as morning sunlight glistened off the rooftops of the Great Mosque. Even the sight of this stunning architectural achievement couldn't lift Hasdai's flagging spirits.

A silk sleeve brushed across a brocade vest. The brooding Foreign Minister raised a hand, rested it beneath the lightly-bearded chin, and sank into a world-weary posture. He appeared lost in disturbing thoughts. Solomon couldn't remember ever seeing his cousin looking so unsettled.

"I sometimes wonder if the Caliph has distanced himself too far from his people," reflected Hasdai.

"I still love the old city," Solomon admitted. "What Córdoba lacks in grandeur is compensated for by its soulfulness."

Hasdai turned and stared with a blank look in his eyes.

"Al-Zahra," he signed. "I fear it may one day lead to our downfall."

"Given his reputation, I'm sure Umar made a lot of personal enemies," Solomon ventured, in a rather obvious attempt to remind his preoccupied cousin about the reason for his summons.

Hasdai understood the ruse. Disregarding his weariness, he summoned strength from a reservoir deep within himself and, as he turned to face Solomon, his steely eyes left no doubt that his attention had returned to the ongoing predicament.

"We're looking into a number of suspects. As I mentioned . . . this Galician woman lived with a friend. You'll find her in the *Ajerquia* . . . the Christian suburb east of the city walls. I have an address for you."

"You want me to scour Umar's apartment and then interrogate the roommate?"

"A rather candid way of expressing it, Solomon . . . but, yes. And, there are other suspects and witnesses for you to . . . as you say . . . interrogate."

They turned from the window and walked back across the room. Their path took them past the imposing bookcase, an edifice revealing the richness of a brilliant and disciplined mind filled with wide-ranging interests. Volumes of poetry, philosophy, and scientific knowledge unknown to the rest of Europe had a place on shelves constructed from aromatic cedar, books embellished with ebony, tortoise-shell, and pearl inlays. Stacked halfway to the ceiling were books bound in leather and embossed with glittering silver, lapis lazuli, malachite, and gold. They were written in four languages: Arabic, Hebrew, Latin, and an edition of one rare botanical work, a copy of the invaluable lost manuscript composed in the original Greek.

"You will be well compensated for this assignment," promised Hasdai. "Perhaps enough to free you from your work as a translator. Not only that. You will earn the Caliph's eternal gratitude."

"I thought I'd already earned that."

An awkward silence ensued.

"We can't rest upon our laurels," Hasdai countered, breaking their brief quietude.

This comment reinforced what Solomon always suspected. The gratitude of rulers and politicians is often short-lived. That May morning proved no exception.

Solomon went over to a table inscribed with intricate arabesque designs as the transitory nature of gratitude led him to consider further possibilities for compensation. On a chess board fashioned from a striking combination of ebony, sandalwood and aloe in-laid with gold, pieces stood aligned like two opposing armies, figures carved out of translucent rock crystal and their red marble foes. This must be a present from a grateful Caliph to one of his most trusted advisors. My kind of reward, Solomon mused. Two silk-covered floor cushions, placed on opposite sides of the chess set, provided comfort for the players. The translator stood admiring the setting, warding off feelings of envy with acute observation.

Hasdai joined him as they surveyed the board.

"Chess is called The Sport of Kings, Solomon. Do you know why?"

"I imagine you're about to enlighten me."

This comment elicited a smile.

"Players in this game, like rulers in real life, must always make the correct choice. From out of the wealth of endless possibilities each move presents, players must select only one. They make a wrong move and they will be forced into a corner and their room to maneuver becomes limited. One needs to exercise clear-sightedness and wisdom if they wish to succeed."

Solomon knew this soliloquy was intended for his benefit.

"It appears Umar failed to make the correct choice somewhere along the way," he offered.

"Umar made a number of wrong moves," Hasdai corrected him.

It seemed clear a match had been left in progress, so Solomon studied the players' previous moves. He couldn't help himself. His hand reached down across the chess board in the direction of one of the pieces.

"Hands off, Solomon!" ordered Hasdai. "The Caliph and I are engaged in a game."

The poet stopped his forward motion.

"Looks like somebody is being trounced," Solomon observed. "I thought I'd offer the Caliph some help."

His cousin offered a second smile, this one more like a benign grin.

"You can help by staying out of affairs that aren't your business."

"Sorry."

"For what it's worth, it's not the Caliph who needs help."

This rare admission of imperfection humanized Hasdai in Solomon's eyes and he experienced a sudden surge of empathy for his older cousin. Hasdai's return to more important matters quickly broke the spell.

"You'd better hurry. The body is decomposing rapidly and you have to interview Umar's wife, and his brother, the Muwallid Hafsun, and the roommate of this Galician entertainer."

Solomon decided to make one last attempt to evade the mission. He so desperately wanted to concentrate on his poetry. He suspected it would appear self-serving, but he felt compelled to express himself.

"Why me, cousin? Can't you have someone else look for this . . . . Galician woman?"

"I chose you for this mission because you speak Latin and you have amazing skills of observation and memory," explained Hasdai. "Most of all I chose you because I trust you."

"What does my speaking Latin have to do with it?"

"This investigation may require a journey to Galicia."

"The savage north?" asked Solomon, in disbelief. "You're sending me to the savage north?"

"Only if it's absolutely necessary."

Solomon didn't respond so Hasdai, recognizing the limits of his younger cousin's familial loyalty, decided it was time to abandon any pretense of understanding. His patience deserting him, the Foreign Minister utilized the most reliable tool in his vast arsenal of persuasion: pure political power.

"You're going to do as I say." demanded Hasdai. "You have no choice in this matter. Do I make myself clear? '

Solomon felt his cousin's enmity begin to pierce through his emotional defenses. He realized that he was left with two essential choices; willingly accept his fate or find himself begrudgingly enduring its vicissitudes. No sense feeling sorry for himself, he reasoned.

"As you wish," he agreed.

"Maybe the scenery will inspire new poems," Hasdai suggested, attempting to lighten the tenor of their conversation.

Solomon didn't appreciate this comment though he knew it was well-intentioned.

The Foreign Minister removed a gold signet ring from his finger and handed it to Solomon. The nascent investigator inspected the insignia and quickly recognized the royal seal etched into the surface.

"Take it," said Hasdai. "This ring will insure your safe passage and give you unlimited access anywhere in Andalusia,"

Hasdai's ebullient nature resurfaced as he smiled and waved his cousin towards the door: "Go and find the Galician woman . . . " he shouted, summoning new energies. "Find her and bring her back to me so that justice may be served."

Solomon bowed his head in submission and walked to the entryway. Pausing at the doorway, he looked back to his cousin and offered a good-natured farewell.

"Good luck with the interrogations," Hasdai continued before offering a warning. "Be careful. There's a murderer on the loose."

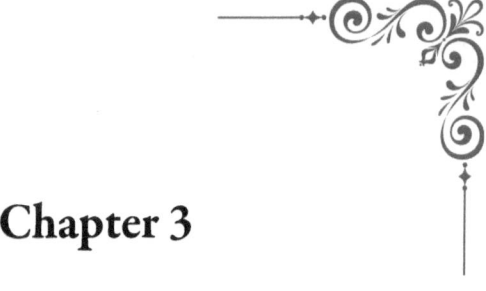

Chapter 3

Solomon left the office of the Foreign Minister clutching a thin piece of cotton fiber paper. There was an address written upon it. He didn't need directions to the scene of the crime. Umar's notorious love nest had always been al-Zahra's least kept secret. Lust nest was a more apt description, he thought. But Solomon understood only one address mattered. It led to the residence of the Galician woman, and her roommate, in the Christian suburb east of the old city.

His older cousin always seemed to keep one step ahead. In his most honest moments, Solomon realized Hasdai was two or three steps ahead of him. In spite of his innate intelligence and erudition, the Foreign Minister operated with the instincts of a street merchant. This rare combination inspired fear in some minds, but it was always a source of awe and wonder for the poet-turned-investigator.

The Tangerine still guarded the entry, no doubt listening through the doorway. Solomon gazed into the man's dark eyes, smiled, and without uttering a word he shuffled back down the polished marble hallway in the same direction he'd traveled less than an hour earlier. A sudden premonition came upon him. He suspected that he and the Tangerine would meet again sometime in the future. He'd have to put this hunch to the test although his intimations of things to come, the mystery of unfolding events, had served him well in the past.

He thought of Layla and how what originally seemed destined to be nothing but a brief encounter had blossomed into an ongoing friendship in which she became his confident. This turn of events was unpredictable, but he sensed from the first time he met her that they would be seeing each other on more than one occasion. Who would've guessed that a lost manuscript would provide an introduction to a courtesan and that their relationship would endure beyond that unique situation.

Solomon's thoughts returned to the Tangerine. Would he see him again in the course of this investigation? Would he remember the man's name, he wondered. As he walked on, his mind became preoccupied with thoughts of the mission. The translator felt grateful he was only pursuing one of many potential suspects though interviewing others. He hadn't even considered how many culprits there might be. Hasdai had done the math and it had obviously placed him under a great deal of pressure.

That lost manuscript, Solomon thought to himself, wondering if they believed he possessed magical powers, the ability to make everything just as it was before Umar met his tragic demise. He supposed he should've been thankful they thought so much of his abilities, only sometimes he felt their expectations of him were unrealistic. True he possessed excellent powers of observation and he could be quite determined, but he wasn't alone in possessing these traits. He believed he'd been chosen for his previous mission because he could be trusted to be discreet regarding Hasdai's deeply held secrets. His cousin had just confirmed that fact. The Caliphate is fragile, Solomon repeated to himself as he continued down the corridor. This wasn't reassuring, but he knew Hasdai's words to be true.

WHEN HE FINALLY LOOKED up, Solomon discovered someone approaching from the far end of the hallway. The youthful-looking figure came closer, and he recognized that it was Ahmad. Unlike most Arab men with their smooth-shaven skulls, tiny ringlets of oiled black hair sprouted from Ahmad's scalp. Shaving the head, a style introduced a century earlier by Baghdad courtier and exile Ziryab, whose widespread influence over many aspects of Andalusi culture had outlived his death, didn't appeal to Ahmad. He didn't flaunt his curly black locks with excessive pride, but he seemed determined to maintain his individuality.

Ahmad refrained from wearing the turban as did a majority of Andalusi men, but he also rejected the high, multi-colored skullcap, the *Qalansuwa*, favored by the male population. He'd dispensed with the practice of wearing rings on every finger, another popular mode of ornamentation, although a tell-tale white circle of skin indicated he had once worn one.

Ahmad adhered to a unique sense of style.

With almond-shaped, brown eyes and an oval face, Ahmad's clean-shaven visage presented a hint of feminine features. At social events and political functions, Ahmad exuded an easygoing and charming nature in sharp contrast to Solomon's aloofness. Ahmad stood out in a crowd while Solomon attempted to remain in the background like the proverbial wallflower. The two men shared a history, knowing each other from mandatory attendance at countless official functions. Ahmad remained the only male Solomon had ever described to himself as elegant. This accurate and honest description, based on firsthand observation, had nothing to do with attraction, sexual or otherwise, at least not on the investigator's part.

No, there was more to it than that.

During an increasing number of public events requiring his presence, Solomon found countless officials stealing looks in his direction, sometimes even staring at him. He was never sure why, but he often stared back hoping to create feelings of discomfort and anxiety in retribution for the intrusions. He sometimes felt tempted to stick out his tongue or engage in some other outlandish or childish behavior, but refrained from doing so because he wanted to avoid embarrassing Hasdai, whose role as the kingdom's Foreign Minister demanded that the poet maintain a degree of restraint. There was also a personal shortcoming. He remained too timid to act out his fantasies. He often wondered if his perceptions were some sort of paranoid delusions.

Ahmad also endured the public gaze of strangers; albeit, for a far different reason. Both women and men found the stylish young Arab captivating. His unique look attracted attention, but Solomon sensed that this wasn't Ahmad's intention. Ahmad was simply being Ahmad.

They commiserated about their fates on many social occasions. Feelings of annoyance created a bond shared in common. Solomon learned to put on a brave front, one that compensated for his reserved inner nature. Ahmad considered the attention unnecessary, but he accepted it as the price to pay for displaying his dazzling persona. They shared another unspoken, perhaps unrealized bond. Both were both stuck in mid-level careers and each lacked the ambition to rise higher.

Solomon continued to observe Ahmad and then moved over a couple of steps to share the walkway. His Muslim counterpart, dressed casually in a loose fitting, white cotton tunic with matching baggy trousers and leather sandals, appeared lost in his own thoughts, ready to pass by without looking up.

"Hello, Ahmad . . . how are you?" Solomon asked.

The beautiful Arab registered a look of surprise, but quickly regained his poise as he flashed a mouth full of gleaming white teeth.

"They're sending me to North Africa to gather intelligence."

That makes sense, thought Solomon. He knew the Fatimids were among the list of possible suspects.

"I may be journeying to the Christian stronghold of Galicia," Solomon offered.

"They make demands, don't they?"

"Yes, they do," he agreed. "You'll have to off those curls."

"I'll just shave the sides of my head and wear a fez."

Nervous laughter arose in both men, and it made Solomon feel uneasy. Each had been chosen for a dangerous mission and there was a chance one or both of them would find themselves in mortal danger. Their weak attempt at joking was meant to shield them from these thoughts.

For his part, Ahmad wished that Solomon had passed him by without making contact, but he'd learned long ago how to play the eternal social game of personal niceties and deception. In his case, constant practice turned it into something of an art form.

"May Allah bring us back safely to our beloved Andalusia," invoked the Arab.

Ahmad appeared rattled and his normally self-assured persona, one he'd worked hard to develop, appeared to have deserted him. Even the light-hearted banter failed to hide his unease.

"Is everything all right, Ahmad?" Solomon asked. "You seem upset."

"It's just that . . . I don't fancy being sent to Tangier."

Solomon wondered if this was another deception, but he also knew how to play the game.

"I can't say that I blame you," he offered sympathetically. "That city has always been a hotbed of political intrigue."

They parted with cheerful goodbyes and Solomon's thoughts returned to his impending adventure. He admitted to himself that he felt terribly conflicted. A part of him dreaded the idea of a possible journey to what he considered the savage north. Another aspect of his being found the idea of a new adventure both stimulating and mysterious. His original intuition had proven correct and, this new assignment offered him a chance to solidify his gains. He'd been able to dispense with the patronage of his older cousin, but he still relied upon the money earned from his translations to help him fulfill necessary financial obligations.

Another successful investigation might create an opportunity for him to leave behind his day job to write poetry full time, enabling him to fulfill his deepest desire. Sleuthing Umar's murder offered a chance for him to help his people maintain their unprecedented success while securing his own personal financial freedom. A dark cloud may have fallen over the Umayyad Caliphate, but his personal future appeared quite bright. At least that's what Solomon Levy chose to believe.

SOLOMON STOOD OUTSIDE on the second of al-Zahra's three tiers, monumental terraces cut into a huge natural spur of the Sierra Morena mountains, east of the fertile Guadalquivir river valley. The vast blue sky, bright sunshine, and a hint of a cool breeze began to restore his sense of well-being. He breathed in the fresh air and surveyed his surroundings.

The new city, laid out in a roughly rectangular plan, stretched a mile and a half from east to west and almost two miles from north to south. Caliph Rahman III chose the name Madinat al-Zahra for his fairy tale like city. It meant "The Resplendent One," paradise on earth, and was intended as a modest precursor of the heaven awaiting all true believers of Islam.

Nonbelievers shared in the opulence of his earthly bliss. They were meant to. The liberal minded Caliph, following in the footsteps of his Umayyad predecessors, strove hard to maintain a multi-cultural meritocracy. Remain loyal—whether Muslim, Jew,

Christian, or some other persuasion—and this magnificent world is yours to enjoy.

Above and behind Solomon's vantage point, the Caliph's magnificent white palace overlooked the city while dominating the upper terrace. White flags, gently waving above a comfortable cocoon protected by the new Alcazar, the Army headquarters with its strategically placed training ground and enormous stables, sailed high above clusters of luxurious Umayyad family villas and those of successful merchants and high ranking officials.

White flowers blossomed in unbroken rows of almond trees planted along the top of the mountain and their scented blossoms created a white carpet along the ground where they'd fallen. The effect was dazzling, luring the eye up past the bright, white buildings. The Umayyad family was obsessed with white and they had good reason to be. For this former Syrian family, the color signified distance and separation from Baghdad's ruling Abbasids, wearers of black clothing, flyers of black flags. Their bloody coup left Rahman I the sole survivor of Islam's second Caliphate family, eventual successors to the Prophet Mohammed. The Abbasids thrust the solitary young nobleman into exile along the shores of North Africa where destiny enticed him with an opportunity to seize power on the Iberian Peninsula.

The two families maintained an ambivalent relationship.

The Abbasids moved their center of operations from Damascus to Baghdad, transplanting the heart of Islam to the lands of ancient Mesopotamia and the Fertile Crescent. It was in Baghdad that the philosophical and scientific works of the Greeks were being collected and then translated into Arabic, thus preserving the learning of that ancient European culture for future generations. The Umayyads privately refused to recognize the Abbasid Caliphate's legitimacy, but remained hungry for the literary, artistic, and cultural influences of Baghdad.

Solomon had wanted to begin his interviews among these Umayyads and their villas in order to question Umar's wife, and then his brother; but, Umar's decaying body dictated his agenda. His first order of business was to go to the nephew's trysting place at the bottom of the mountain so he sought out his driver.

The one-time teamster, waiting patiently with gnarled hands and a receding hairline, made his living with the aid of a healthy Balearic mule and a well built, two-wheeled cart whose design harkened back to Roman times with eight-spoked radial wheels attached to a fixed, straight axle. Cart making was a lost art in the Arabian world where a nomadic culture, dependent upon the camel to transport goods, had little use for the technology. This was a strong indication that his driver was Ibero-Roman, a member of an indigenous older culture that intermixed with Romans over a six hundred year time span and a people who still used this mode of transportation in the numerous suburbs surrounding the walled city of Córdoba and in the wider streets al-Zahra, the Caliph's emergent city.

They began their descent, but the driver stopped the mule at a crossroads. A goods-laden caravan of North African camels impeded their progress so the old man halted his cart, allowing the procession to pass and turn up a service road. Solomon vented his displeasure because the slow pace of the heavily-burdened animals irritated him no end.

"Come on," he cried out. "I don't have time for this."

The driver, hearing his complaint and sensing his impatience, turned to assess him. The leathery, weather-beaten face, a result of decades spent outside in the blinding Andalusian sun, registered disbelief. The shrug of his shoulders and relaxed body language conveyed a what am I to do approach to the inconvenience.

He's surprised by my apparent lack of self-control, Solomon thought.

"Umar's body is decaying," he explained before realizing his driver had no idea what he was talking about.

As the caravan passed, and the cart's two wheels creaked back into motion, it began to dawn on Solomon why he'd been rushed out of Córdoba and thrust into an awaiting cart to answer a mysterious summons by the Foreign Minister. Horses would've been commandeered by the military in response to news of Umar's death. As a result of uncertainty, not knowing if the murder resulted from a personal attack, a political feud, family jealousy, or even the opening salvo of an invasion by rival Fatimids from North Africa, the Caliphate cavalry had been mustered into action and placed on high alert.

At that very moment, mounted troops were patrolling the streets of al-Zahra.

Chapter 4

Inside the luxurious villa of Umar abd-Rahman a cupola made of glass, surrounded by white stucco mortared over brick, brought morning light down into a well-maintained reception area. The walls stood painted a soothing aquamarine; but, at that moment in time nothing could bring peace to the two individuals who stood facing each other. Gold lettering, an elegant calligraphy rendered in Arabic script along the surface of these aquamarine walls, might just as well have been absent. The exquisite calligraphy drew no interest from these two.

Nuzha, Umar's only wife and the mother of his son, Ali, dressed herself in an elegant silk tunic, dyed yellow with saffron. Bands of decorations, in this case exotic birds, appeared at the upper arms. She stood without attendants by her side, stoic and aloof. Her husband's concubines lived in regal splendor beyond arched portals leading deeper into guarded apartments, but she was the de facto ruler of this realm. By custom, Nuzha should have been escorted by one of these mistresses and overseen by a eunuch guard. She'd dismissed them with no protest.

The man named Hasan, brother of Umar, wore a long and flowing white tunic with widespread sleeves and a loose fit. Beneath it were hidden hips disproportionately wide in comparison to his upper body. Nuzha disliked her husband when he was alive. She detested his brother Hasan even more. At least Umar loved his son and showered affection upon Ali. Her observations of her

27

brother-in-law led her to believe that the only thing Hasan truly loved were his horses.

Still, her husband's brother had brought her news of Umar's demise, not that Nuzha felt surprised when hearing of her husband's murder. She thought that it would seem curious if she didn't appear interested in the circumstances surrounding the event, perhaps it might seem even a little suspicious.

"How did it happen?" she asked.

"I'm not sure," Hasan answered in an agitated voice. "It was a dagger, but I don't know who wielded the weapon or why they would want to murder Umar."

"You've reported this to the authorities?"

"Of course," he replied. "It's the first thing that I did."

"You will be questioned again," Umar's widow told him.

Hasan frowned as he considered the possibility.

"Nuzha, surely they can't suspect me ... "

"They will suspect all of us," she replied, wondering why Hasan would think that he wouldn't be a suspect. "I imagine Shaprut will be in charge of the investigation."

"The Foreign Minister?" questioned Hasan. "A Jew?"

"He is the Caliph's most trusted advisor."

Nuzha was correct on both counts. Both she and Hasan would be prime suspects in the investigation into the murder of Umar abd-Rahman. It's not hard to imagine that Nuzha had been driven by Umar's numerous liaisons and rude behavior towards her to the sort of madness that resulted in such an act. One need only understand her anguish and reflect upon the humiliation she had been forced to endure. She attended social functions with her husband, and men found her charming and cultivated and captivating. Umar chose to ignore his wife at these events as he spent his time casting his eyes about in search of his next conquest. Nuzha had been worthy of a happier marriage, but she bravely endured her sad fate for the sake of her son. Maybe time, and Umar's indecent proclivities, had finally taken a toll upon her tortured soul.

Hasan also made no secret of the fact that he and his brother were not on the best of terms. He only tolerated Umar because his brother provided the necessary capital and contacts for their horse business. Even though they were business partners everybody knew there was little love lost between them. Umar's son Ali would inherit his father's share of the business, but it wasn't unrealistic to think that Hasan might attempt to buy the boy out. Perhaps killing Umar provided a means for the surviving brother to ingratiate himself into Nuzha's life. Hasan made no secret of his admiration for his brother's wife.

They were both suspects, but there were others.

"He told me he was spending the night with a Galician *quyib*," Hasan told Nuzha..

"You think she murdered Umar?"

"Things might have gotten a little rough . . . "

It was Nuzha's turn to frown. She lowered hers eyes, shaking her head in disbelief. She'd heard the rumors dozens of times. She had hoped for more from her marriage, but she'd always been disappointed. She'd longed for a happy marriage, but her own union had never given her pleasure.

At first, she was convinced that it was her pregnancy that led Umar to seek out other women beyond the harem he'd gathered around himself. Her husband's frequent absences after the birth of their son had disproven this theory and left little doubt in her mind that she would have to endure a sad and frustrating marriage. An attractive and cultivated woman deserved better, she often thought to herself. She decided to dedicate her time to studying music and writing poetry and most of all to nourishing the relationship between her young son and herself.

"I must prepare for mourning," she told Hasan.

As the man of squat stature turned to leave, he remembered there was something that he wanted Nuzha to consider. Something for the widow to think about as the future unfolded.

"Your son will need a father," Hasan told her, stepping in closer.

Nuzha took a step back before replying: "You know how I feel about you."

"Keep me in mind, Nuzha."

"Leave me in peace, Hasan."

NUZHA SAT FACING A gilded mirror. She rested in her toilette room dealing with conflicted emotions, settling into a room designed with indoor plumbing to enhance bathing and grooming. She began to prepare herself to take on the appearance of mourning.

For Nuzha, a facade of grief allowed her to offer a convenient mask to Andalusi society, one that would help hide her true feelings. She felt uneasy deep down in her soul. She gazed into the mirror and found herself frowning. Nuzha resented having to wear traditional mourning clothes and presenting a false front when she would rather dress in a manner that reflected her true self. The death of Umar could not hide the fact that she viewed herself as an impressive woman. She'd capitulate, but only for the sake of Ali.

In her heart, she almost felt grateful that her husband had met this fate. She had borne Umar a son, a male heir, and that's all he'd wanted of her. From the moment of Ali's birth, he scorned her. His countless liaisons and numerous concubines were a constant reminder that her status as his first and only wife meant nothing to him. Now, she could devote her full attention to her son without any of Umar's unreasonable demands or his ongoing desire to get his hands on her dowry. He'd never accomplished that bit of thievery.

Nuzha smiled to herself.

She dabbed a cotton cloth into a basin of water and, gazing up into the mirror, she closed her eyes and began to remove black kohl eyeliner from an oblong face. Opening her eyes as she wrung out the cloth, Nuzha noticed a couple of wrinkles, small lines developing at the edges of those orbs, the first signs of aging. She wasn't a girl anymore, neither in body nor in spirit.

Ali will be heartbroken at first, she thought to herself. For all his many faults, Umar was a good father and he loved his son. She hoped, Allah willing, that the boy would one day grow into a man and the years would help erase his father's memory. That was her fervent hope for the future.

She dipped the cotton cloth into the basin of water a second time, wringing it out and rubbing the soft cloth along her arms and legs, over her entire body to remove the scent of jasmine perfume. This sensuous touching of her own skin made her bemoan the lack of another's touch.

This privation led her to resent Umar and his chosen lifestyle all the more, but this would soon be a memory. Perhaps not forgotten, but a memory nonetheless. Nuzha then cleaned the henna dye from her fingernails and toenails. She removed the lipstick from her mouth using the dampened cloth. After completing this task and changing her facial appearance, she conformed with an archetype, the grieving widow. She would later change out of the exquisite silk robe into a plain, drab linen tunic and then adopt a veil, an accessory women of her social status weren't given to wearing either in private or in public.

The veil, she thought, what an inconvenience.

While Nuzha contemplated the inadequacies of the mourning ritual, one of Umar's concubines entered the room. Fatima, considered by many to be more attractive than the wife, lacked the advantage of the widow's cultured upbringing.

"I should follow your lead and prepare for mourning."

"I appreciate your support, Fatima."

The concubine, named after the daughter of the Prophet Muhammad, entered further into the room. She placed her hand upon Nuzha's shoulder and gave it a gentle squeeze. Umar's wife turned her head and looked up at the woman with an enigmatic smile. This was the first time the concubine had displayed kindness towards her. How sweet of Fatima, she thought, and the compassionate act began to heal the widow from her feelings of isolation. She reached up and placed a palm gently upon the concubine's hand.

"I should go change my clothes," said Fatima, as their two hands disengaged.

"So must I," replied Umar's widow.

Nuzha looked back into the mirror one last time before rising to leave the room. She found a tear forming in the corner of one eye. The emotions beginning to well up inside of the widow were not caused by love for her dead husband, but only from concern for her only child, her son Ali. Nuzha would do anything for Ali. Had she resorted to murder and blocked out all traces of memory?

Nuzha wasn't sure.

Chapter 5

At the southern edge of al-Zahra, where suburbs gave way to rows of lavish apartments, an adroit Iberian driver found his designated street and deftly veered a two-wheeled cart around a corner without slowing down to reduce speed. Solomon grabbed a tight grip on his seat and fought successfully to maintain his balance. Three blocks later they came upon an armed guard stationed outside the front door of Umar's apartment. The weather-beaten driver halted his cart and the investigator jumped down.

The nervous sentinel's fingers found the handle of a short sword, but he froze in place when Solomon shoved the Foreign Minister's impressive signet ring in front of his pudgy face.

"I'm under orders from the Caliph," he explained. "I need to inspect this apartment."

The stout guard grunted something unintelligible and allowed him to pass.

Solomon opened the door and crossed the threshold. A month of grunts like that guard's and he'd be a candidate for admittance into one of Córdoba's many asylums, he told himself. This clever interior monologue, a stream of consciousness often indulged in, but one best kept to himself, came up short against a strong sensation. An odor of decay assailed him and he knew beyond a doubt that he'd found himself in the presence of death and decomposition.

He held his breath for an instant, realized the futility of this approach, and then cupped one hand over his mouth and nose.

Even this proved ineffective so he gave himself over to the olfactory invasion, grateful that he hadn't eaten anything earlier that morning. The Caliph's sweet-smelling oranges had lost their appeal.

Solomon scanned the extravagant apartment. Green divans, set back against vermillion hued walls, were accented with soft pillows covered in yards of silk and chenille. This room must've required the yield of an entire mulberry orchard. He laughed at his own joke, but again second thoughts regarding the timing of his unintended mental dexterity assailed him.

This was serious business.

Be silent chameleon mind, he admonished himself.

Umar's hookah rested nearby, a pipe with a long flexible tube connected to an ornate chamber where smoke cooled by passing through water. Solomon wondered if this particular device had been used for smoking molasses based *shisha* tobacco. More likely Umar preferred hashish.

A few tiny particles of charcoal, heated to cook the tobacco or hash to a temperature that didn't burn it but still produced smoke, had fallen to the floor off a metal screen placed over the tobacco bowl. He removed the screen and inspected the bowl. It proved empty and clean and offered no evidence revealing what type of substance pleasure-seeking Umar favored.

An embossed and gilded goatskin tapestry hung from the near wall suspended between stucco cornices. The scene depicted sexual imagery suggesting nefarious erotic adventures. This apartment feels contrived for unbridled indulgence, he thought

Solomon experienced a tightening in the pit of his stomach.

In this ostentatious chamber he sensed the presence of the dark side of human sexuality. Human appetite ruled by compulsions. This wasn't a setting in which to pursue a natural physical attraction, or a satisfying act of compassion, or even a co-mingling awareness of mutual creaturely comfort. Healthy sex seemed out of the question in this gilded lair. The absence of windows in the apartment heightened the effect.

He must visit Layla, he thought, suspecting his confidant could shed more light on the nature of Umar's preferences and perversions. He decided this would have to wait until after he questioned Umar's widow and the Galician woman's roommate.

A round bed, fit perfectly into the center of the room, left him wondering if the divans were reserved for additional party-goers or perhaps a group of voyeuristic cronies. His mind returned to the present as Solomon looked down and found Umar lying prone, stretched out on the bed's silk sheets. A triangular shaped, double-edged iron dagger protruded up from out of his heart at a slight angle. The cold finality of death put an abrupt end to his musings so he endeavored to view the scene with the detachment of a surgeon.

He observed no signs of a struggle. That seemed odd to him. Either Umar was familiar with his attacker or somebody had taken advantage of the element of surprise.

Red blood.

The metallic scent of iron filled the air.

Solomon felt ill as his stomach turned queasy, ending his surgeon's fantasy.

The dagger, its tarnished handle sticking out from Umar's once pulsating heart, mocked the Umayyad Caliphate's ideal of peaceful co-existence. Celtic symbols, inscribed on the knife handle, made it easy to believe the Galician woman committed this murder. Did somebody plant this particular weapon in Umar's body to point a finger at Galicia, he asked himself. This type of knife could be purchased in many of the bustling markets of Córdoba and al-Zahra; a novelty perhaps, but easily acquired. Then again, maybe that Galician woman or Christians inspired by the idea of a Reconquest of Muslim Andalusia were responsible. The size of the dagger handle was inconsequential, either a man or woman could've grasped it without difficulty.

He had an inkling that his cousin, the Foreign Minister, had already examined Umar. This stood to reason and explained how Hasdai had known the time frame of bodily decomposition. Poor Hasdai had probably been up half the night. No wonder he appeared perturbed, not his usual good-natured self. Solomon wondered who else might have seen the corpse before him. Hasdai didn't mention any names so he could only venture a guess. The Chief of Police was likely to have been to the apartment and perhaps the Caliph himself, though that was unlikely.

He turned his attention back to the body.

Even in death, Umar retained his handsome good looks, bearing features similar to the Caliph: pale skin covered facially with a silky red beard. The nephew, unlike his uncle the reigning monarch, didn't dye his red hair and beard to color them black. Some said the Caliph adopted this vanity to appear more Arabic. The heritage of Caliph Rahman III's mother Muzna, a captive slave concubine and Christian from Navarre, in the region of the Pyrenees, suggested as much.

The Caliph's grandmother, Iniga, daughter of King Fortun Garces of Navarre, also contributed to his Hispano-Basque heritage, making Rahman III only one-quarter Arabic. Maybe even less when one considers that Rahman I's mother, two hundred years earlier, was a north African Berber concubine taken to Damascus for the pleasure of Caliph Hisham ibn Abd al Malik's son, the Arab general Mu'awiya ibn Hisham who distinguished himself in the Arab-Byzantine Wars.

Ironic, thought Solomon, how a ruler with strong European and African bloodlines masquerades as an Arab Islamist to preside over the most enlightened kingdom on the Continent. The illusions that make life worth living never failed to amaze him. This mental

THE GALICIAN WOMAN 37

conjecture, albeit interesting, had little bearing upon the investigation. Stick to the facts and the evidence before your eyes, he reminded himself. Stop the meandering history lessons he mumbled, castigating himself for being distracted. No time for a wandering mind even though it was often his greatest pleasure.

His attention turned back to the dead man's body. Umar surpassed Rahman III in both height and weight. Alive, he weighed a hundred pounds more than his uncle. The physical resemblances between the Caliph and his nephew ended with the pale-toned skin and, if Solomon remembered correctly, striking blue eyes. Thank God somebody had closed Umar's eyelids. He bet it was Hasdai. Two shiny gold dinar coins rested in the victim's eye sockets like miniature suns. These coins hadn't traveled far from the Caliphate's new mint.

Had he been overpowered it would've taken a group of men to subdue Umar. The lack of evidence of any kind of a major struggle led Solomon to consider once again the possibility that Umar either knew his attacker intimately or the perpetrators used the element of surprise. He'd been told Umar possessed a fearless temperament. Reckless is a more accurate description, he speculated. Umar, confident in his strength and physical prowess, dispensed with the necessity of traveling with a bodyguard. He thought of himself as invincible.

Solomon looked closely at the dead man's hands.

Like many men in mid-10th century Andalusia, Umar loved jewelry and especially rings. A keen-eyed connoisseur of lapidary artistry, all eight fingers were adorned with precious metals and stones: gold, silver, diamonds, sapphires, garnets, and emeralds. There were a couple of gemstones Solomon didn't recognize, but this shortcoming wouldn't have any bearing on his investigation. He couldn't begin to calculate the wealth that Umar's jewelry represented. A small fortune, he guessed. Umar retained all his fingers and rings so that ruled out robbery as a motive. This wasn't an opportune thief's plans gone awry.

Solomon's mind drifted back to happier times when he and the nephew rubbed shoulders in Rahman III's court. He suspected Umar might've been one of the Caliph's favorites if he hadn't been betrayed by a lack of moral restraint. Umar lived in the upper echelons of the Andalusi world, but his rendezvous apartment required a descent to the lowest level of the city, both physically and spiritually. Solomon had never witnessed anything quite like this apartment with its aura of perversion.

He focused his eyes once again on Umar's stiff body. Coagulated blood encrusted the dagger and spilt over past the garments of the Caliph's nephew, creating a crimson swatch on the pastel blue sheets. He began to poke around, but the scene of the crime proved disappointing.

No evidence of a major struggle. This fact kept bothering him.

He continued searching the apartment.

When Solomon wrote poetry it grew out of his love of using words to describe experience. It required a degree of concentration, but this was different. This investigating business demanded a heightened level of diligence. He needed to reapply himself, look for small details and meaningful clues and then think about their significance. His powers of observation came to the fore as he continued his search.

Something soon caught his eye.

A delicate wisp of long, silky hair glimmered in the late morning sunlight. Using his thumb and index finger, he plucked it off the floor like a thread and peered intently at the fiber. The brilliant copper strand left little room for doubt in his mind. The Galician woman had paid a visit to the scene of this crime.

He retrieved the thin roll of paper from his coat pocket and unfolded it. He concentrated on an address in the Christian suburb, repeated it a few times to himself, and then felt confident enough to deposit the details into his memory bank. He folded the paper into four equal sections, unfolded it again, and tucked the strand of hair inside. He carefully refolded the paper and returned it to his pocket.

This could be a bit of incriminating evidence, but don't make too much of it, he told himself. It seems too easy. The hair, well there was little doubt she'd come to Umar's apartment, but a dagger with Celtic symbols inscribed on its handle seemed too obvious. The strand of hair might have also been planted he realized in a moment of mental clarity.

Then he discovered the ring.

He found it at the base of a porcelain amphora, a five-foot high, double-handled vase whose swollen belly rested beneath a narrow neck and large open mouth. He knew that amphorae had been used for grave markers in the ancient world, but a connection between this practice and his discovery seemed unlikely. He picked up the thick, gold band and examined it closely. On the inside of the ring, he found an inscription etched into the metal.

It read: *Yours in Eternal Embrace.*

Before Solomon had time to consider the significance of these words, he heard a loud disturbance coming from outside the apartment. He pocketed the ring and returned to the front door to discover what might be causing the commotion.

AT THE ENTRANCE TO Umar's apartment, Solomon found a man arguing with the corpulent guard.

The investigator stepped outside: "Who's this?" Solomon demanded of the guard.

"He claims he's Umar's brother, Sir."

"My name is Hasan, and I demand to see my brother."

Solomon raised his fist and displayed the signet ring.

The sibling of the dead man quieted down, but he continued to protest his lack of admittance through body language, shifting back and forth and then sideways before he commenced muttering unintelligible words. No tears in his eyes. The man appeared stoic rather than grief-stricken. The investigator wondered if the theatrics, and the man acting rattled, were a charade enacted solely for his benefit.

He took a closer look at the actor and observed how Hasan resembled a pear. His upper body, slight in the arms and shoulders, gave way to gravity as his torso expanded, unlike most men, at the hips. The rotund brother awaited Solomon's initial inquiry while the investigator reflected upon his own good fortune. The victim's brother had come to him. Now he wouldn't have to seek him out for questioning.

"What are you doing here, Hasan?"

"I've returned to spend time with my brother before they come to take him away," Hasan explained. "I never should have left him."

"You discovered the body?" Solomon asked although he knew the answer to this question from his audience with Hasdai.

"Yes, and I reported it right away."

"It's all right," the investigator told the guard. "Let him pass."

The guard hesitated, then stepped aside as a sneering Hasan strutted inside.

Solomon closed the apartment door behind them and continued his questioning.

"I'm investigating Umar's murder under orders from the Caliph," he explained without divulging anything about his own background or his connection to the Foreign Minister.

"Tell me what you know about this tragedy, Hasan."

"I came to see my brother shortly after midnight. My brother likes to engage in nocturnal liaisons and sleep late into the morning, but on this day we had an important business appointment early in the morning." Hasan paced nervously as he considered his response to Solomon's question. He stopped abruptly and turned to face the investigator.

"Umar told me he was going to attend a party last evening and then spend some time with one of the entertainers. He said he'd send her home after he'd had his way with her and he told me that I should come over just after midnight and spend the night.

"Had his way with her?" Solomon asked.

"Those were the words he used."

Solomon didn't doubt this choice of words given Umar's reputation. Something bothered him. He searched around the room casting his eyes back to the prone figure of the Umayyad ruler's nephew lying on blood soaked sheets.

"There's only one bed in this apartment," he pointed out.

"We pull two of the divans together," replied Hasan. "We've done it before."

"You say that you and Umar had important business," Solomon reminded the brother. "What was the nature of your business?"

"We understood a dozen pure Arabians were available for a good price."

"I assume you're referring to horses?"

"Umar and I *are* . . . " Hasan hesitated for a moment, and then an expression of genuine sorrow, and the pain that it registered, changed the look on his face. "We *were* partners in a breeding operation. It may have only been a side interest for my brother, perhaps nothing more than a diversion. I, however, love these animals. They're incomparable. The most beautiful creatures in Allah's entire creation"

"What happens to the business now that Umar is dead?"

"His share becomes a part of the inheritance," answered Hasan.

"I see." replied the investigator, making a mental note to check further into Muslim laws of inheritance.

"No matter what you think of him . . . I know his reputation . . . Umar didn't deserve this unholy death."

"So where were you before you came here last night?" Solomon inquired.

"Home alone."

Solomon considered the response and realized there was no way of proving it's veracity. It's a convenient alibi, he reasoned. One that's been used a thousand times before. One that Hasan would have used had he plotted his own brother's murder and been lying in wait for him when he arrived home from the party. For all he knew the entertainer might have been an accomplice. He decided to press on with his questions.

"Did you notice anything unusual when you arrived last night?"

"That Galician woman killed my brother," Hasan shouted, ignoring the question. "I swear by Allah that I will hunt her to the ends of the earth and make her pay for this crime."

Hasan's eyes protruded from a weary face; his garlic breath overpowered.

Solomon took a step back.

You may have to travel to the ends of the earth to find her, it occurred to him. If so, we may be crossing paths. "You didn't answer my question," the investigator reminded him. "Was there anything out of place?"

"What makes you think I have to answer your questions?" Hasan sneered as his nostrils flared in anger. "Just because the Caliph chooses to employ Jews at the highest levels of his government doesn't mean he can force his own family to answer to them. There's no law that says I have to answer your questions."

Solomon flinched. He knew that a majority of Andalusia's Muslims, following the example of Rahman III, maintained an attitude of toleration, and even respect, for their Jewish and Christian counterparts. He also understood that there were some not so agreeable, including some in the Caliph's own family. Hasan was evidently one of them although for some reason he had cooperated at the beginning of the questioning.

"No, you don't have to answer my questions, but your reluctance to do so in the murder investigation of your own brother makes you a prime suspect, doesn't it?"

Annoyed by the brother's attitude, the investigator wondered if one of the empire's thousands of Ibero-Roman converts to Islam would react the same as somebody with bloodline connections to the royal family. He doubted it. Hasan seemed perturbed; maybe Solomon had touched a nerve.

"Sounds like you have something to hide," Solomon goaded.

"I didn't notice anything," Hasan replied. Umar's excitable brother avoided eye contact while nervously adjusting his clothing. "I was too upset."

"So why have you returned?"

"I've already told you. I want to spend time alone with my brother before the family arrives to claim his body and prepare him for burial."

He found himself disliking Umar's brother, but Solomon decided that he should respect the brother's request. He would have wanted the same consideration if it were one of his own family members.

"As you wish, Hasan," he consented. " I may need to ask you more questions, later."

"As you wish . . . " mimicked Hasan.

Solomon ignored the brother's sour attitude and took his leave, but he couldn't help feeling that Umar's brother might be hiding something from him. Sure he had answered the investigator's questions, but only reluctantly and with a vehemence disproportionate to the situation. Was there a vital clue or piece of information that he was withholding? Solomon had collected two pieces of physical evidence, but didn't know if they would lead him to the murderer of the Caliph's nephew.

Solomon only knew one thing for certain.

He did not trust Hasan.

Chapter 6

Solomon sat next to the old muleskinner, back on the weathered bench seat, as the flick of a switch and a sudden shout caught the mule's attention. The cart lurched forward and they began to retrace their route across the city.

His driver pulled away from the scene of the crime just as something new occurred to the investigator. He wondered how the brother knew that the Galician woman was the entertainer who had visited Umar's apartment. In the heat of the moment, he hadn't thought to ask. Solomon often wished his mind operated more quickly. He suspected cousin Hasdai would not have made the same mental mistake. He didn't feel like returning to confront the dead man's brother so he allowed the matter to rest. There was another reason that he dismissed the idea of returning to ask the brother about the woman.

A new and disturbing thought had arisen in his mind. Has anybody considered suicide he wondered as they raced back through the suburbs. The investigator doubted that anybody other than himself had thought about the possibility; and, even he doubted it was a plausible explanation. The angle of the dagger in the dead man's chest argued against it. Given Umar's temperament it seemed unlikely. Solomon decided to dismiss this possibility as the cart continued to rumble towards the heart of a vibrant city: past public baths, popular libraries, hospitals, public schools, and sacred mosques with their beloved minarets.

The driver steered his cart around al-Zahra's main square where the city's principal fountain, one of hundreds found throughout the lush, green metropolis, spewed a stream of water high above the embellished figures of twelve different quadrupeds, each animal incrusted in gold leaf with eyes fashioned from embedded precious stones.

Lavish al-Zahra, a sight to behold.

They slowed their speed as the cart rolled down a wide, paved street past dozens of store fronts and outdoor markets where they found themselves surrounded by al-Zahra's animated crowds. The song of life pulsated in their blood, infusing the city with energy and vitality.

Arab, European, Asian, and African shoppers offered a visual kaleidoscope of world fashion with long, flowing multicolored tunics woven from a variety of cloths and silks, all displayed in a multitude of colorful designs and topped by an assortment of headgear, including swirling turbans worn proudly by dark-skinned North African Berbers.

They drove past stalls displaying an array of fruits, vegetables, nuts, and berries—myriad shapes, textures, and hues—offering an endless variety of flavors appealing to the culinary diversity of the Andalusi palate. The investigator found his appetite returning. He asked the driver to pull over and stop so that he might buy a loaf of leavened bread to assuage his hunger.

They continued at ground level, on the southern and largest of the three terraces, in a city burgeoning with thousands of new arrivals. Higher wages attracted migrating artisans and laborers from North Africa and the East. They came for construction jobs, a thriving market and commercial district, an official center for artisans, and State controlled workshops: armories for making arrows, chain-mail, spears, and leather tack for the cavalry.

Large numbers of people had taken advantage of an added incentive. The Caliph's program of subsidized housing acted as another magnet attracting ambitious newcomers staking their claims in the nascent city whose dazzling array of domestic and imported products had created one of the world's first consumer societies.

They passed the Caliphate's gold mint, the first in Europe since the Roman empire. It had been relocated from Córdoba, three years earlier. Solomon remembered the two shiny dinars resting atop the dead man's closed eyelids as he chewed on crusty bread. A few blocks later, as he finished his last bite, they began their ascent.

Solomon trained his sight on al-Zahra's remarkable middle terrace where a small army of craftsmen and laborers engaged their energies in transforming a once barren hillside. From this perspective, he could see the scaffolding on the magnificent Great Hall, under construction for the reception of foreign dignitaries. Nearby gardens would house colorful aviaries. Already completed were the homes of lesser government officials, orchards of fruit trees, flower and vegetable gardens, ponds, fountains and water sculptures, an impressive aviary filled with tropical bird species, and a well-stocked zoo.

Madinat al-Zahra remained a work in progress more than a decade after the initial start of construction. Even in its unfinished state, this product of the ruler's visionary imagination—his religious and political desires—indulged and overwhelmed the senses.

Solomon remembered hearing from a reliable source, namely his uncle Isaac, that during the beginning of construction ten thousand men, with two thousand mules and four hundred Arabian camels, were required to haul marble and jasper and other costly resources into the city. These materials, including more than four thousand columns, about four times as many as used in the Great Mosque, were brought to al-Zahra from Carthage and other ancient cities.

Paved streets spared the populace the indignity of sucking in the swirling dust stirred up by dromedaries.

Solomon and his driver tried to focus.

Their route led up through a tree-lined avenue skirting fragrant rose gardens where gurgling fountains served as centerpieces to provide the musical sounds of water splashing. Fountains of all types were highly esteemed and functioned as a key architectural element in al-Zahra, a green oasis fed by a series of long, underground pipes and massive aqueducts carrying life-giving waters from the mountains located ten miles north of the city.

They rode on past stucco covered homes whose rare exotic plants and trellises, ripe with overhanging grapes and tangerines, created a riot of color. A peacock wandered aimlessly while birds warbled and sang in the trees overhead.

They continued the ascent.

Though Al-Zahra was meant to complement and not conflict with Córdoba, Solomon felt the upstart city's opulence trumped good aesthetics, an extravagance not quite satisfying to the soul. Most visitors experienced the opposite intended response, a sense of amazement and admiration for al-Zahra's magnificence and wealth. The strength of his personal sentiment kept Solomon firmly planted in his beloved Córdoba.

At least, for now.

THE RIDE FROM UMAR'S apartment to his opulent villa on the upper terrace of al-Zahra gave Solomon an opportunity to reflect upon his mission. He removed the ring from his pocket and examined it closely. If this belonged to Umar, the man must've worn two rings on a single finger, he surmised. Back at the apartment he'd inspected the dead man's fingers after discovering the ring. He didn't find a telltale trace of light skin where the band blocked out sunlight. Maybe he hadn't worn it for long.

Perhaps the ring was planted on purpose, he now thought. A ploy, like the dagger, to throw authorities off the trail of the real murderer. A further study of the ring offered a small clue. Unlike the dagger, the outer surface of the gold band remained smooth with no Celtic symbols incised into the metal.

Does this mean something? he wondered.

Don't jump to conclusions, he told himself. There might be no connection between the dagger and the ring. Either could've been purchased in the bustling markets of Córdoba. Maybe a maid servant lost her ring while cleaning the apartment after one of Umar's notorious wild parties. Or, maybe it was a token in exchange for a night of pleasure. Who knew how long the gold band had been sitting at the base of that atrocious amphora.

He slipped the ring back into his pocket.

Something else bothered him, and it had nothing to do with physical evidence. Perhaps Umar, unable to integrate his dark side, to live with it instead of within its obsessive grip, had taken his own life. Solomon had dismissed the idea earlier, but it had involuntarily returned for consideration. This possibility still seemed unlikely because Umar's braggadocio didn't suggest the type of man who'd consider suicide. He suspected the Caliph's nephew was a victim of foul play or perhaps a crime of passion.

This unnecessary destruction of life challenged him to stop clinging to his fading youthful idealism. What a strange madness, he thought to himself. Even in this culture of tolerance, where Muslims, Christians, and Jews live in relative harmony, the eternal rebirth of evil in the human soul continues to manifest itself. How sad to witness a kingdom under siege from the dark side of life, especially a land where a meeting of minds and a melding of communal pursuits had led to cooperation between different peoples. Compromises made by all in the interests of the common good.

Was cousin Hasdai correct? Would he ever stop being right? Were the absence of pogroms and persecutions reason enough to accept a degree of partial inequality? Were there degrees of evil? Was evil itself relative? Solomon possessed no answers just a growing list of questions, perhaps unanswerable. No wonder he'd felt an initial reluctance to take on this assignment despite the rewards it offered.

What if the Galician woman is the murderess, he asked himself. If this were true, it meant that Hasdai had every right to enlist his services to find her and bring her to justice. Somehow, they needed to make their shattered world whole again.

He remembered Hasdai's heartfelt plea: "Andalusia is the light of Europe . . . we cannot allow it to be extinguished." A sudden stop jolted him from his reflections.

Solomon braced himself, physically and emotionally. He'd arrived at the extravagant villa of Umar abd-Rahman.

Chapter 7

Two eunuchs stood guard outside the domed domicile. Solomon looked them over. Bodies and minds scarred, they lived a breed apart. But most still appeared masculine. He had found eunuchs capable intellectually and they made strong, commanding bodyguards. These two human geldings, powerful physical presences outfitted in military regalia, stood hairless in a posture of rigid attention.

Almost four thousand eunuchs resided in al-Zahra, a small but significant minority. Most worked as palace guards, provided security for harem women and children, or labored as civil servants staffing the vast Caliphate political bureaucracy. Many of these eunuchs came manufactured from the slave market in Verdun, France, a conduit for captive European unfortunates sent down to the Iberian Peninsula.

Solomon had once found the word "manufactured" quite odd when used in a human context, but it had become part of everyday vernacular in Andalusia. Since eunuchs were bought and sold in marketplaces, he finally came to realize that the reference wasn't so far-fetched. Some eunuchs were slaves carried off in childhood or orphaned in wars. Since they no longer retained family connections, the Caliph became a father figure to many of them. Others were boys with family ties whose poor, struggling parents believed they insured a better life for their offspring by allowing the practice. The great numbers of eunuchs holding high administrative posts or working

as bodyguards for the most distinguished families in the kingdom
reinforced parent's belief in the efficacy of the system. Although
the practice made merchants in the business wealthy men, including
many Jews, most sensitive Andalusis referred to it as the "hideous
trade."

Solomon stepped down off the cart and approached the two
guards.

After he had explained the nature of his business, the tallest of
the eunuchs led him down a long walkway towards a front entrance
built in a style favored by Umayyads, a horseshoe shaped archway.
He observed luxuriant green foliage along the footpath. It provided
a vivid contrast to the villa's white-stucco exterior.

They entered the premises. Like most Muslim villas, the
reception area opened up inside into a light and airy interior with an
expansive sense of space. Arched portals led deeper into the seraglio's
guarded apartments where, the investigator knew, the concubines
and children of Umar lived lavish and well-cloistered lives.The tall
eunuch disappeared through an archway on the far side of the room,
leaving Solomon free to gaze at regal splendor.

He studied the walls while he waited, walls painted a soothing
aquamarine and flashing brilliant gold lettering, an elegant
calligraphy rendered in stylish Arabic script. He read words arranged
from right to left, written in the same direction as his native Hebrew.
No mistaking the patron of this masterpiece; the sentiment paid
homage to Umar abd-Rahman.

The distinct script, and the accuracy of its alignment, revealed
the graceful hand of the compositor. Solomon's own refined, legible
handwriting, a skill highly sought after in the translator's field, gave
Solomon a deep appreciation of this calligrapher's immense talent
and extraordinary expertise. The aspiring poet stood lost in a
moment of aesthetic arrest, his mind and senses elevated to a blissful
gratefulness for the writing's sheer rhythmic beauty.

No wonder Andalusi's call the practice of calligraphy "The Golden Profession," he mused. Although Solomon loved the art of calligraphy, he considered himself a second rate talent. He'd once aspired to the profession, but his skills were no match for his desire. Hasdai suggested he study Latin instead. Since he didn't possess his cousin's pedigree, born into a wealthy family in Jaen and first son of a successful father who encouraged his every aspiration, Solomon took the advice and applied himself to mastering a language other than Hebrew and Arabic. All the while he wondered why his mother had married beneath her station, leaving him the poorer cousin. After mastering the *lingua franca* of the Roman Empire, he took a job as a translator, a practical livelihood to support himself while he pursued his poetic avocation.

Solomon appreciated Hasdai's support. Nobody thought less of him because he loved to read and write poetry. Quite the contrary. Like the moon orbiting the earth, the intellectual life of Andalusia revolved around the central hub of poetry. Ancient Bedouin warrior poets had set a high standard for integrating fierce courage with imaginative sensitivity. In his most honest moments, Solomon realized he'd been gifted with only half of the equation.

The polyglot poet in his soul found a professional niche translating Greek scientific and philosophical works from Arabic into Latin. A tri-lingual education wasn't unusual among his generation of translators. In their milieu, translation wasn't considered a mechanical or even an uncreative process. The goal was to create a new scientific vocabulary suitable for Andalusi's secular disciplines.

Writing poetry had to remain a deep yearning for the time being. Only now Solomon believed that he might be close to realizing his dream of writing verse full time. His eyes focused on the stylized curves of the letters. Such bliss. Only a handful of men in Andalusia wrote script at this level of proficiency.

He soon became lost in a mild euphoria.

It wasn't meant to last.

WHEN SOLOMON FINALLY reoriented himself, he discovered two pair of eyes staring in his direction. Tradition dictated that Umar's wife be questioned in the presence of another woman. Over the years he'd learned that much about Muslim society, along with a few other rules of etiquette.

Time to put on his investigator's hat.

Both women dressed in simple white, linen tunics and the lack of decorative silk robes with accompanying jewelry suggested to him that they were already given over to mourning. The absence of tears evoked his curiosity just as they had with Hasan. None of the family appeared visibly upset by Umar's demise, and he was already inclined to dismiss Hasan's theatrics as an intended deception.

Another clean-shaven eunuch, his face a mask displaying no emotion, stood guard on the far side of the room where the arched portal framed the entrance to the villa's living quarters. The sound of children's laughter floated in the background, coming from rooms he knew he'd never be allowed to enter let alone view.

Solomon's eunuch escort politely dismissed himself and returned to his post outside. The investigator turned his attention to the women. Both were veiled, a custom not widely practiced in the cities and towns of Andalusia, this being the prerogative of men. Primarily dark-skinned Berbers, but also upper class women who usually refrained from employing them except on special occasions. Other segments of society hadn't yet adopted the veil as an accessory to their wardrobes.

One of the veiled women stepped forward. Solomon felt certain she was Umar's one and only wife. He knew her name to be Nuzha. The second woman, undoubtedly a prized concubine, remained quietly in the background. Nuzha offered no greeting. Perhaps she failed to recognize him from past social gatherings.

"We're preparing to leave so that we may claim my husband's body."

Only vague outlines of the woman's nose, mouth, and chin appeared behind the thin layer of gauze. Her eyes, without the usual kohl accentuation, burned with an intensity Solomon found unnerving. Neither woman seemed to be wearing perfume, another sign that they had begun a period of mourning.

"I'm sorry for your loss," he began sympathetically. "I need to ask you some questions about your husband."

"I bore Umar a son, a successor," she said abruptly. "That's all he wanted from me."

Solomon experienced a brief shock. This isn't going to be easy, he told himself. He decided it might be best to use an approach as straight-forward as the widow's opening salvo.

"You know about the other women?"

"I'm not a fool."

"Jealousy is a powerful motive."

Nuzha laughed in his face. Even through the veil her spray of spittle found its way to his cheek. Nothing veiled about this woman's personality, he thought. He found this disconcerting. She'd always appeared gracious when he'd encountered her in the past.

"The time Umar spent with other women was Allah's blessing to me," she told him with a smirk. "I disliked my husband."

"Hated him?"

"Hatred is also a powerful motive, but I didn't hate him. "

"Did you fear him?"

"Everybody feared Umar."

"The other concubines in the harem," he continued. "How did they feel about Umar?"

Instead of returning his gaze and looking him in the eye, Nuzha's eyes moved slowly down along his right arm, past the wrist. He followed their path until they came to rest on Hasdai's signet ring. She'd seen it before at some social gathering and quickly realized that it belonged to the Foreign Minister.

Now she understood why they'd sent a Jew to interview her. Maybe they suspected that Umar was murdered by a Jewess? It wasn't an impossibility. It was well known that Umar didn't discriminate against women because of their religion or ethnicity. He selected his women solely on the basis of physical attraction.

How did the harem feel about Umar? Was that the question he'd asked her?

"You're wasting your time," Nuzha answered. "We all felt the same."

Umar's concubine stepped forward. She'd been standing discreetly in the background listening to the interchange of questions and answers, so quiet Solomon had almost forgotten her.

"She speaks the truth."

"So any one of you might have murdered Umar?"

"To what end?" asked the newcomer.

"That's what I'm trying to determine," Solomon replied. "Once I know that, I'll know the identity of Umar's killer."

The two women exchanged glances before the second woman answered.

"It doesn't matter to us now that he's gone."

"Now, if you don't mine," Nuzha said. "We have a body to claim."

Solomon was beginning to realize he'd have a difficult time finding a rational witness to shed light on Umar's murder. Feeling frustrated, he thanked the women and excused himself. As he began to leave the reception area another question occurred to him.

He spun around quickly and directed his question to Umar's wife.

"Will your son inherit his father's wealth?"

"That depends upon the wishes of the Caliph."

Was she telling him the truth or what she thought he wanted to hear? He put a check mark by his mental note to research Muslim law on the subject of inheritance.

"Will that be all? I must attend to my son. I'm not sure what to tell him," Nuzha confided. "About his father, I mean."

Solomon had a hard time believing that this woman could ever be at a loss for words.

"Yes, that's all for now," he replied. "I'm sorry for this inconvenience."

He left the villa without uttering another word.

SOLOMON FOUND BLUE sky and sunshine giving way to high clouds. A cool breeze played upon his cheeks. He thanked the eunuch guards and found a familiar looking couple dozing at the cart. He decided to leave the old muleskinner and his Balearic counterpart to their reveries, opting for a short walk to give himself time for a little cold-blooded thinking.

He felt perplexed, emotionally uncertain.

He'd rubbed shoulders with Nuzha at official state functions arranged by the Caliph's chief-of-staff. He'd known the woman as a warm, charming, intelligent, and educated individual. He'd heard she studied music and wrote poetry. She'd always carried herself with a sense of grace and dignity.

Although the name Nuzha meant pleasure in Arabic, the woman he'd just questioned seemed distant and mean-spirited. He mulled over the dichotomy and decided to give Umar's widow the benefit of the doubt. They were all reeling under pressure generated by tremendous stress. How could any of them keep a semblance of balance when the status quo had been completely overturned, the result of a singular disruptive act. They all seemed to realize, at some deep subliminal level, that Umar's murder threatened Andalusia's fragile peace.

Solomon found himself entertaining many questions, but he lacked convincing answers. He found it easy to identify a list of potential suspects, difficult to pinpoint clearly defined motives. At least his investigation wouldn't be impeded by major religious observances. Ramadan, Passover, and Easter had all recently concluded. Muslims and the *dhimmi*, "The People of the Book," believers in the Torah and the Bible, were all available to answer his questions. The investigator saw this as a remarkable concurrence of events given the shifting lunar calendar. He believed the mild spring weather also worked in his favor.

Now what, he asked himself.

He did possess an address. It led to the Christian suburb east of Córdoba's walled inner city.

It led to the abode of the missing Galician woman.

Chapter 8

S olomon instructed his driver to disregard the shorter route across the northern suburbs of Córdoba. If he was being followed, perhaps by Christian spies from the north who were dreaming of reconquering Muslim Andalusia, it would be easier for him to elude them in the crowded, familiar streets inside the walled city. He told the old teamster to stop on the south side of the old Roman Bridge, an engineering marvel spanning the Guadalquivir River atop sixteen solidly constructed arches.

One of the main entryways into Córdoba, the bridge had required rebuilding by the conquering Muslims, two centuries earlier, to renew access across the river. The Visigoths, who'd made the city of Toledo their Iberian capital, lacked interest in this city by the river, allowing superior Roman ingenuity to fall into disrepair.

As Solomon disembarked, he gave his driver instructions to return to the exact same location, at sunrise on the following morning, after the first call to prayer. That's when he planned to report to Hasdai and receive the Foreign Minister's next set of instructions.

For a brief moment, he contemplated giving the old man a gold dinar for his services. He decided against it. He knew the driver's compensation wasn't his responsibility and it would already be quite generous given the immense resources of the Caliph.

His gaze turned towards the great river. Ancient Córdoba stood on the north bank of an unusual bend in the east-west waterway.

Cargo boats, moored downstream, used the navigable freshwater port as a hub for thriving import and export enterprises. The Guadalquivir flowed south to Seville and Cadiz, then out into the Atlantic Ocean and beyond.

The investigator crossed the heavily guarded span on foot and passed through the Gate of the Bridge, a massive stone archway leading into the walled inner city, a heavily congested area covering two square miles. Most of Córdoba's quarter million residents lived and worked in the twenty three suburbs outside these walls as an expanding population spilled out into the surrounding countryside.

Solomon heard the groans of a waterwheel in the distance. It supplied water along a gently inclined aqueduct to the Old Palace and its lushly maintained gardens. As he walked on, the waterwheel came into view on his left, just inside the gate.

He felt a pang of disappointment as he entered the city, sensing he stood little chance of finding the Galician woman anywhere inside the capital. A journey north seemed inevitable, an unanticipated and unwelcomed incursion into his poetic endeavors.

Solomon usually returned home from al-Zahra through the Almodovar Gate. Located at the western city wall, this gate was flanked by towers on both sides and linked by a parapet walkway. One of nine portals built by Emir Abd al-Rahman I, this route led directly into the Juderia, the thousand year old Jewish Quarter. This is where the investigator made his home, as had thousands of Jews since before the time of the Romans.

This assignment dictated a different direction.

He continued on past the Great Mosque.

Despite his fall from grace, Solomon felt certain Umar's body would be transported for burial to the Royal Cemetery, in Córdoba. First he'd be washed in scented water and wrapped in sheets of clean, white cloth. After funeral prayers, in the square of the Great Mosque, he'd be taken to the cemetery and laid to rest on his right side, facing Mecca. At the gravesite, any display like tombstones, markers, flowers, or mementos would be discouraged. The entire ritual would be conducted with dignity, thus preserving the impression that the status quo remained in effect despite the circumstances surrounding Umar's passing.

Solomon went through the Mosque's main square, walking past a fortress-like edifice with forty-foot high outer walls finished in cinnamon-colored, unadorned stucco. He had always heard the inside of the unprepossessing Mosque was breathtaking in contrast to its non-descript exterior. As a non-Muslim, he'd never been allowed the opportunity to see for himself.

This Mosque was reminiscent of Syrian architecture and the Mosque at Damascus, harkening back to happier times for Andalusia's Umayyad rulers. The Córdoba structure was later extended south towards the river by Rahman II and his son, Muhammad. On its northern side, Rahman III would soon construct a new minaret after demolishing the existing tower, built sometime during the late eighth century. The footprint of the structure continued to expand in proportion to the rate of conversion to Islam.

Like al-Zahra, the Great Mosque remained a work-in-progress.

Although Solomon's small refuge from the world was located only a dozen blocks northwest of this architectural wonder, he headed in a northeast direction along a circuitous route leading to the old Christian suburb. He passed the covered market, the *Alcaiceria*, where vendors busied themselves trading silk and other textiles and then he continued through a lively area of makeshift stalls and craft workshops.

He knew the route by heart.

He'd spent his entire youth exploring the streets of Córdoba.

Entering a maze of twisting streets teeming with locals, he found the merchandise of the walled city's ground-floor shops spilling out into the street. The greater part of the city's business of living was conducted outdoors. It had always been that way. He took a deep breath and pushed his way through the ever-present crowd, keeping his purse and the precious piece of paper he'd been entrusted with, now protecting a single strand of red hair, hidden from view.

SOLOMON WALKED ON THROUGH this warren of narrow, cobbled streets, angling northeast along the butcher's street and then the coppersmith's street. He held his breath as he passed the fish market, exhaling deeply when he felt well clear of smells he personally considered malodorous. Though he sometimes envied them, he knew that he could never have earned his living as a fisherman

Leaving the walled city through the New Gate, Solomon entered the *Ajerquia*, the oldest extension of Córdoba outside the walls. This suburb, also known as the Eastern Wing, covered an area larger than the walled city itself. A population of Arabized Christians, called Mozarabs, lived in this part of town. Vague memories stirred within him, memories of the times he and his young friends had ventured into these streets as young boys to explore a beckoning, if not taboo, world beyond their personal environs. He felt more cautious now, lacking in the fearlessness or perhaps foolishness of his youth.

He stopped to ask for directions..

Then he continued on his way, wondering if his next set of questions and observations might yield new clues or at least new insights into the mystery behind Umar's murder. He entertained little hope that the Galician woman would be waiting at home to answer questions upon his arrival. His thoughts turned to her roommate. What could she tell him? What would she tell him? Would this Mozarab Christian woman help or hinder his investigation?

Solomon had no way of knowing.

WHAT'S HAPPENED TO Lia, the young woman wondered.

Worrying and feeling confused, she paced the floor. Why hasn't she come home? She asked herself this question, but her mind could find no answer to quell her concern. Struggling to make some sense out of her roommate's absence, the woman continued to pace back and forth inside the sparse living room of a small house in the *Ajerquia*, the old Christian suburb of Córdoba.

An image of her friend and roommate and fellow entertainer appeared in her mind. Lia with her deep green eyes, pinkish white skin and sensuous red hair accentuated by copper streaks when the sun decided to cast its rays her way. The olive-skinned and amber-eyed woman had trusted that Lia could take care of herself, but now she wasn't so sure. Her worst fears began to assail her, rising to the surface of her mind like a coiled serpent ready to strike and poison her being with untold doubts.

Had the Galician woman, with the voice of an angel, become prey to the Devil?

Lia had accepted an invitation from the Caliph's nephew Umar. Had the risk been too great? There were rumors of what it cost to be a recipient of the nephew's lavish rewards, rumors of unwanted groping and indecent proposals. Should the woman have protested her friend's decision more vehemently?

She continued to pace back and forth across the floor.

She began to blame herself. "It's all my fault," she heard herself whisper aloud. The thought that this might be true began to terrify her. It made her feel like a stranger to herself. It made her feel sick inside as her stomach became nauseous. She searched for another explanation to assuage her guilty conscience.

Lia had told her that she was homesick. She wanted to sing for the scion of the royal family and collect her reward and return to far-off Galicia, gladly returning to her younger siblings and their family farm. The land would be paid off and Lia would be free of the burden that had led her to venture into another culture and way of life.

It had all seemed so innocent, thought the Mozarab. But that thought didn't soothe her queasy stomach. It only made things worse. She should've warned her roommate even if doing so made her seem unsympathetic.

She stopped pacing and stood erect in the middle of her living room. The Christian woman spread her arms out wide as her body took on the form of a cross. This was the stance Andalusi Christians assumed when they prayed. Arms outspread, a human cross emulating the Redeemer's crucifixion. Sara silently invoked a prayer as she softly chanted a heart-felt plea for her Lord to protect her friend's well-being. Where can she be, the woman wondered anxiously as she dropped her arms to her side and went to her roommate's bedroom and entered that domain.

A candle had burned down on the dresser next to Lia's bed. The woman would replace it, an act of faith to demonstrate that she believed with all her heart that everything would be resolved and her doubts and fears would be revealed as unnecessary worries, mere phantoms of her mind.

The snake retreated.

The Mozarab ran her fingers lightly over an embroidered silk tunic that rested on a footstool. She missed her fair-skinned friend, a woman as melancholy as the misty, rainy countryside that she had described so many times and with such deep longing.

She calmly dismissed the fears from her mind. The situation was out of her hands and events were beyond her control so she embraced what Bishop Racemundo had always referred to as "the peace that passeth understanding."

She realized she hadn't yet eaten. She left Lia's bedroom and passed through the living room on her way to the kitchen. She found dates and figs and oranges sitting in a large bowl on top of her kitchen table,. Somehow, she couldn't bring herself to eat. Her stomach hadn't yet settled. Perhaps a cup of water would suffice.

What's happened to Lia? she wondered again.

The question refused to go away.

Chapter 9

Solomon entered a neighborhood of deteriorating streets and dilapidated houses. It provided a visible example of how the once dominant religion's fortunes had declined since the rise of Muslim culture on the Iberian Peninsula. Wealthier Christians, a decided minority, favored villas outside of the *Ajerquia*, down along the shoreline of the Guadalquivir. In the Eastern Wing, outside of the walled city, commercial enterprises tended to be less significant: vinegar making, soap making, cobblers, and plasterers. Solomon's assignment led him past the straw market and the mat market and finally into an area of tiny squares and meandering streets.

The afternoon sun, positioned directly overhead, somehow found its way into the narrow street to beat down upon the back of his neck. Despite his discomfort, he continued searching until he found the dwelling that he was looking for in the middle of a block of attached one story houses. All of them exhibited similar degrees of decline.

After arriving at his destination, Solomon took a close look around.

Solomon found no guards posted outside the Galician woman's residence, but he did spy a pair of misplaced Arabs eyeing the house from a shaded doorway on the far side of the street. Were they waiting to see if the Galician woman returned home? Were they tailing him? He felt a twinge of paranoia. If he were to hazard a guess, he'd presume these men worked for the Chief of Police.

Seeking comfort, he gazed down at the signet ring. It guaranteed his safely most anywhere in Andalusia. He looked back across the street and discovered the two men had vanished. His eyes searched up and down the roadway. The two were completely out of sight. He returned to his task, but not before making a mental note of the occurrence. It seemed the Galician woman wasn't the only one capable of disappearing.

Time for a small precaution. He stuck a small sliver of clove into his mouth to freshen his breath. He sucked on its pungent yet sweet outer layer for a moment and then began chewing on the nail-shaped flower bud's fibrous pulp.

Solomon rapped on a weathered door.

Bare wood, visible beneath flaking blue paint, provided ample proof of the dwelling's lack of maintenance. To be fair, he reasoned it might be caused by a lack of resources and not desire. The entry indicated as much; a plain flush door without panels or molding and devoid of a transom. He knocked again, and then Solomon waited.

The door finally opened.

An attractive young woman stood looking up into Solomon's eyes. He judged her to be about his own age, late-twenties, perhaps a few years younger. With dark hair and full, moist lips, she could've passed for a Jewess or an Arab woman. Chestnut brown hair, with the barest hint of reddish tones, might have cascaded down along the nape of a slender neck, framing a sweet face, if she hadn't pulled her long strands up and tied them at the back of her head with a simple, wooden clasp.

Solomon spoke to the woman in Arabic because he assumed that she was also conversant in the language. He would've been surprised if she wasn't: "I'm investigating the death of the Caliph's nephew and the disappearance of your roommate."

The woman remained silent.

Solomon observed her closely and realized the thread of hair he'd found in Umar's apartment didn't match hers. Beneath dark brows, the deep-set eyes still gazed up at him, holding his attention for a moment. Those amber-colored orbs held flecks of green and brown. Her only jewelry, a pair of pearl earrings, also caught his eye. They complemented a white, floor length linen tunic under which, he imagined, she wore pants and a chemise. She can't afford cotton, he observed. Certainly not silk. This made him wonder who had given her the pearls. An absence of perfume, almost essential to Arab and Jewish women, added to his initial attraction. Something about her unpretentious and unvarnished beauty appealed to him.

This isn't going to be easy for her, he told himself.

"May I come inside?" he asked with a quiet voice.

She hesitated and then opened the door slowly, retreating to the interior of the residence where she turned to face him.

"Are they connected?"

"The death and the disappearance?" he asked as he closed the door behind himself. "That's what I need to find out."

"I'm Sara," she said, introducing herself.

"Solomon Levy. I'm afraid I have to ask you some questions," he told her. "It's official business."

"I understand."

She doesn't really, he thought.

"When did you last see your roommate?"

"Last night, after our performance," Sara answered. "She stayed behind to visit with the audience. It wasn't unusual."

"You're a Christian and a *qiyan*?" he asked.

"You seem surprised."

"It does seem a bit contradictory."

"We have to make a living." she explained. "Times are difficult for Christian singers and dancers so we entertain at public gatherings and private parties."

Times are only difficult for some Christians, he reflected. Others are quite prosperous. The most successful Christian men accrue harems like their Muslim counterparts. Maybe this Sara is a bit naive. Or, maybe she's a talented actress.

"We share the gifts that God has blessed us with," Sara continued. "Bishop Racemundo has given us his permission. Our spiritual leader is a wonderful man."

"Yes, he is," Solomon agreed. "My cousin, the Foreign Minister, works closely with the Bishop."

His attempt to impress her didn't elicit a response.

"Did your roommate have any ongoing contact with Galicia? he asked. "I'm thinking especially of Santiago de Compostela."

"I don't recall anything," she answered with a vacant stare.

Solomon couldn't help noticing the dwelling's whitewashed walls, devoid of the intense colors decorating Arab interiors. He found the lack of a popular influence interesting, if not odd. Very little attention had been paid to the inside or the outside of the dwelling, a telling commentary on this *qiyan's* approach to spirituality. The interior life given precedence over the material realm. He felt like he had entered a cloistered world.

Solomon knew that Christ had said: "The kingdom of heaven is within you."

He also knew that the former Jewish prophet had shared a divine paradox, the other side of this equation: "The kingdom of the father is spread upon the earth and men do not see it."

He sensed that this woman's perspective contrasted with his own upbringing and the impetus to find God's hand not only in the wings of angels but also in the prosaic world of everyday life. Had the Christians turned their backs on a more earthly spirituality. He decided he was better off returning to secular concerns.

"You said she failed to return home last night," he began. "Did you notify anyone?"

"No, I trust her to know what is right for herself."

"Think she spent the night with the Caliph's nephew, Umar?"

"We're cautious," Sara told the investigator. " It was unlike her to go with a man, even a member of the royal family," She felt the weight of a guilty conscience, but it wasn't a complete lie she rationalized. It just wasn't the whole truth. She reasoned that she could come to terms with having committed a venial sin because it didn't entail damnation of her soul.

"Perhaps her curiosity outweighed her caution."

This comment drew no response.

Solomon began to wonder about the woman named Sara and her seeming lack of emotion regarding his inquiry; she appeared aloof and disengaged. Maybe she's in a state of shock. He deliberated about how to proceed and concluded it might be best not to press her too hard.

He turned his attention back to a room furnished with only the barest essentials. A low couch and an armchair occupied the wall behind the entertainer. He waited for an invitation to sit. When it wasn't forthcoming, Solomon continued looking around the apartment. His eyes discovered a table with a bowl of fruit, set back against the opposite wall, surrounded by three chairs. Did this signify an occasional visitor for prayer meetings or music practice or both. A plain wooden crucifix, devoid of the usual effigy of the redeemer, hung on a narrow wall between two bedrooms.

In one corner, he spied the most popular musical instrument of the Arab world, a pear-shaped, five stringed 'ud with an angled headstock fixed atop a short, fretless neck, and a spruce body with three sound holes surrounded by intricate geometric designs. He knew that finely-crafted 'uds like this one had originally possessed four strings. Finding himself strangely attracted to the Christian woman, he seized an opportunity to impress her with his knowledge and perhaps open her mind to his inquiries.

"Did you know that Ziryab brought the five-stringed 'ud from Bagdad a century ago?"

"Every dedicated musician knows Blackbird's contribution," Sara retorted.

Her words were delivered like a slap to the face.

Solomon quietly studied his new acquaintance. Too bad she isn't more friendly. At least she knows the courtier's nickname. He wished they'd met under more favorable circumstances. Given their vastly different worlds, they probably wouldn't have met at all if Umar was still breathing. Should he tell her he was glad that Ziryab had introduced the idea of multi-course meals to Andalusia as well as the use of toothpaste and deodorant. No, he didn't want to sound pedantic.

"We're musicians and dancers . . . a breed apart," Sara tried to explain. "You probably wouldn't understand."

Solomon had always admired those who made a living using their artistic talents. He knew from firsthand experience the sacrifices it required to make this dream a reality. He'd tried himself and failed many times with his poetry.

"I might understand what you're speaking of," he revealed to her in the quietest of tones. "I make my living as a translator, but my passion is writing poetry."

"I see," she said, her voice softening. "So why are you investigating a murder?"

"It's a long story," he told her. "I'm afraid I don't have time to explain."

Solomon watched as she bit down on a fingernail, caught herself engaged in this nervous habit, and then lowered her hand self-consciously to her side. He felt a part of her wanted to aid in the investigation, another part seemed to be wary of him. He sensed her reluctance but continued the questioning.

"Tell me about her . . . this Galician woman."

"She called herself La Gallega. She possessed the voice of an angel and always sang one or two songs in her native Galician tongue."

"I've heard they were haunting."

"She transported her audiences to another realm."

She may have transported Umar to another realm, he reflected. Only not with her voice. La Gallega still felt more like an apparition than a flesh and blood person to Solomon's way of thinking. This is all too vague, he told himself. He was hoping to discover something out of the ordinary, a distinguishing detail that set the Galician woman apart from all others. So far he hadn't had much luck and he felt frustrated by his lack of progress.

Solomon decided to change his approach.

Time to dig deeper.

"I need a name," Solomon said as he stepped in closer to the Mozarab woman. His eyes locked on hers and he refused to look away. He knew that she might interpret his behavior as mean-spirited, but he needed answers to help give impetus to his investigation.

"Her name is Lia."

"How would you describe . . . Lia?"

"She's somewhat melancholy. There's a sadness about her . . . she really missed her family farm in Galicia."

"I need a physical description as well."

"I don't know. She's average height with red hair and green eyes."

The red hair might help, he thought.

"Anything else?" he asked curtly. "Did she have a distinctive birthmark or something?"

Surprised at the sudden change in Solomon's demeanor, Sara clenched her teeth. Had she said or done something to upset him. It seemed like he was angry with her. She decided to do her best to cooperate with the investigator. His last question had served as a reminder, triggering something in the young woman's memory of her roommate. This gave her the opportunity she desired.

"Actually, there is something," Sara offered as she stepped in closer to shorten the distance between them. Trying to overcome her fears, she looked up into the investigator's eyes. "Lia has a discolored area, a splatter of purple on her left forearm."

Solomon witnessed Sara begin to bite one of her fingernails again. She caught him staring and quickly dropped the hand to her side before sharing her thoughts: "If she killed Umar, I'm sure she had a good reason."

"I need to find her so I can discover what that reason might've been."

"She wore a ring with a black stone," Sara volunteered. "She told me it wasn't really a precious gemstone. Some kind of wood or . . . I don't know."

"Sounds like jet lignite. It's called it *Azzabâǧ* in Arabic," he told her before elaborating. "Basically a form of decayed wood, a minor gemstone. It's been around for thousands of years."

The Galician woman can remove the ring from her finger so the black stone isn't much help. Solomon caught Sara glancing at him for a brief moment before she lowered her eyes. She seemed afraid to look him in the eye now and this made him wonder if she might be hiding something from him. Give him a little bit of information, but hide the most relevant details.

"What else can you tell me?"

"Lia used that word, *Azzabâǧ*. She learned Arabic quickly. It's because she's a musician and a singer . . . she has an excellent ear for language . . . and, she certainly had the desire . . . she wanted to save her family farm. That's the reason she left Galicia and came to work here in Córdoba."

"Mind if I have a look inside of the bedrooms?"

"Yes, I do!" she exclaimed before hurrying over to plant herself firmly in the middle of a doorway.

The negative response stunned Solomon. After getting over the initial shock, he wondered if her protest was based upon his impending invasion of her privacy or if maybe there was something she was trying to prevent him from seeing.

"I'm afraid you don't understand," he explained, softening his tone. "I'm conducting a murder investigation."

"This is our home," she asserted. Sara felt this stranger had gone too far. His demands for information were becoming unreasonable.

"I'm sorry, but I have to insist."

Sara suspected that he wasn't sorry at all.

She reluctantly made way for him and then followed him into one of the two bedrooms. Solomon chewed on the fragments of the shredded clove as he began to look around the room.

"This is my room," she told him.

Not the room he wanted to inspect, but he decided to appear interested. A half-burnt candle lay upon the nightstand next to a single bed, little more than a wooden frame and straw mattress covered with a linen bedspread. He assumed the three-drawer dresser contained her clothing as well as personal articles. He felt like he'd entered a cloistered cell whose simplicity bordered on austerity. Solomon continued looking around and discovered two embroidered silk tunics. They were folded neatly and placed on top of an unadorned footstool.

He turned and found her staring at him.

"The silk tunics are used in our performances."

All of their money goes into costumes and musical instruments, he observed. No wonder they live in such poor circumstances.

"I'd like to see the other bedroom."

Solomon slipped the spent clove into his pocket and followed Sara into the sleeping quarters of the Galician woman. He still didn't think of La Gallega as Lia. That seemed much too personal for a woman he hadn't yet met. Although the second bedroom was much like the first, he observed only one of the exquisite silk costumes. It lay folded on a footstool identical to the one in Sara's bedroom. He considered the second costume and wondered why it might be missing.

"Did you carry a change of clothes to use after your performances?" he asked.

"Yes," she replied. " Our costumes are very costly so we have to take good care of them."

The Galician woman might've changed before disappearing, he surmised. He made a mental note of this possibility. He'd write it down later so he wouldn't forget. Solomon took the lead and left the bedroom since it offered no additional clues to aid in his investigation,.

Back inside the living room, he turned to face her:

"Is there anything else?" he implored. "Please."

Solomon didn't like pleading with a stranger, but he didn't have much to go on.

Sara stood before him with arms spread out wide as her body assumed the form of a cross.

"What're you doing?"

She closed her eyes and mumbled something unintelligible under her breath.

"What're you doing?" he asked again.

She didn't bother looking at him when delivering her answer: "I'm saying a prayer for Lia."

Is she, he wondered. He studied her posture. She remained almost motionless except for her mutterings. So this is the stance Christians assume when they pray. Nothing like Muslims, who get down on their knees to prostrate themselves before Allah. Certainly not like us Jews, swaying back and forth if at all.

"Nothing else you can tell me?"

Sara finished her prayer before dropping her arms and answering.

"That night, before we went on stage, she said she was expecting a visit from a man."

"A man?"

"She said he was very dear to her."

A new scenario unfolded and it made perfect sense to the investigator. The Galician woman killed Umar and then her lover, or former lover, helped her to escape. Or, her lover killed Umar and then the two escaped together.

How plausible, yet it seemed unlikely.

What the hell is going on, he asked himself.

Even though Solomon had his back turned to her, he felt Sara's eyes studying him. He turned around quickly in order to put his intuition to the test. His eyes met hers for an instant before she turned away in embarrassment. Since the time he was a young boy, his mother had sworn he had eyes in the back of his head. This was her way of explaining how he sometimes knew things without knowing how he knew them. His mother claimed he possessed a gift. Solomon sometimes knew the world without seeing it. His mother called this a sixth sense.

As he watched Sara brooding, he felt some mysterious form of attractiveness beyond religion, ethnicity, or culture exerting a strong magnetic force. Biology overcoming surface inhibitions. He found himself liking this woman. He didn't know why. He suspected that she felt some kind of fascination as well.

"Why don't we sit down" she said, offering the invitation he'd been expecting earlier.

She led him to the couch before sitting down in one corner. Solomon sat in the opposite corner. They turned to face one another.

"I'm sorry. That was rude of me to refuse your request," she said.

"I guess I was a bit harsh earlier," he admitted.

"Lia felt homesick. I think that's the key to her disappearance," Sara said offering an opinion as well as a smile. She seemed more sure of herself as she moved over closer on the couch while directing her gaze into Solomon's eyes. The nervousness in her voice had also vanished, her tone almost soothing as he attempted to gauge her responses to his questions. The effect was almost hypnotic. She is an entertainer, he reminded himself.

"You think that could've led to such a drastic act?" he asked, his voice suggesting uncertainty. "Maybe she became a bit unbalanced?"

"I don't honestly know," she admitted. "For Galicians the longing for home is a kind of sickness."

He appreciated Sara's helping him in his attempts to understand her roommate's personality, but missing a distant homeland seemed a thin motive. Not the kind of pressure leading to an act of passion. There had to be more to it.

"Do you think her naivety led her to believe Umar would lavish gifts upon her? The reward for a private concert, for merely singing and nothing more?" he inquired. "Maybe he lured her to his apartment by pretending to accept such an arrangement before . . . "

Solomon paused.

"Before?" she asked.

"Before he had his way with her," he replied, remembering how the dead man's brother had described his intentions.

"I don't know. I suppose it's possible," lamented Sara, cringing at the idea of such a thing happening to her unsuspecting roommate.

Of course it's possible, he thought. She might've been quite naive or perhaps really desperate. Although he wanted to stay and talk more with this young woman, Solomon suspected questioning Sara further would yield little in the way of a motive or new information. There were possible clues: the splotch of purple, the missing costume, and the person dear to her.

"I'd better go now," he said as he rose from the couch. "Thank you for your cooperation, Sara. I really appreciate your help."

Solomon made for the front door and discovered she'd followed behind.

Sara stepped in closer, surprising him.

She gazed up into his eyes while gently caressing his forearm with her fingers, brushing it ever so lightly. He hadn't seen it coming. So much for a sixth sense that wasn't always functional. He had no trouble settling for five in this instance. And then he wondered if she was conscious of what she had just done.

Her unexpected gesture led to a brief epiphany as Solomon realized how the sense of touch can be the most compassionate of all. He began to understand how one can imagine all sorts of things about a person they don't know well, traits that they may or may not have perceived accurately; but, if that same person touched you their warmth conveyed itself directly through the body to the soul.

Solomon had no clue what Sara might be thinking of him, but her gentle touch felt like an enticing hint of things to come. Then again, he might be imagining a scenario that had no basis in reality, conjuring up a future that would never come to pass. He wondered what she'd think about his library and his poetry, but he'd had given up trying to impress her.

"Be careful," she counseled.

"I shall . . . "

She's quite the enigma, he thought. Perhaps she knew something he didn't. Something she hadn't shared with him. Something she was afraid to tell him. He didn't expect to find out what it might be. The time had come for him to leave. Solomon wondered if he'd ever see this woman again as he stepped outside into the bright sunlight and the woman named Sara closed the door behind him.

Chapter 10

Solomon had one more stop to make before he returned home to review in his mind what he'd learned and to write up some notes. He'd return to al-Zahra, in the morning, to make his report to Hasdai. He hoped that those investigating other leads had fared better than himself. If he were to venture a guess it would be that the brother or the widow were somehow involved in Umar's murder, but he possessed no solid proof to back up his assumption.

His route took him back into the old walled city and led him to a long established neighborhood bordering the Juderia. Beyond patio gates, two-storied, white-washed houses rose up below red-tiled rooftops. Many of the well-cared for homes belonged to families who'd inherited them, passed down for generations dating back to the very beginnings of Córdoba.

Everybody knew where ibn Hafsun lived. He was one of Córdoba's wealthiest citizens. Solomon arrived at his destination and found the gate unlocked. He entered, closed the gate, and walked past a gurgling courtyard fountain. The sound of water added a soothing background ambience, one the investigator sorely lacked at his own place of residence.

He used a brass door knocker to announce his presence and, as he waited, he found himself hoping that this next interview would be productive. Even crossing suspects off the list would be a step in the right direction. He didn't see the point of talking with a Muwallad, but orders were orders. Hasdai had proven many times in the past that he usually knew best. When the door finally opened Solomon found himself staring at a silver-haired man servant wearing a black cotton tunic. The contrast was dramatic.

"I'd like to speak with ibn Hafsun," he told the man. "I've been sent by the Foreign Minister."

The servant raised an eyebrow before noticing the signet ring "Wait here, please."

A few minutes later, another man came to the door. This dark haired man looked younger than the servant, probably in his late forties or early fifties. His lavish silk tunic, a long and flowing brilliant red garment, with wide sleeves and a loose fit, sported intricate bands of black geometric patterns at the upper arms. Below the tunic he wore leather ankle boots

"I'm ibn Hafsun," he said. "You wish to see me?"

"Solomon Levy," replied the investigator. "I was sent by the Foreign Minister to ask you some questions."

"I'm surprised the venerable Shaprut has any interest in me," the man replied, his steely blue eyes revealing nothing. The Muwallad smoothed his tunic as the hint of a smile creased his lips.

"Please, follow me."

Solomon entered the house. The old servant, who had been standing off to the side and out of sight, quietly closed the door behind the two men before disappearing into another room. Hafsun led the way through a lavish reception area lined in the round with carved benches surrounding a wool rug whose exquisitely detailed patterns suggested a foreign origin. Solomon guessed that it had been woven in Persia, but he wasn't an expert. It might have been India.

Bright colors danced along the white walls and off cream-colored floor tiles: yellow, green, blue, and violet. Solomon looked up and discovered the source of this marvelous effect, a stucco cupola supporting half a dozen stained-glass window panels.

Hafsun turned and smiled. He must have believed that the investigator was impressed by the trappings of success. He continued walking down a hallway towards the back of the house. Solomon followed and the two men shortly entered an elegant sitting room. Two oversized, upholstered chairs sat facing each other on either side of a round table made from deeply grained imported wood. There were no crucifixes or religious pictures on the walls, nothing to suggest that Hafsun wasn't a convert to Islam. Then again, he sat in chairs and not on pillows set upon the floor.

"Would you care for some refreshments?" he asked, and then he paused briefly for effect. "I'm sorry, what did you say your name was?"

"Levy. Solomon Levy," replied the investigator. "No thank you."

Hafsun clapped his hands loudly and the servant came running. "We'll have coffee."

The servant bowed submissively and quickly left the room. Another brief smile appeared on Hafsun's face. Clearly he was enjoying the encounter. "Please sit down," he said. Solomon took a seat and his host circled around the table and sat down opposite him. The investigator thought about how he should frame his first question, but the Muwallad spoke out before he had the opportunity to proceed.

"You probably think that I inherited this house," he began. "Actually I purchased this property using a part of the fortune that I've earned working in the spice trade. Like your people, I saw an opportunity to profit from the business."

Solomon nodded, knowing that many Jewish merchants had also grown wealthy importing spices into Andalusia. If they weren't deemed more valuable upon arrival in Tunisia, or Egypt, they were sent on to the high priced Andalusi markets.

"I maintain contacts in Alexandria where I keep a second home," the Muwallad continued. "It puts this house to shame I dare say. In

Egypt, I trade inexpensive pick-ups for spices like black pepper and nutmeg."

"'Pick-ups?'" inquired Solomon. He'd never heard the term.

"Sorry," laughed Hafsun. "Pick-ups are cloth made from waste silk spinnings."

"Oh, I see."

Solomon admired the Muwallad's ambitious nature. He often wished his father had been more successful in his chosen field. Toviyah Levy had also possessed a nose for business which is why he decided against joining the many Jewish artisans of Córdoba who had involved themselves in glass blowing and metal working. Like Hafsun, Solomon's father had entered the textile trade. He started a family enterprise in league with his two brothers. Only they weren't nearly as prosperous as their Muwallad competitor. They'd achieved a modicum of success with their dyeing and weaving business, but had never advanced their interests beyond the domestic marketplace.

Solomon had absolutely no interest in textiles and, least there be any doubt, he pursued his artistic and intellectual interests with a decided passion as soon as he realized that his family wasn't beyond sacrificing his creative energies and God-given talents to keep the business running in perpetuity. He had no intention of playing Isaac to his family's collective Abraham.

Fortunately, he had an ally. The opinion of his distinguished cousin Hasdai wasn't to be taken lightly so the family relented. Solomon's younger sister, Miriam, wasn't as lucky. She was brought into the fold as the firm's bookkeeper. She didn't seem to mind since the position allowed her to keep her finger on the pulse of the business.

Solomon refocused his attention on his host who seemed amused at his visitor's lack of concentration.

"What is the nature of your business, Levy?" asked Hafsun, abruptly changing the subject of the conversation "What is it that the Foreign Minister wants to know?"

"There's been talk that the Muwallads aren't happy," said Solomon. "Rumors are circulating that they may be inclined to revolt."

Hafsun jumped out of his seat to confront Solomon. His piercing eyes met the investigators and he stared in anger for a moment before speaking. Solomon could feel the man's discomfort and he understood his host was clearly upset.

"Who is it that says such things?" Hafsun demanded to know.

"I'm sorry," Solomon apologized. "I can't divulge that information."

The servant reappeared with a silver tray. There were two small cups of steaming coffee, a bowl of sugar, and a spoon resting upon its surface. The man set the tray down on a side table, bowed politely, and then he exited the room leaving the two men to themselves. The interruption had given Hafsun time to regain his composure. He gestured to Solomon.

"Are you sure you won't join me?"

"Actually, I think I will," the investigator replied.

Solomon was beginning to tire. He wasn't used to this present line of work. His energies were flagging and it was important that he concentrate. He also reasoned that a more sociable attitude might help him extend the interview so that he might learn something of value from Hafsun. He knew he'd already struck a nerve.

"Sugar," asked Hafsun as he made his way over to the side table.

"I think not."

Hafsun brought over a cup of the aromatic liquid and handed it to Solomon. He went back to the side table, spooned sugar into his cup, and took the coffee with him to his overstuffed chair. He sat down and turned to the investigator as the smile returned to his lips. He paused, clearing thinking about how much he wanted to reveal.

"I apologize for overreacting," he began. "Inciting revolt would be a treasonous act against the Caliph. I assure you I am quite content although I cannot speak for others. Why seek me out? Because of my great uncle? I admit he was a bit of a rogue and a thorn in the side of the Umayyads. Did he convert to Christianity. I don't know. Was he buried as a Christian? Again, I'm not sure. What people like to forget is that by the time he died, some thirty years ago, he had pledged his allegiance to the Umayyads."

"He returned to the flock?"

"You might say that," Hafsun agreed.

Solomon sipped his coffee before offering a response.

"Yes, we're aware of all of that," he replied soberly. The investigator felt like he was finally beginning to get the upper hand in his dealings with the Muwallad. He eyed Hafsun suspiciously, waiting for his host's response.

"Is the Caliph feeling insecure," asked Hafsun as he raised an eyebrow. "If so, he might look for traitors among his own family. I've heard rumors that someone in the royal family covets the throne. One of his nephews perhaps."

"Who might that be?" inquired Solomon as he stood up from his chair and took a final sip of his coffee. He waited, but there was no response from the Muwallad so he walked over to the side table and placed the ceramic cup down on the silver platter next to the bowl of sugar. He turned to Hafsun and repeated the question.

"Everybody knows that Umar abd Rahman and his clique of elitist Arabs are not happy with the Caliph's desire for equal opportunity for all regardless of any affiliation other than loyalty to his Caliphate."

Solomon reflected upon Hafsun's phrasing of "are not happy." Clearly not the words of a man who knew that the Caliph's nephew had been murdered. Either that, or the Muwallad was a good actor. The investigator wanted to tell him that Umar had been murdered so that he could gauge the response, but he knew this approach was unwise. Hasdai would have advised him to share as little as possible with any of the possible suspects.

"The Umayyads treated us cruelly," said Hafsun, the long pause in the conversation making him uncomfortable. He sighed deeply. "It would be understandable if some wished that harm would come to the Caliph. There may even be some who are in league with the northern Christians. As for me, I've made my peace."

The Muwallad rose from his chair without waiting for a response.

"If you have no further questions," he said with no hint of a smile.

Had the Muwallads, acting independently or in alliance with the northern Christians, enlisted the help of the Galician woman in a scheme to overthrow the Caliphate? It was a possibility. If they had, Solomon believed that they had done so without the help of Hafsun. He found the man's story credible and felt somewhat like an intruder in this house. Solomon disliked this part of his assignment, the need to question people he considered innocent and perhaps completely uninvolved in the events he was investigating. Solomon took a step towards the doorway.

"Wait please," requested Hafsun. He came around the table to speak to Solomon. "I don't care much for politics or religion. If rumors get around that I might be involved in some sort of plot against the Caliphate, whether they're true or not . . . well, you understand."

Solomon couldn't fault the man on that score since he was similarly inclined to minimize his involvement in those two spheres. And, yes, he understood that it might prove detrimental to the man's business to be linked to a conspiracy. The investigator saw a chance to make amends so he offered Hafsun a warm smile and then, quite spontaneously, he bowed politely.

"I'll be sure to tell the Foreign Minister that you cooperated."

Chapter 11

Solomon turned the door key clockwise inside an iron lock. He knew immediately that the lock had been tampered with and quickly realized that his front door had been left slightly ajar. This bothered him. Although his library of books held no apparent monetary value, they meant the world to the investigator. It was a part of his life that felt irreplaceable.

He pushed the door open and entered, expecting to find his comfortable living quarters just as he'd left them. A sudden shock and a feeling of violation and a sense of revulsion all washed over him at the same time as he found the living room in complete disarray. The furniture had been overturned and an important collection of books and papers lay scattered haphazardly on the tile floor in a room doubling as a library and private study.

"What the hell is going on," he cried aloud.

His hand reached instinctively inside his vest pocket and he withdrew the ring. As he rubbed its smooth gold surface between his fingertips he couldn't help but wonder if the shiny object he'd discovered in Umar's apartment might explain the chaos surrounding him. Is someone searching for this ring? he asked himself. Nothing appeared to be missing. Not that he owned much of value.

Solomon looked at the inscription inside the band before pocketing the object.

He made a beeline for the bedroom.

He flung open the door to his wardrobe and gazed silently at his most valuable possession. The gorgeous sea wool tunic, with a woven gold and iridescent fabric made from fibers harvested from a unique mollusk, had been a gift from the Caliph for past services rendered. His thoughts raced.

They would've stolen this precious coat to sell on the black market. It took many years to collect enough mollusk fibers to create even one tunic. This wasn't a random act of thievery. The perpetrators were definitely targeting him and he now believed Umar's ring held a clue to their identity. He wondered how the ring inside of his pocket fit into the mystery of Umar's murder.

He remembered that two men had been watching Sara's house. Had they returned to continue their surveillance after he'd left? He'd forgotten to look for them when he re-entered the street. Another lapse on his part. Maybe he wasn't cut out for this investigating business. Was it possible they'd tailed him to the Christian suburb and later ransacked his apartment while he'd spent time questioning the Christian woman Sara about her roommate? How did they know where he lived? So many unanswered questions.

He heard loud knocking at the front door.

This noise startled Solomon, but he managed to gather his wits. He closed the wardrobe door and left the bedroom to encounter the source of the unwelcomed interruption. Once inside the living room, he realized he'd left the front door wide open after entering the apartment. He looked out across the room, to the open doorway, and felt another invasion into his once predictable life. At the threshold, staring at the mess in total disbelief, stood Hasdai Shaprut.

HASDAI LOOKED SPENT. His slumped shoulders and sagging jawline revealed the extent of his travail. Touched by compassion,

Solomon felt an ache in his heart as his beleaguered cousin crossed the room while surveying the damage.

"What happened here?"

Solomon fished inside his pocket, withdrew the gold ring, and held it up for inspection.

"I think they were looking for this," he explained, though he knew full well he was just guessing. "I found it in Umar's apartment."

"You think it points to the murderer?"

"Perhaps it does," he replied. "I'm not sure yet."

Hasdai stepped forward and extended his outstretched arm with an upturned, open palm: "The ring will be safe with me."

"Why would I leave it with you?" Solomon asked. "That would deprive me of an opportunity to see if it fits on one of the Galician woman's fingers."

"Point well taken," acknowledged Hasdai. "I'm glad to know that you've finally come to terms with the importance of this assignment."

Solomon didn't bother to mention the strand of hair. It seemed inconsequential. He returned his desk back to an upright position and reset its chair while Hasdai helped by placing volumes, written in three languages, back on the shelves of a bookcase the intruders had left standing

"There's been a change of plans," Hasdai informed him. "You're leaving for Galicia in the morning."

Solomon stopped tidying up: "What," he responded incredulously. "Tomorrow morning?"

"We have no time to waste. News of Umar's murder is all over al-Zahra and it's spreading here to Córdoba. It makes our investigations more difficult."

Solomon replaced the cushions on his sofa while taking in the news.

"You're sending me to Galicia . . . to the savage north?"

"She's gone," said Hasdai.

"Gone?"

"Fled the city," responded Hasdai, thrusting out his arm and waving his hand in no particular direction. "We think she has an accomplice."

"How do you know this?" asked Solomon.

Hasdai ignored the question.

"You'll need an escort," declared Hasdai, "We've assigned you one of the Caliph's elite Slavic Guard, one of The Silent Ones, only this one's not silent like most of them. He didn't come to our land as an adult mercenary, but as a young slave. I'm told he has an ear for languages and he was hand-picked for this mission by General Naja, the Caliph's Chief of Staff.

"You're sending me with a single bodyguard?" Solomon grimaced.

"It will be difficult enough for you to keep a low profile in Galicia. This soldier is worth a dozen others and his Arabic is quite good. I believe he wants to emulate the General, become a Slavic freed slave and rise through the ranks to a position of eminence. We'll provide horses for the ride north. You may still be able to overtake her."

"Why don't you sit down, Hasdai," Solomon suggested. "You look exhausted."

The Caliph's Foreign Minister accepted the offer and sank down into the furniture's soft fabric while the nascent investigator continued restoring order to the room while updating his cousin on his progress.

"I've talked with Umar's wife, Nuzha. And, I've questioned his brother, Hasan," he reported. "They're not very cooperative. Ibn Hafsun seems unlikely, but the Galician woman's roommate Sara told me that our suspect was expecting a man very dear to her. He may have helped her to escape."

"I'm growing weary of politics, Solomon," Hasdai confessed, abruptly changing the subject of their conversation. "How's your Grandfather? I was preoccupied earlier in the day and forgot to ask."

"He's become more eccentric . . . possibly senile."

"We have asylums where he'll be treated with understanding and compassion."

"Yes, but the family considers that a last resort."

"I understand," Hasdai said with genuine sympathy. "Have you written any poetry lately?"

He keeps changing the subject on me, Solomon moaned to himself. This particular change evoked a touchy subject because the younger cousin felt unsure of himself in the presence of his former patron. Cousin Hasdai, benefactor of Jewish poets and scholars in communities throughout the world, deserved an honest response since his largess had once provided a small stipend allowing Solomon to continue pursuing his dream of publication. He'd often wondered if his cousin felt motivated by admiration or merely compelled by a generous kindness.

"I'm working on some poems inspired by my time in Granada."

"Perhaps the journey north will also stimulate your muse."

"The trek's poetic possibilities might prove more interesting than a search for a missing person."

"Try to summon more enthusiasm for this mission, Solomon," the Foreign Minister advised.

He wants me to summon more enthusiasm. He's not the only one growing weary of politics. Try to be fair, he told himself. Hasdai is a Jew working for a Muslim, albeit the most powerful Jew in Andalusia working for the most powerful Muslim in all of Europe. He reports directly to the esteemed ruler of the empire; but everybody knows their relationship goes deeper than religion or ethnicity.

Hasdai Shaprut might be Rahman III's most trusted friend. And, Solomon knew why. His older cousin's deep devotion to his community had demanded personal sacrifices. The Nasi led by example, serving the Caliph's desires because this pragmatic approach assured the well-being of his people. He gathered the leaders of his community together and rallied them around the sovereign. Although he served in a dependent position he was regarded as an equal by the Caliph's most trusted advisors. As Foreign Minister he had enough clarity of vision not to abuse his great influence but to use it for the benefit of the Caliphate. Solomon stood wondering if he could entertain such a selfless existence. He pressed his lips together. He knew which direction his loyalty, and his travel plans, were pointing. They would take him on a journey to the savage north.

"I don't lack enthusiasm, cousin," he finally responded. "It's just that there're so many suspects, all with good motives for killing Umar, that this Galician woman seems a longshot."

A wan smile was the Foreign Minister's only response.

Hasdai's a difficult man to read, Solomon thought to himself. He's dedicated to the Caliph, sometimes to the point of ruthlessness. At the same time he's sympathetic, encouraging those of us less talented than himself. The vagaries of human nature never ceased to amaze Solomon. Now this unanticipated assignment loomed. The far off reaches of Galicia where time for inspiration would be hard to come by in the midst of a murder investigation.

Tangerine, the ebony-faced African mercenary, peeked his head inside the front door, the safely of the Foreign Minister paramount on his mind. Solomon smiled to himself as he remembered anticipating the guard's role in the unfolding drama, and he was certain they would be seeing each other once more.

Hasdai regained his strength and rose from the couch to issue final instructions.

"Your *salibqui* escort will have a horse waiting at the Almodovar Gate one hour after sunrise. That signet ring on your finger remains the key to opening doors in what might otherwise be a hostile environment. My Christian friends, in León, have agreed to your safe passage through their kingdom."

"Problem is they don't have any control over murderers and thieves along pilgrim routes in their lands," Solomon replied, unable to hide his anxiety. "That concerns me."

"We're counting on you, Solomon."

"I know."

"I took the liberty of checking with Bishop Racemundo," Hasdai said, reaching inside his cloak and bringing out a rolled sheet of cotton paper stamped with an embossed wax seal. "You'll need this introductory letter to the Bishop of Santiago. You can also use it, if need be, when you encounter officials of the Caliphate as you journey north. Racemundo wishes you God-speed."

Hasdai handed his cousin the document, walked to the front door, and then he turned:

"Take the Mozarabic pilgrim route. It joins the Via de Plata route, in Mérida. Your guide has already been provided with a map."

Always one step ahead, the investigator couldn't help but thinking.

"I'll post a guard so your home is secure while you're away."

"Wait a minute," Solomon blurted out.

His appeal stopped Hasdai dead in his tracks.

"I almost forgot. I told the cart driver to meet me at the Roman Bridge at sunrise."

Hasdai thought about this minor complication for a moment.

"I'll see that somebody meets with him in the morning to tell him that we won't require his services until further notice."

The Foreign Minister disappeared through the doorway leaving Solomon alone to straighten up the apartment with little time to contemplate an uncertain future. It's all happening so fast, he thought. . . leaving at dawn and don't have a handle on this case . . . need to know more about Umar and the suspects: the brother, the wife, and especially the enigmatic Galician woman.

He found himself hoping his older cousin was discerning in the assessment of the Slavic mercenary he'd assigned to protect him on his impending journey to the savage north. The Foreign Minister claimed the man was intelligent and spoke almost fluent Arabic. One of 'The Silent Ones" He found it hard to believe.

Solomon felt lost and a little unsure of himself.

It was time to pay a visit to Layla.

Chapter 12

The room smelled of men, earthy hormonal warriors. At the far end of the barracks, a powerful soldier stood alone packing leather saddlebags with clothing and personal belongings. His *saqaliba* counterparts, kidnapped from Central and Eastern Europe or enslaved in wars to serve in the Caliph's army along with professional mercenaries for-hire, were watching and guarding the streets of -al Zahra and neighboring Córdoba. Most of these men were of Slavic origin, bought to Andalusia by Radanite Jewish merchants along the Volga trade route.

The Umayyad Caliph Muawiyah I initiated the practice when he settled an entire army of five thousand Slavic mercenaries inside of Syria in the mid-7th Century. Subsequent Andalusi Umayyad Emirs, and now self-anointed Caliph Rahman III , continued the practice on the Iberian Peninsula.

Jalal had been signaled out for a special mission, selected from among a thousand men known throughout the kingdom as "The Silent Ones." Most of these Slavic soldiers lived apart, demonstrating little interest in learning the Arabic language or assimilating themselves to the dominant Muslim culture.

Unlike his fellow soldiers, Jalal took a keen interest in learning the language of the Andalusi elite. He spent his weekends with an Ibero-Muslim woman, a convert to Islam, and she supported his aspirations. She tutored the warrior, teaching him the basics of reading and writing Arabic script as well as venturing out with him into the markets for a little practical application.

The blond-haired, muscular Slav took a smooth vellum map and secured it at the top of the full saddlebag. He had been told by General Naja, the Caliph's commander-in-chief and a fellow Slav, that the drawing had been prepared by the Foreign Minister. The map indicated the routes he must follow, the roads and trails that would take Jalal and his charge all the way to far-off Galicia, if that proved necessary. He was already familiar with some of the terrain having gone on maneuvers along the Camino Mozarabic earlier in the spring.

Jalal considered what else he might pack.

Warm clothes and his seal-skinned raincoat were a necessity.

What about his personal sword, he wondered. No, he'd leave the inscribed blade behind and give it to his woman for safe-keeping. He'd take a military issue sword instead. An extra pair of boots would have been welcomed, but he didn't have room for them.

Jalal wasn't worried about the dangers he might face on this mission. He possessed a strong and disciplined body and mind. Death had no hold on his emotions.

He wondered about the man he would be escorting.

All that he had been told was that the man had the absolute trust of the Foreign Minister and he was a translator who lived in the Jewish Quarter of Córdoba. A woman had vanished and their mission was to find her and bring her back to al-Zahra. Jalal had been ordered to keep these details to himself. He was also led to understand the assignment could be cancelled on a moment's notice. The soldier was told to await further instructions from the General.

Jalal closed the flap on the leather saddlebag and tied it down securely. He felt good about his future prospects. If the Caliph's Chief-of-Staff and the Foreign Minister were involved he'd likely be rewarded with a promotion to a higher rank if the mission proved successful. That was how Rahman III's Caliphate operated throughout the political administration and the armed forces and the society as a whole. By the middle of the 10th century, this ethic had helped create one of the greatest cosmopolitan kingdoms in the world.

More important, to Jalal's way of thinking, was the possibility of earning his freedom.

General Naja had begun his army career as a slave and had proven his worth. He'd been rewarded with promotion after promotion until he had achieved the ultimate honor when chosen as the supreme commander of the Caliph's army. Along the way, he had been granted his manumission. His wasn't an isolated case. The opportunity for a life of freedom was the carrot that enticed both men and women to proclaim, through words and deeds, their loyalty to the Umayyad Caliphate. Throughout Andalusia, slaves and eunuchs who had proven themselves trustworthy had risen to positions of power. Many had also been granted their freedom.

Jalal's spirits were buoyed by the thought he one day might be joining them.

He waited patiently, even hopefully, for his call to action.

Chapter 13

Twilight, an eternal marriage of day and night, found Solomon returning to the Muslim half of Córdoba. He reflected on the simplicity of the mathematics. Jews and Christians each lived in one quarter of the city, the Muslim victors possessed two quarters. His people's share hadn't changed since Roman times. The Christians, on the other hand, had basically been displaced. They'd lost half a city during the fateful invasion of 711. This geographical distribution mirrored a populace about one-half Muslim and the other half a mixture of Jews, Christians, and foreigners. Of course, the boundary lines weren't that easily defined. Some neighborhoods were more integrated than others.

Like the one Solomon was visiting when he turned down an urban alley between tall, two-storied buildings designed to block out the scorching summer sun. The narrowness of these streets magnified the intimacy of sound which led to heightened conversations, only the investigator now walked alone.

A short block later, Solomon arrived at a wooden gate. Beyond it lay the courtyard leading to Layla's house. He found the latch and smiled to himself. She never locks the gate, trusting soul. Stepping quietly through the cool, green courtyard where brilliant red geraniums bloomed in terra cotta pots, he gathered his thoughts and walked up to a door painted a bright indigo. He rapped four times in succession and wondered if, after such a long absence, she'd remember their secret code.

The door swung open: "I've been expecting you, Solomon."

"What?"

"Bad news travels as fast as good."

"How did you find out so soon?"

"Come inside," cooed Layla, "It's getting cold."

She closed the door and locked the latch. She wasn't that trusting, definitely not naïve. Solomon eyed the way she swayed her hips as he followed her into a well-appointed living room where scented candles illuminated the impending darkness, their low flames casting shadows along brightly painted walls. Everything about her seemed unique, especially the soft, sultry sound of her voice.

She hadn't changed her look, hair still jet black with subtle highlights of orange-red henna dye, pulled back off her forehead and woven into a thick braid falling down her backside to her waist where an indigo ribbon was deftly tied around three inches of hair splayed out at the end of the plait.

Layla's tasteful tattoos, stylized arabesques also painted with henna, adorned her index fingers and the back of her hands a quarter of the way up her smooth-skinned forearms. There were more designs along the top of her small feet and on the sides of her delicate ankles.

More impressive were intricate, swirling lines dancing subtly across her forehead above dreamy indigo eyes. They created a visual spell as they continued downwards before coming to an end on her prominent cheek bones. Layla's body had been transformed into a work of art and Solomon knew it had taken her hours to produce the mesmerizing effect.

He remembered getting lost in those patterns and losing track of time. He remembered the dress, long flowing folds of silk dyed indigo to match eyes accentuated with black kohl eyeliner, the neckline of this garment cut in the shape of a keyhole, Layla's trimmed lower than most with fabric as smooth to his touch as her soft, supple skin.

More intimate memories rose to the surface of his mind: their first meeting when he'd begun his search for the lost manuscript, her connections with underworld characters and book dealers, some respectable, others not so scrupulous. It might seem unlikely that Solomon had a courtesan as a confidant, but their introduction had been arranged by Hasdai to help expedite that quest.

Solomon had found her worldliness a bit scary at first, but also attractive . . . seductive even. So, why had he resisted her advances?

So much time since he'd been here in her nest, yet everything felt as familiar as a warm sunny day. The deep-cushioned sofa and walls painted in popular vermillion hues mimicking her personality, passionate yet comfortable. Exquisite attention to detail revealed a sense of grace offset by stylistic nuances. Here he was again, gazing at her left ankle where half a dozen gold chains jingled a subtle rhythm, in time with her footsteps, while she walked as always in bare feet.

Solomon didn't have time to dwell on more particulars.

"How did you know I'm investigating Umar's murder?"

"Friends in high places tell me things." Layla reminded him. "Al-Zahra doesn't keep many secrets."

"That's why you've chosen to remain in Córdoba?"

The courtesan offered a smile in-lieu of an answer. Solomon had long since given up trying to understand how Layla knew so much. Her friends in high places might even include the Caliph. He knew only one thing for certain. He needed her help.

"I've got witnesses and some possible motives, but I can't prove a thing," he confessed. "Can you shed some light on Umar? Why any of this might make sense?"

Layla reached out and took Solomon by the hand.

"Come, sit down."

She led him over to the sofa and sat him down. Releasing his hand, she joined him on the soft cushions and moved in closer, so close he felt her hips rubbing up against his own, her flesh pressing into his. He felt a charge of energy as a strong current surged through his body. He took a deep breath and swallowed hard, hoping to hide his excitement and obvious discomfort.

"Are you hungry?"

"I had grilled vegetables and couscous from a street vendor," he replied. "Anyway, I can't stay long."

Layla picked up her cue and returned to the investigator's original question:

"Umar could be charming, but he also liked to play rough."

"What do you mean?"

"A little too much wine and he turned aggressive, sometimes violent."

Solomon had always thought of sexual intimacy as a tender sentiment, albeit capable of rising to heights of intense passion and sensuality. But he wasn't totally naive.

"Was he a sadist?"

"I've heard Rahman III is worse. It's just a rumor, but they say a slave girl who showed displeasure at being kissed by the Caliph ended up permanently disfigured. He had his eunuch's burn her face with a candle." Layla patted Solomon's knee and gave it a squeeze. "There's more. Another time at al-Na'ura, the Caliph's villa on the river, his executioner, Abu 'Imran Yahya, was called into a room where eunuchs were holding a young woman begging for mercy. The Caliph shouted insults at her and then ordered the executioner to behead the woman."

Leave it to Layla to pass on gossip's most salient details. She had a reputation as a raconteur and relished shocking her audiences with disturbing stories. A heartfelt laugh seemed to rise up from out of her belly, making Solomon even more uncomfortable.

She thought him completely naive and inexperienced in the ways of the world. She'd told him that more than once, but he never knew when she was being serious with him or just kidding. She'd also said his innocence was what made him so appealing to her. That and his huge brown eyes and long lashes.

"What's so funny?" Solomon asked.

"When I told you about the Caliph your eyes grew as big as watermelons."

Solomon grumbled.

And Layla delighted in her teasing.

SOLOMON DISCOUNTED most of the stories he'd heard about the Caliph. Powerful men are often the subject of jealous innuendos and countless fabricated tales, he reasoned. Only one story he'd heard interested him because it actually seemed plausible. It also shed light on Caliph Rahman III's chosen successor and contained little shock value.

Given these circumstances, he found it difficult not to believe the story of Marjan.

He'd met this woman socially and understood that she was originally a Christian slave. They had both attended official gatherings and Solomon found her refined and resourceful. Her status as one of the Caliph's four legal wives gave the story added credence. He knew that she'd emerged as Rahman III's favorite through a bit of clever trickery.

The Caliph had once, the story was told, decided to spend the night with Fatima, a wife of noble lineage known as "the Great Lady." Marjan told Fatima she wanted to spend that night with their husband and offered a great sum of money to buy the opportunity. Fatima agreed, but she then made the fatal mistake of signing a document recording the sale.

Marjan spent the night with the Caliph.

The following morning she showed him the document.

From that day forward the ruler refused to visit Fatima and her status was substantially weakened. Marjan became the Caliph's favorite wife and the recipient of lavish rewards. She bore Rahman III two daughters and three sons. One of the boys, the wonder child al-Hakam, appeared destined to inherit the Caliphate.

"Maybe all the stories you tell are exaggerated, Layla." Solomon contended.

"Who knows what goes on in those villas in al-Zahra and those along the river?" she asked bluntly. "Do you?"

Her pointed barb carried deeper implications, revealing a darkness he rarely considered.

"You dance at their parties," he groused. "You tell me what goes on."

Layla raised a slender finger to his lips.

"Hush," she whispered. "No need to get angry, darling . . ."

It was his turn to laugh. Solomon tucked his chin down towards his chest and quietly chuckled to himself lest he offend his hostess. He found arguing with Layla difficult. Totally disarming, Layla always had him at a disadvantage. He often felt envious of her worldliness and the depth of her emotional intelligence. He didn't know how the former slave girl had secured her manumission or the details of how she'd gained her freedom. He'd always considered the question too delicate to broach. Not wanting to open old wounds the subject might engender, Solomon took a cautious approach to this aspect of their relationship.

He knew Layla meant "night" in Arabic, and she almost always performed at night.

Maybe her parents had felt an intimation. If they were still alive, they might be surprised to learn that she attended classes during the day at The University of Córdoba. It wasn't hard for him to imagine Layla flirting with her professors and shocking them with her uninhibited approach to life. Her personal history must have made her unique among the eleven thousand students pursuing a higher education at one of the world's most prestigious institutions.

For independent women like Layla, attending classes at the University would've been as natural as breathing oxygen. In Andalusia, almost all of the gynecologists and pediatricians were female graduates of Córdoba's internationally renowned Medical School, rivaled in Europe only by the School of Medicine at Montpellier, in southern France. Both institutions, at the forefront of science based 10th century medical knowledge, also maintained impressive research faculties.

Solomon knew one reason for employing women doctors to attend to childbirth and early childhood diseases lay in male jealousy resulting from the custom of maintaining harems. The desire for privacy, and the need to exclude competing men, meant limiting contact to desirables. More important, in Solomon's estimation, were empathy and physical dexterity. He'd once listened with rapt attention as a Jewish gynecologist described her childhood obsession. As a young girl she loved dissecting dead chickens.

Layla's aspirations, fostered by the cultural milieu, didn't surprise him.

"Have you been listening to me, Solomon?" she asked, poking him hard in the ribs.

"I'm sorry," he apologized. "I got caught up in my own thoughts."

"What kind of thoughts, darling?"

"Nothing important," he said, side-stepping her inquiry. "I'll tell you later."

"I answered your question, Solomon When I dance at parties, the outer world almost ceases to exist. I'm aware that men stare at me, they probably mentally undress me. That's their problem. When I dance nothing else matters. Some may find me uninhibited and exhibitionistic," she continued while waving her hand in the air with a distinct flourish. "That doesn't bother me because I pretend nobody's watching. When I finish performing, I'm very particular about whom I relate to. I usually leave the parties early, but others don't. They always ask me to stay. I always refuse. Do you know why?"

Solomon shrugged his shoulders, thereby admitting his ignorance.

"They often have wild parties," she told him. "Sometimes they get completely out of control and I don't fancy group participation."

Layla's revelation disarmed Solomon and left him speechless. She knows of the darkness, but its allure doesn't entice her into giving up her hard earned individuality. This thought helped him find his own moral bearings.

"The last person known to have seen Umar alive is a Galician singer," he informed his confidant.

"Sexual intimacy with Umar often resulted in lavish rewards."

"I don't think this Galician woman was the type."

"You know nothing about her, Solomon."

"A little," he hedged. "I spoke with her roommate."

"Galicia, huh," quipped Layla. "I'll bet they're sending you north to track her down and bring her back."

"You're uncanny."

Solomon sometimes wondered if Layla possessed mediumistic powers. He knew she'd experienced many hardships at an early age, but behind her mask of bravado he sensed a sensitive woman. Take a gentle approach, he told himself. Appreciate this special friend, and don't ever forget that softness overcomes hardness just as water wears down the most impermeable rocks.

As much as he needed Layla's friendship, Solomon desired it as well. He valued her role as a guide to various disreputable venues and also appreciated her insights into a wide spectrum of human nature.

Better yet, her fun loving nature offered a practical counterpoint to his sometimes serious disposition, thereby creating a shared affability.

They genuinely enjoyed each other's company.

He often wondered if she loved him. Maybe it was just the idea of him. They were so different. Layla was a virgin in the original sense of the word, a woman who didn't need a man to support her. She possessed an independent streak although it was very clear that she enjoyed the company of men. Some men, at least. Solomon knew that she was very selective about whom she offered her friendship to. Hadn't she just told him so.

Layla rose from the sofa, hips swaying slowly and sensuously as the anklets produced a rhythmic tempo. Indigo eyes gazed briefly into brown. She circled the room and the cadence increased as she blew out all but one solitary candle, fashioning a more intimate ambience.

SOLOMON'S FAVORITE courtesan had created a dreamlike world built by the mysterious light of a single candle. Its flickering revealed that a gentle draft of air had entered the room. Wavering shadows conveyed the impulses of the night as Layla quietly returned to the couch and lowered herself down beside the investigator. Only this time she moved in closer.

In the soft candlelight, Solomon began to relax. He took a breath, inhaling Layla's perfume, and the fragrance of roses transported him as his mind began to wander, a victim of unwelcome pressure seeking escape. Incense wafted in the air. He knew it burned, pungent yet sweet, in Layla's bedroom. Olfactory overload weakened his defenses, giving rise to sensuous thoughts.

Solomon felt slightly unnerved and a bit overwhelmed.

He'd only once seen Layla's boudoir. At the end of one long, agreeable evening, she'd invited him to spend the night. He'd had second thoughts so he declined her generous invitation, but only at the last minute. He often wondered if he'd made a mistake.

Layla decided to give the reluctant translator yet another opportunity.

"You'll be gone a long time," Layla whispered as she inched ever nearer. "I can ease your burden."

Her attractive offer made it difficult for him to resist her advances. It would've been easy to go bed with Layla, but in the aftermath she might have desired more from their relationship and he might have wanted less. Although Solomon wanted to press his body against hers and feel the wonder of her warm, inviting flesh, he still wasn't sure they were meant to be lovers. And he didn't want to risk losing a friend and a confidant.

"Don't tempt me."

"But I want to tempt you, darling."

"You're making it hard."

"I want to make it hard," she laughed.

Was the dual meaning intended, he wondered. Of course it was, and this was his conundrum: Solomon wasn't naturally inclined towards asceticism, yet he didn't want to spend *that* night with Layla. What a dilemma. His inner nature inclined him towards a sensuous and deeply felt enjoyment of the natural world.

This appreciation of the prosaic aspects of life was a trait he shared in common with his hostess, an unspoken bond. They both valued the importance of small details: texture, color, scent, verbal nuance, and a wide range of other sensory particulars. Solomon found it a necessary component in his poetry and translations. These aspects of everyday life, the kind most people habitually dismissed, intrigued his poetic soul.

Layla had helped him cope with the changes his new life demanded following that initial investigation into the whereabouts of a lost, *read* stolen, manuscript. When he felt doubtful she listened to him and encouraged him to continue writing poetry. She served as a sounding board and soul mate. They'd grown close, yet he still felt uncertain about their long-range prospects.

Layla's sisterly side, the willing helpmate, had filled a void in his once solitary life. He knew she felt eager to initiate him into mysteries deeper than the sophomoric relationships he'd accepted with woman at the University and during his subsequent professional life, but he wasn't quite ready to take the plunge.

He began to understand why this was so when his mind turned to thoughts of Sara, the Christian woman he'd encountered earlier in the day. He suspected she might be part of the equation. She might be why he'd declined Layla's invitation. Layla's was a dancer, a storyteller, and an actress. How could he know when she wasn't onstage, not playing a role. Sara, on the other hand, seemed genuine and sincere and guileless.

Then again, maybe that's what Solomon wanted to believe. Maybe he'd read her incorrectly. Maybe Sara had also woven a spell and all his thoughts about her were illusionary. Perhaps he just wasn't ready to cling to a new lover, any lover. Frustrated and recognizing his confused state of mind, it seemed the time was ripe to depart.

Solomon rose from the sofa and smiled down at Layla.

"I can't stay." he told her as he walked to the door.

The dancer forced a weak smile, but he knew that look of disappointment. It stung his heart. He paused at the threshold to reconsider. She must've sensed an opportunity because she stood up and followed him to the doorway. Please don't make this more difficult, he said to himself.

As if reading his mind and knowing the anxiety he felt in his heart, Layla quietly encircled her arms around his neck, stood up on tip-toes, and planted her soft lips against his cheek. He found that this soulful, platonic, and heartfelt expression brought him emotional satisfaction.

"Take care, Solomon." Layla advised. "May you be safe from every harm."

This was the second time he'd heard the sentiment that day. It echoed similar words he'd heard earlier at Sara's house. He found the coincidence unsettling, so unnerving that Solomon couldn't find any words to offer Layla as a response.

A half-hearted smile and out the door he went. Through the courtyard, past the potted geraniums, quickly closing the gate behind himself. Street lights illuminated the pavement. He knew sleep would be impossible.

His mind was racing. So many unanswered questions and so much left to do before his journey north. He found himself nervous and excited and fearful all at the same time. During the course of that one day his life had become a mass of confusion and he wasn't really sure about anything.

Solomon decided to walk the wall, a chance to mull things over.

Chapter 14

A full moon illuminated the Roman Wall surrounding Córdoba as Solomon strolled along a path wide enough for two chariots to pass each other. Built as fortifications after the Romans captured the city, in 206 BCE, the ten-foot high wall completely enveloped the urban nucleus, a protective measure inspired by a combination of practicality and paranoia, and one providing the reluctant investigator a rare view of an ancient city first settled by Carthaginians centuries before the birth of Christ.

He felt too tired to circle the entire wall.

He began his trek on the southeast perimeter near the closest of the city's arched gateways. A nearby aqueduct brought water down from the Sierra Morena mountains and distributed the life giving liquid through iron pipes for the city and its twenty-three suburbs, making possible the development of a world attuned to sounds of water: gurgling fountains, irrigated lush gardens, and the healing waters filling hundreds of public baths.

Since it took an hour to circle the entire wall Solomon dispensed with the north side where the Old City, once safely ensconced within the barricade, spilled out into surrounding suburbs, residential areas with mosques, markets, and industrial zones devoted to weaving, leatherwork, jewelry making, furniture making, gardens, bath houses, and cemeteries. These spread imperceptibly into a countryside of market gardens, and the *munyas* or country villas of the wealthy, situated along the southern slopes of the mountains, far below a rich mining region which provided the city with important reserves of coal, lead, and zinc.

Solomon passed a semi-circular tower and continued south towards the river.

Sailing in the night, along the Guadalquivir, boats laced with glowing lanterns resembled fireflies gliding along a liquid silver ribbon. Moonlight illuminated the sides and rooftops of the Great Mosque, an almost mystical presence in this European Islamic city. From its minaret, a soothing voice sang the 'Isha, an evening call to prayer, the final summons of the day. Before retiring for the night, Córdoba's devout Muslims took time to honor God's presence and to pray for guidance, mercy, and forgiveness.

Five calls to prayer were evoked daily from just before sunrise until sunset.

Solomon first heard these enchantments as a young child. With no context in which to associate the words drifting into the porches of his ears, he simply enjoyed sweet, melodious sounds, like echoes in a canyon, an appeal he later learned was intended to remind listeners to acknowledge a mysterious presence, both hidden and manifest. As an adult, he still preferred releasing these words from their religious references so he might enjoy the evocative resonances of pure sound.

He walked on, his attention directed across the Guadalquivir. Along the river's southern bank, where the Roman Bridge spanned the waterway, the area remained cleared of settlement. It lay like a fallow field since the Córdoba revolt of 818, when many of the Christian insurgents who revolted against Emir al-Hakem were crucified during an uprising crushed by three days of massacre and brutal pillage.

Many of the survivors chose a self-imposed exile, most relocating north to the Christian enclave in Zamora, where these followers of Christ became important middlemen in the lucrative olive oil trade connecting the two disparate cultures.

The former Secunda district had been razed and left in ruins as a necropolis. Times had surely changed, mused the investigator as he contemplated a sparsely inhabited section containing an old cemetery, a leper colony, and a few scattered *munyas*. The most celebrated of these villas was *Munyat Nasr*, attractively situated along the banks of the river.

Originally built by one of the counsellors of Emir Rahman II, a hundred years earlier, it became the home of the famous musician and courtier Ziryab, "Blackbird" as he was known among his inner circle and acolytes. By the 10th century the villa was back in the hands of the Caliph who often used it to house visiting notables like the distinguished envoys arriving from Constantinople a year earlier, in 949, with a priceless botanical manuscript.

Solomon's walking meditation allowed him to stop and pause briefly, turning inward to once again contemplate Umar's murder and the nature of evil it revealed. It must be a contagious disease, he reasoned, spreading its disastrous effects subliminally. Those inclined to that particular form of madness, the acting out of their destructive fantasies, drew strength from the manifestations of uncontrolled impulses by others of their ilk. Lost souls creating a world of pain and fear and terror.

Not a pleasant thought he reflected as he resumed his stroll.

Beyond the Great Mosque, on the far side of the Roman Bridge, a dozen mills employed waterwheels, taking advantage of the river and the power of its currents to grind grains into flour to feed a growing, hungry populace of Ibero-Romans who were converting to Islam in droves. Solomon's eyes focused on a mill called *Albolafia*. Earlier that day, when he'd entered the walled city, he heard it creaking and straining as its massive wheel pumped water from the river to irrigate the lush gardens of the Alcazar.

This old royal citadel opened to his view.

The Alcazar once functioned as the political center of Andalusia long before the vision of Madinat al-Zahra entered Caliph Rahman III's fertile imagination. The impressive, old fortress contained various palaces built by previous Umayyad rulers along with a variety of buildings serving different administrative functions, the Umayyad family cemetery, and the exclusive Caliphal baths inherited from the Romans.

Its six gates included the Bab al-Sudda, near which the administrative bureaus were located and executions took place. Solomon soon spied the terrace built above this gate, a platform from which the Caliph viewed the esplanade between the Alcazar and the river. Along this route parades were still celebrated and the corpses of enemies exhibited for public viewing. After his unprompted mind conjured up the disturbing image of decapitated heads hanging from the Bab al-Sudda, he flinched and hurried onwards.

Al-Zahra glimmered in the distance at the far end of a wide boulevard winding its way three miles south, curvaceous as a sinuous snake. This roadway was illuminated by street lamps, dazzling globes glowing like a loose string of luminous pearls while the new city's dark corridors of power continued to suck Solomon into a maelstrom beyond his control.

He felt slightly lost despite an innate confidence in his own abilities, incapable of escaping this fateful development in his life and unable to put any distance between his emotions and the sense of despair Umar's death stirred in his mortal soul.

Compelled to look reality in the face, he realized he'd been compromised, pressed into an assignment he originally wanted to refuse. But, there was so much at stake: the future of the Umayyad Caliphate, the well-being of his own people, and an opportunity to realize his deep and private, selfish yearning to write poetry full time.

At least with the lost manuscript an intellectual challenge presented itself. This unexpected mission and a potential search for an enigmatic, missing woman, in the far off reaches of the savage north, hit Solomon straight in the gut. Even worse, it felt more like a punch below the belt.

Why so glum? he asked himself.

These circumstances provided a rare opportunity to consolidate his good fortune.

Can he be trusted? Solomon wondered if the bodyguard might have been enlisted to spy on him and send reports back to Hasdai and the Caliph.

He breathed a deep sigh, but it brought no relief.

Stop this internal chatter and these infernal questions, he admonished himself. He would have to conquer his irrational fears if he wanted to succeed in the investigation. He'd experienced a similar predicament, once before, and emerged unscathed. But that was a manuscript, he reminded himself.

His walk brought him to the Almodovar Gate.

Outside these gated walls, buried in the hallowed ground of the Jewish cemetery, lay his deceased ancestors, relatives who had once led vibrant lives inside the walled city, generations who had come and gone for almost a thousand years, since the time of the fall of Jerusalem, seventy years after the birth of the Christ.

Solomon hoped he wouldn't be joining them anytime soon.

GAZING OUT ACROSS HIS beloved Córdoba, Solomon marveled at the city's hold on his soul. This city, the jewel of Europe, sparkled inside his imagination like a multi-faceted diamond: intricate, comforting, iridescent, alluring, enchanting, refined, historic, and so much more. He suspected others entertained these sentiments, but he wondered if their emotional involvement ran as deep as his own. The vast, yet intimate city spread out before him like a languid lover. His view included the city inside the old Roman walls and the mushrooming city suburbs beyond.

Sweet Córdoba, home to a hundred thousand souls. More populous, prosperous, and artistic and scientifically brilliant than any city in Europe and perhaps the entire world.

Grandmother Córdoba, once home to prehistoric peoples and Carthaginians.

Mother Córdoba, lavishing gifts upon her spoiled children: luxurious villas along the banks of the Guadalquivir with indoor plumbing; patios, gardens and fountains creating oases of protection against urban congestion and the blistering summers; cool, narrow, paved streets known for their cleanliness and lit at night to dispel the darkness after sunset; five hundred public baths, scattered throughout the city, promoting personal hygiene and bodily cleanliness; trash disposal containers situated at strategic locations throughout the city and massive sewers used to reduce human waste; impressive libraries, both public and private, containing hundreds of thousands of volumes; bookstores to encourage literacy; public schools fostering the mandatory education of children and young adults (as well as private Jewish and Christian academies), the most accessible and distinguished University in Europe; and, tens of thousands of dwellings to house the beneficiaries of all this affluence.

Compassionate sisterly Córdoba, a helpmate offering hospitals and asylums to care for the sick, feeble, and aged, with well-regulated pharmacies dispensing life-saving herbs, tinctures, barks, twigs, and prescribed medicines made from crushed minerals.

Divine Córdoba, promoting the spiritual well-being of the city with her five hundred mosques as well as countless cathedrals, churches, and synagogues inspiring peaceful co-existence among an assortment of religious affiliations and multiple ethnicities.

Industrious Córdoba, whose denizens enjoyed access to an unsurpassed variety of goods, a seemingly endless supply provided by domestic and import markets. A vast, enterprising city where thousands of looms clattered, spinning cloth into cotton, linen, silk, and brocade, velvets, and felts; where world famous leather craftsmen created everything from shoes to wall-sized tapestries; where ceramic and porcelain warehouses sold exquisite merchandise; where glass-blowers, ivory carvers, bookbinders, woodworkers, and metalworkers flourished. A thriving metropolis where street markets offered shoppers a cornucopia of imported goods, dominated by those arriving from China and India: textiles and teas, spices and dyes.

Generous, abundant Córdoba whose variety of agricultural goods, introduced by the new regime, was astonishing: oranges, lemons, limes, watermelons, figs, pomegranates, almonds, bananas, artichokes, eggplants, spinach, sugar-cane, and more. Herbs and spices abounded: cumin, caraway, coriander, fennel, mint, parsley, cloves and nutmeg. There were cash crops such as cotton, flax and silk. Vast wheat fields fed a growing, healthy populace feasting on dietary staples like couscous and pasta.

Córdoba, the lover, opening her arms wide to embrace the artistic and learned elite of the world, drawing them to her bosom and nourishing them with unsurpassed mental and monetary stimuli. All valued and appreciated for their contributions to the cultural life of Andalusia and for giving the Umayyad Caliphate a reputation renowned throughout the world as the intellectual and scientific center of the European Continent. Córdoba, lover of poets and patrons, a city where the finest wordsmiths and translators were honored with lavish stipends from the Caliph's personal coffers as well as private patronage.

Regal Córdoba, Queen of Europe, one of the greatest cities of its epoch, rivaled in splendor only by Baghdad, Constantinople, and upstart al-Zahra. A magnet attracting intelligent, industrious, and intrepid individuals from London to Paris, from Mumbai to Beijing. They came and went, attracted by the magnificence of Rahman III's court and the opportunities for upward mobility, increased social status, successful careers, and the accumulation of wealth. Solomon, and many of his educated, well-traveled countrymen understood this splendor existed at a time when most of Europe wallowed in filth and illiteracy. It was the same throughout much of the world, and this only served to enhance the city's reputation and its allure for citizens and outsiders alike.

Solomon guessed he'd never unravel the mystery of Córdoba, and this didn't seem to matter. He found his love affair with the city emotionally and physically satisfying and he never ceased enjoying an aesthetic appreciation of her bounteous and pleasing nature. He told himself maybe one day he could shape these impressions into a poem to satisfy his secular soul, composing a paean to his beloved city.

Maybe one day if he actually returned safely from the savage north.

NOT SURE IF HE WOULD return to the city he cherished, Solomon found himself soaking up impressions like a sponge. The crisp night air, the aroma of grilled mutton wafting up from below the wall, the sounds of footsteps as guards policed the streets providing security to local residents, all these sensations filtered through a full moon's soft yellow lens.

That same moon, floating directly overhead in a cloudless sky, cast a magic spell over the city; but, Solomon remembered how the dark power of the moon becomes strongest when the lunar sphere is wholly round. He thought of how passions and crime rise like ocean tides when this phase of the moon positions it directly opposite the sun, its waning inevitable. An ominous sign or merely a coincidence, his journey beginning during this inauspicious time.

Solomon wondered if any of these thoughts would be useful to him in the savage north. He possessed too many reservations with too little time to analyze his options or properly prepare for the journey. Even though he tried to muster his courage for the morning departure, he still felt uneasy. Descending the steps of the Roman Wall, he wondered if he could sleep.

LYING IN BED WITH EYES half-shut, Solomon's thoughts turned to Sara. He found the Christian woman attractive and her spirituality struck him as quite refreshing, almost soothing to his earthy, profane soul. He began to speculate about the roommate, the mysterious Galician woman. What was her name . . . Lia? Would he find her attractive as well? Would he find her at all? Knowing the need for sleep was imperative, he turned over on his side and closed his eyes.

He settled deeper into his bed, but his sense of anticipation made it impossible for him to doze off. What if he did find her, this Galician woman who seemed more apparition than substance. Umar's death had already overturned the generally peaceful social reality and Solomon wasn't sure he could maintain his composure in this whirlwind of events or find any semblance of inner peace amidst the storm of outer happenings.

"Learn Latin," Hasdai had counseled him. "It will open many doors for you." It had, but sometimes he wished he hadn't listened to his elder cousin. His knowledge of Latin was opening a door he'd just as soon keep closed, a door leading into the unknown.

Solomon's feelings were conflicted.

How could a part of him dread the journey to Galicia while another part of him experienced a compelling sense of excitement about this opportunity for adventure? Perhaps his mind was filled with too many preconceptions about the savage north while his heart felt a certain receptiveness towards this unexplored mystery. Layla always advised him to follow his heart. He decided to take her advice.

A new mystery had taken hold of his imagination.

Solomon finally gave in to mental fatigue. He slept for a few hours and then woke up to the night. More thoughts ran through his rattled mind. Better pack warm clothes for the journey north and don't forget your oiled silk rain-proof cloak. It will be cold and dank and dreary. He heard it rained in the lands of the Peninsula's northwest even during the month of May. Might as well leave his cork-soled shoes behind. They would be of little use in the misty, wet north.

All very shadowy, he told himself. Especially this vanished woman. He wondered if the assignment would take him closer to her or further away. He so desired sleep. Embrace emptiness, he repeated over and over in an effort to entice the words to melt into his soul. Embrace emptiness he kept saying to himself. Allow all worldly concerns to drop away. Easier to tell himself what he needed to do than to accomplish the deed.

The word empty entered Solomon's mind, only this time as a visual presence. He saw each of the five letters lined up in the correct sequence before they began drifting apart from each other. Soon the letters were floating off into space in no discernable order. Then, the letters began to expand and dissolve, leaving behind only a trail of vapor. Solomon's head sank into the soft pillow.

The nascent investigator sighed and then he drifted down into a deep dreamless sleep.

Chapter 15

They rode together along a narrow path under a cloudless blue sky. The Slav appeared familiar with the rugged terrain so Solomon allowed him to take the lead. His new acquaintance guided a powerful, white Andalusian mare up a steep incline while leading a sure-footed Majorcan mule packed with two-week's provisions,.

The investigator followed sitting astride a second mare, the animal Muslims preferred for warfare because stallions had proven less dependable during the intense heat of battle. Though high-spirited, he found no difficulty controlling the movements of his chestnut colored mount.

Solomon wasn't an inexperienced rider, and he had plenty of recent practice on his search for the lost manuscript, a botanical work by Greek physician Dioscorides detailing the medicinal use of herbs in the ancient world. That assignment took him down to Málaga, on the Mediterranean Coast, and then inland to the city of Granada and the home of an old book collector living in the ageless Jewish quarter.

He remained behind, content to let his bodyguard continue in the lead. They'd left Córdoba behind hours ago. Not a pilgrim in sight since entering the Camino Mozarabic pilgrim route to Mérida, a trail whose origins lay to the southeast in the aforementioned Granada. As the investigator learned on his earlier mission, the city was noted for its abundance of pomegranates.

For citizens of Granada and the surrounding countryside there was more to the picture than just the growing of their glorious pomegranates. The fruit, with its hundreds of seeds, symbolized fertility and abundance which is how they viewed the land itself and the local water and the climate. For Muslims, the fruit was also a symbol of beauty for it was said to give attractiveness to those who ate it.

Solomon had eaten more than his share while engaged in his first assignment. During that mission Solomon had also been rewarded with a stay in the port city of Málaga where he had an opportunity to explore and enjoy "the Old Roman Sea," spending time on a shoreline that robust Empire had once taken sole possession of.

The Camino Mozarabic offered Granada's Catholic sojourners, a tiny minority of the city's population, a shortcut through mountains leading them to Santiago de Compestela where they hoped to encounter a sacred relic, the remains of St. James the Apostle. Legend has it that St. James preached the gospel in Iberia as well as in the Holy Land. After his martyrdom, at the hands of Herod Agrippa, his disciples carried his body by sea to Iberia, landed at Padron on the coast of Galicia, and took him inland for burial at Santiago de Compestela.

The trail from Granada angled northwest instead of directing these pilgrims due west to Seville, the more popular rallying point for beginning the six hundred and fifty mile test of faith and endurance. It offered Córdoba's Christians an alternative route as well, lopping miles off the arduous trek to Galicia.

For Solomon, and his bodyguard, it provided a necessary shortcut, one that increased their hopes of overtaking the Galician woman. He still couldn't convince himself to call her Lia. That could wait until he met her in the flesh.

Still no sign of pilgrims as they continued on a deserted trail.

Solomon remained at the back of the tiny caravan, bringing up the rear. This gave him an opportunity to observe his mercenary escort. The Slav wears his hair long, unlike Arabs or eunuchs, he noticed. He wondered if this was encouraged by the military, but he doubted it. Maybe the soldier was intent on expressing his inner nature, and his superiors turned a blind eye. Hasdai indicated the man was held in high regard. If he did possess an independent streak the two of them might share something in common.

Solomon began to sense he was traveling with a kindred spirit.

Perhaps they would make a good team after all.

He studied his companion's military attire. The Slav's tunic, tight in the body and sleeves, included a full skirt ending at the knees. Over this, he wore a short red cloak, a style the military borrowed from Christians. Wool leggings were tucked into tall riding boots made from oiled leather, a kind of leatherwork which made Córdoba's artisans famous even before the arrival of the Muslims.

The mercenary didn't wield a scimitar, but rather a broad, heavy sword of tempered steel whose blade rested in a protective scabbard of purple velvet and upon which the military dispensed with the usual filigreed and jeweled mountings. Its well-balanced gold hilt wasn't enriched with colored enamels or set with gems, nor were the crossbars embellished with inlaid arabesques of precious metals depicting floral designs and intricate geometric figures. These absences signaled its military origin.

Solomon hadn't yet seen the blade, but he guessed an Arabic text would be inscribed along its surface. He wondered if he'd have an opportunity to view the words, to decipher their meaning, and to decide if they presented a key to understanding the man's personality.

THEY SPENT ANOTHER hour traveling through difficult terrain. Solomon began to wonder if overtaking the Galician woman on the trail was a realistic proposition. He decided to keep his misgivings to himself. No sense voicing his lack of confidence in the mission at that early stage of the search.

The Slav halted their progress so they might all enjoy a brief respite, and the erstwhile translator was grateful because his hip muscles were getting sore from spending so many hours in the saddle. He had the luxury of traveling at his own pace during his very first mission, but he didn't feel comfortable taking the lead in his present situation.

The two men dismounted by the side of the trail in an area shaded by pine trees.

They tethered the horses and mule to the branches of a tree.

Each one collected a soft leather pouch from his saddlebags, loosened drawstrings to open it, and then extracted the contents in small handfuls, nourishing themselves on dried figs and dates. The Slav's pouch also contained candied pumpkin and ginger slices which he shared in exchange for sugared orange wedges and candied cherries.

Although Solomon knew the swap was sweet for sour, he declined to think less of the mercenary for taking advantage of the trade. They remained on the ground, eating their provisions and savoring delicacies concocted in a wide variety of textures and colors; some of the flavors were quite tart while others tasted sugary to the investigator's palette.

Solomon took a closer look at his tall, muscular companion whose round face and high cheekbones looked natural beneath smooth, straight blonde hair. His tan complexion accorded with the outdoor life of a soldier. Exposed to the elements, the once pale skin carried more reddish than brown pigmentation, divulging his escort's Slavic origins.

Solomon seized an opportunity to open a conversation.

"Did you know Arabs refer to a certain kind of white colored bean as *Saqalibiya* which translates as Slavic."

"I've heard that," responded the mercenary. "No idea why."

"They say the bean reminds them of the color of a Slav's hair."

"Like mine," came the reply. "Makes perfect sense."

The soldier wasn't offended. They we're off to a fine start. His vocabulary sounded rudimentary, but his diction was excellent. Solomon munched on a ginger slice while pondering the direction in which he wanted to steer the conversation. He opted for simple comradery.

"How are you known?"

"My name is Jalal."

"I'm called Solomon Levy."

Solomon judged Jalal's age as late twenties or possibly early thirties. He reflected on what else he and the Slav might share in common. Slavs were thought to be courageous and violent. Solomon didn't think he possessed those traits himself. Maybe there was something impersonal. A moment of concentration and then it came to him. The Caliph's personal guards, the silent ones, were despised by other segments of Andalusi society because most were illiterate and made no attempt to learn Arabic. Even though Jalal didn't fit the mold, as a Slav he would have been stereotyped.

Solomon was acutely aware of his own people's history and how Jews had often been denigrated by others. Perhaps there did exist a mutual bond between the two of them. Meanwhile, Jalal was doing some sizing up of his own.

He'd been briefed by General Naja.

Solomon was a city man, a translator whose life was full of books and poetry. However, he didn't appear to be a weak man, either mentally or physically. He presented a stark contrast to the mercenary with his olive-toned skin and everything dark: thick black eyebrows, curly brown hair, and pupils the color of roasted peas. He didn't appear apprehensive and actually looked quite comfortable out in the woods close to the natural world.

Jalal could've done worse than this assignment. If the mission proved successful a bright future might be on the horizon. Thousands of Slavs had been brought into Andalusia from eastern Europe. Despite their unfree legal status, many attained wealth and became influential members of the ruling class, some gaining the status of freemen. And, freedom, above all else, was the mercenary's primary goal.

"Where are you from, Jalal?"

"I have no memory of it."

"What about your family?"

"I suppose they're all dead."

"You're a Slav, but you wear your hair long. You don't appear to be . . . I mean, you're probably not . . . "

"Castrated? No. I was brought to Andalusia as a boy and put to work in the army barracks right away. I've always been around soldiers. It's the only life I know."

"They groomed you for the military?"

"I've been circumcised, and I have a girlfriend." Jalal added, ignoring a question whose answer he deemed self-evident. "Anything else you want to know?"

An awkward beginning and Solomon held himself responsible.

He was one of a small number of professionals who translated Arabic into Latin while working alone; the usual modus operandi was two scholars working in tandem. The basic procedure had one scholar translating aloud from the Arabic text into the vernacular and for the second to translate this into a Latin draft.

Solomon completed this process by himself and also encountered opportunities to translate texts from Latin into Hebrew. His desire to work alone deprived him of a social contact during the process and he suspected this might be one reason he sometimes felt uncomfortable at social gatherings. Another explanation might be a certain receptiveness to his poetic soul which generated a passion for exploring unique ways of experiencing and expressing his impressions of the world.

He stole a glance at the mercenary.

Solomon felt himself trespassing, entering an emotional no man's land. Perhaps he'd been prying too deeply into his escort's personal life. He certainly didn't appreciate it when the process was reversed. He decided to end the conversation before any antagonism developed between them.

"We should be going."

Chapter 16

They took a short detour, a side path leading them into a forest clearing. Jalal had been there once before on maneuvers and decided it would be a good place for them to make camp for the night. A circle of small boulders, with dry ashes scattered about inside its center, formed a fire pit they could utilize for their own needs. The mercenary dismounted and began to look around. Solomon climbed down out of his saddle and joined him.

"There have been deer through here," Jalal said as he sank to one knee. "See these droppings? I see undigested seeds in the pellets. Probably red deer. We saw small herds of them when we were here on our drills."

Solomon took a look at the scat before smiling at his escort. It gave him a comfortable feeling knowing his escort possessed an intimate knowledge of the local terrain and helped dispel any fears he might have harbored about spending so many nights sleeping under the stars.

They unloaded the pack mule and took the saddles down from their horses. As the Slav pitched a small one-man tent, ten yards out from the trees, the investigator carried his portable lodging closer to the canopy. Neither of them paid much attention to the other.

Solomon wondered if his companion relished this assignment as his mind entered a mental territory Jalal had visited earlier. A successful mission meant a possible promotion and the opportunity to move up through the ranks, maybe even freedom from slavery though he couldn't imagine Jalal had been treated badly by the army. The Muslims maintained a strict code regarding the treatment of slaves, and they fared well when their master's adhered to it. Jalal's master, the entire Caliphal army hierarchy, had probably been generous so it would be natural for him to cherish dreams and personal ambitions.

One day, Jalal might even be commissioned a general and command his own men. This wasn't too far-fetched an idea. Berbers, Christians, and other non-Arabs had often been selected to lead the Caliph's powerful armies into battle. Loyalty to the Caliphate garnered substantial rewards; and, the army taught its men this virtue from the onset.

Solomon was pitching his tent under the canopy when he heard Jalal shouting at him.

"What?" he yelled. He looked over at Jalal and gave his escort a questioning look.

"Stay away from the trees. There are ticks in these woods," explained the mercenary. "If one latches onto you, turn its body counter-clockwise to disengage the sucker."

A quick burst of laughter as Solomon played with the image in his mind.

"Is the pun intended?"

"Of course," the Slav replied, joining in the laughter. "Everyone knows ticks feast on blood."

Hence, they're suckers, thought Solomon concurring with the assessment. Jalal possesses a very clever mind. To look at him, one might think he was a muscle bound cretin. Don't judge the contents of a book by its binding was advice Solomon had been taught since childhood.

The soldier helped the investigator pitch his tent out in the clearing before each of them began to engage in separate duties. Jalal gathered wood for a fire while Solomon pitched stakes to tether the animals more securely for the long night ahead

"We need to keep them close to us," Jalal instructed. "Our lives depend upon them."

Jalal had mastered the placement of twigs and small logs, the architecture of building a useful fire. The Slav worked with a quickness and dexterity Solomon had seldom witnessed. The investigator took a fresh opportunity to observe his movements more closely after the mercenary returned with some things he'd retrieved from his saddlebags.

His escort removed a handful of dried fungus from a pouch and tucked it gently into the dried grasses and tiny pieces of kindling gathered at the base of his construction. He took a flake of flint in the fingers of one hand and a piece of mild steel—iron with charcoal added when it had been heated in a forge—in the other. He struck the flint against steel and directed the sparks to the tinder to create a yellow and blue flame inside the fire pit.

Fascinating, but there was more work to do.

Solomon left to go unpack food provisions. By the time he returned dry wood had ignited inside the circle of stones and flames licked the logs like a dog's tongue working a bone. This gave rise to smoke.

"There are bears and wolves out here."

"Bears and wolves," Solomon repeated.

"Don't worry," Jalal said reassuringly as he placed a small log on the fire. "The flames should keep them away."

"Glad to hear it," replied Solomon with a smile on his face. He wasn't terrified of the prospect, but he did maintain a healthy and cautious respect for wild animals.

"Others have been here before us."

"Others? You mean the droppings you showed me earlier?"

"I showed you some droppings, but I've also seen tracks and other signs. Rabbits and squirrels . . . and hawk feathers. The raptors swoop down into this clearing to snatch an occasional meal. Especially this time of year when they're feeding newborns and fledglings."

Once again, Solomon felt fortunate to have such a skilled companion accompanying him. He also realized how unprepared he'd been for the journey north. He would've laughed at his apparent naivety if he hadn't felt so pitiful. He couldn't believe he'd considered making this trip by himself. He suspected Jalal could survive alone in this wilderness by living off the bounty of nature. Solomon knew he would've been easy prey for some hungry bear or a pack of wolves.

They broke open more provisions and devoured their meal. A liter of wine helped them to relax. After dinner, they cleaned up and made ready to settle in for the night.

"This will keep us quite warm," Solomon said as he stepped in closer to enjoy the heat of the fire.

"More importantly, it will keep wild animals away."

He repeats himself, thought the investigator.

"You said you've been here before."

"Last autumn," Jalal said. "We were on maneuvers near Magacela."

Solomon added another layer of clothing, his favorite leather vest, as the sun set and the darkening night brought a distinct chill to the air. He sat down to rest in front of the crackling fire. Sometime later he allowed his gaze wander up to the night sky, a black backdrop for bright planets and millions of milky white stars. The night sky, an eternal presence. An immense and captivating mystery. Something one could count on like the rotation of the planets and the changing of the seasons.

Jalal pointed out the North Star and explained its significance in navigating long distances through the wilderness. He remarked on how lucky they were to be traveling to a destination in that very same direction.

"You're a free man," Jalal stated in a matter-of-fact tone. "What's it like to be free?"

Solomon had never given much thought to this question because being born free he imagined he would always remain this way. He took a moment to reflect upon the question and then he offered his thoughts to a man who didn't share his social status and didn't take his freedom for granted: "I suppose it feels good. I mean it does feel good . . . you can do what you want, when you want, and you can go wherever you want. Sometimes you understand it's best if you sacrifice your personal ambitions for the general welfare of your people and the continued success of the Empire. In that case, you know you've given up a bit of your freedom. That's about all I know about the nature of freedom."

Solomon decided not to elaborate any further and the conversation soon turned to the assignment at hand.

"Had this been an assassination attempt the Asturians might be helping our suspect escape to Galicia," Jalal ventured. "Maybe they're assuring our safe passage as a ruse."

"Good point," Solomon acknowledged.

"Then again, maybe she fled by sea."

"No easy answers."

"Cádiz is the most logical port, but the navy would've been alerted by carrier pigeon. I don't think they had time to make their escape by boat."

"All idle speculation . . . "

The Slav soon realized Solomon had little interest in pursuing a conversation he couldn't close without resolution so he stopped sharing his ruminations and opted for silence.

"Better get some sleep," Solomon suggested, but when he looked over he found his companion already slumbering. That's when he realized a languor created by the day's ride, along with wine and the warmth of the fire and the light of a full moon, had conspired to keep them from crawling inside their tents.

Solomon stretched out on his bedroll and gazed up again at the immensity of endless space. His thoughts soon carried him elsewhere and he began to wonder if maybe he should've taken Layla up on her generous offer.

"I can ease your burden," he remembered her saying.

Layla spoke the truth. Given another chance he might not make the same choice. You're stupid and crazy, Solomon told himself as he sought the solace of sleep.

Sometime, during the middle of the night, Solomon was awakened by the cries of wolves howling somewhere in the distance. As much as the investigator loved nature, and romanticized it in his poetry, this intrusion of wild nature was disconcerting. He experienced a tremor of fear as his mind conjured up a disturbing vision of him and Jalal fighting off an attack by a pack of vicious wolves.

The wolves quieted down and so did Solomon's overactive imagination.

He looked over to discover his mercenary escort hadn't budged at all. He was amazed anybody could sleep through the yowling. Solomon soon fell back asleep himself, grateful for the soldier sleeping peacefully nearby.

LONG PAST MID-MORNING, closer to noon, they arrived at a fork in the road. A narrow side path, perhaps an animal trace, caught Jalal's attention. He reined his horse and slid down from his saddle in a single fluid motion. Kneeling down, he studied two sets of tracks veering off towards the south.

"What's wrong?" asked Solomon.

"I've been following two sets of tracks and they've now turned off the main road."

"You didn't think to tell me?"

"I wanted to be sure it was important before worrying you."

"I should be worried?"

A curious Solomon guided his horse closer to have a better look. Was this evidence of the Galician woman and her lover? Why would they head south? It didn't make sense. Unless they wanted to lead their pursuers off the track.

"What do you think?"

"It wasn't them. These horses were carrying two men, heavy men."

Solomon took a second, longer look at tracks gouged deep into the soft dirt of the trail. They were so obvious. How had he missed this telling bit of evidence? He'd need to hone his observation skills in a hurry. He found his initial displeasure at having Jalal assigned to the mission evaporating.

Once again he'd underestimated his unpretentious escort.

Solomon understood now why his cousin insisted on a military bodyguard with impeccable credentials. Not only because they faced unaccustomed physical dangers, but also to provide a down to earth counterbalance. It wasn't that Solomon was incapable of spotting the tracks. He simply hadn't been looking for signs of the escaping couple. His mind had been preoccupied with thoughts of traveling through the Galician mountains, entering Santiago de Compostela, and his audience with the Catholic Bishop.

He felt a keen sense of disappointment in himself.

He'd have to be more sensible and stop anticipating the future, be more present oriented and allow events to come his way more naturally so he could respond from his instinctual core. Only a deeper, more soulful approach would enable him to meet impending challenges head-on.

Jalal remounted. The mercenary resumed the lead and they rode on through the forest.

They never thought to look back.

AN AFTERNOON WIND SWIRLED dust on a side path of the Camino Mozarabic as a young woman emptied rocks from a pair of leather saddlebags. Long red hair cascaded down her shoulders as she swiveled her head to have a look at her companion. She smiled inwardly, knowing the man to be both brave and clever. This gave her hope that their escape and the long journey back to her homeland might prove successful.

The man stood hurling stones down a hillside, flinging them far from sight.

He's tall and powerful, she thought. Yet, there's a gentleness about him that adds to his attractiveness. Under her breath, the woman uttered a prayer of thanks to express gratitude to her God for bringing this man to rescue her in that dark moment, a time when all hope seemed lost.

This man orchestrated their escape from al-Zahra and Córdoba.

She suspected he was trying to reassure her when he first told her of his plan. Thus far, his ruse had proven successful. They waited and watched and saw their pursuers continue along the pilgrim path without venturing down the side trail. Only then had the woman dared to breathe a sigh of relief.

She wanted to go to the man, to hug him and tell him how much he meant to her, but she understood this was neither the time nor the place for such affection. She needed to conserve her energy and steel her nerves. They still faced many dangers on this arduous journey.

The man turned to smile at her and thought he saw a tear forming in the corner of her eye.

"It's going to be all right," he called to her.

She nodded her head, but somewhere deep inside of this melancholy woman's mind fresh doubts surfaced.

Now what? Lia wondered.

Chapter 17

Solomon and Jalal emerged from the forest into a vastly different landscape of olive orchards, pastures, and agricultural lands that fed a burgeoning, rapidly multiplying polygamous population. Science and medicine and the arts as well as commerce also flourished under the Umayyad rulers while the rest of Europe passively endured a physical and spiritual malaise. This Arab fecundity wrapped itself around Solomon and his fellow citizens of Andalusia like a soft, warm blanket. Now an overriding self-assurance had been challenged, and the murder of the Caliph's nephew felt more like a ripping off of comfortable bedcovers in the middle of a cold, freezing night.

As the two not so self-confident Andalusi citizens continued with their mission Solomon and Jalal found the ride getting easier. They passed through olive plantations, crossed several shallow creeks, and rode past an occasional watchtower, landmarks commanding a wide view of the countryside. They stopped, chatted up the lookouts, and always came up empty-handed. No sign of the Galician woman or her companion. Was she mocking them, laughing at their inability to find any trace of her whereabouts?

They spent a night in relative contentment, resting at a deserted Inn near the center of the hilltop fortress and village of Medellín. The hard earth makes for a difficult mattress night after night so the two men found it relaxing to sleep in a comfortable bed for a change.

They rose early, pushed hard, and arrived on the outskirts of Mérida, late in the afternoon.

The city of Mérida cast its spell over them the moment they saw the bridge.

Sixty-two arched spans crossed over the Rio Guadiana and neither of them had ever witnessed such a marvel of Roman engineering. Annexed to the bridge, on the far side of the river, stood the Alcazaba, an Umayyad fortification built in 835 CE. This brainchild of Emir Rahman II commanded a city which had stubbornly rebelled, for the umpteenth time, only thirty years earlier.

The massive square fortress, with thirty foot high walls and twenty-five towers, was a study in opportunism. Like in many Umayyad structures, the building materials were salvaged Roman walls and Visigoth granite blocks. The entire perimeter was surround by a large moat except on the side overlooking the river.

Inspired by Byzantine models, architect Abd Allah designed a fortified palace serving as Umayyad Administrative offices and as a residence for the local governor. Above all, the Alacazaba filtered access to the city from the Roman Bridge. It also offered shelter to the Arab minority during the repeated local revolts against Umayyad rule from far-away Córdoba. The Emir's troops were sheltered here to quell these disturbances by the local Mozarabs or to carry out raids in the Catholic Asturian kingdom to the north.

The ongoing strife in Mérida may have been a result of the city holding out against the Muslim invasion. If they had offered armed resistance, the city would've met with a horrific fate. The adult males would have been executed and the women and children enslaved. Memories of these atrocities might've etched themselves deep into the local consciousness and been kept alive by stories passed down from generation to generation. Two and a half centuries may not have erased the bitter taste of defeat.

Solomon and Jalal were about to enter a relatively peaceful Mérida as they led their mule across the Rio Guadiana Bridge and arrived at a military checkpoint. They waited in line while soldiers inspected pedestrians and merchants bringing goods into the city. As the queue advanced they had an occasion to view the nearby military installation. Two towers flanked the main gate. From their vantage point they were able to read the proud inscription chiseled into stone above a horseshoe shaped arch, words celebrating Rahman II's patronage of the work.

Solomon decided against using the considerable influence the Foreign Minister's signet ring offered although it meant a chance to pursue an audience with the Caliph's local administrators and a night spent in relative comfort, if not luxury. Knowing spies worked the city, both militant Christian and Fatimid infiltrators, he chose to maintain a low profile. Those seeking to find them would discover their whereabouts soon enough, he reasoned. Better to find refuge in one of Mérida's anonymous caravanserais.

Solomon guessed it wouldn't be long before the trackers became the tracked.

He had no idea they were already being watched.

THEY ENTERED THE WELCOMING caravanserai. Merida's largest roadside inn offered a great opportunity for rest and recovery from an arduous day's journey. Riding through a long, square-walled exterior beneath a high arched portal tall enough for heavily laden camels to pass under, they found themselves in an open courtyard under a deepening azure twilight.

Travelers and merchants mingled in the cool shade of the caravanserai.

The inside walls of this enclosure were outfitted with a number of identical stalls. This series of bays and niches accommodated merchants and their servants, animals, and a wide array of merchandise. The caravanserai provided water for human and animal consumption, for personal hygiene, and for the enactment of ritual ablutions. It also bestowed upon weary travelers the added attraction of an elaborate communal bath.

After arranging for bedding and feed for three animals, the two men replenished their dwindling supplies and opted for separate bed chambers. Solomon looked forward to retiring in peace, left alone to reflect upon personal thoughts; but, first their famished appetites required the sustenance the caravanserais specialized in providing its clients.

Too much time on the trail had dulled their palettes.

They selected from among a half dozen eateries. Surrounded by chattering Iberian merchants, they delighted in a leisurely dinner, course after course, thanks be to Ziryab, of their favorite familiar foods: soup, hors d'oeuvres, lamb and couscous, an array of vegetables, with fruit and nuts for dessert. They drank wine from delicate glassware rather than heavy ceramic or silver goblets, another of the courtier's innovations.

Soon their dinner conversation turned to the future.

"We've worked hard to get this far, and our journey will get more difficult when we enter the frontier zone," Solomon opinioned. "Let's enjoy ourselves in the morning and do a little exploring."

"I'm not sure that'd be wise."

He's questioning my judgment Solomon couldn't help but think. I hope Jalal doesn't think he's in charge here. He decided not to reveal his irritation. He simply wanted to be an investigator in the full sense of the word.

"I want to visit the Roman ruins . . . they might inspire me to write some poetry."

"Are you serious?"

Turns out cousin Hasdai was correct. The change of scenery was invigorating. Sometimes others, especially those closest to us, know us better than we know ourselves. The budding poet inside of Solomon laughed at his own ignorance. The Foreign Minister even suspected he might attempt to turn the mission into a bit of a vacation. Heaven forbid.

"What about our assignment?" Jalal wanted to know, interrupting Solomon's musings. "Don't you want to overtake the Galician woman as soon possible?"

Solomon convinced himself he had time to find her without rushing ahead. He understood most people experience the future like a dimension of time they are moving towards. How could he explain the inexplicable, his sense that the future was moving towards him. He decided not to share these thoughts with Jalal. He won't understand, thought the investigator.

"For all we know zealots might still be hiding her somewhere in the Christian suburbs of Córdoba," he suggested in an attempt to lesson his escort's apprehension.

A pensive Jalal wrinkled his brow as he considered the possibility.

This soldier isn't interested in dawdling, thought the investigator. Too bad his curiosity quotient is so deficient. Better attempt to assuage his doubts.

"If she's in Galicia," Solomon continued, "We'll catch up to her. My cousin, the Foreign Minister, says I have a proclivity for finding missing things."

"The Foreign Minister is your cousin?"

A look of shock came over the Slav's face and the soldier turned away from Solomon to contemplate this revelation in private. When he turned back around, his expression revealed nothing. Jalal's face had changed into an impenetrable mask.

"You didn't know?"

"They told me you're a well-connected translator chosen for this mission because of your knowledge of Latin. General Naja never mentioned the Foreign Minister is your cousin."

At least Jalal isn't a sycophant. All his good-natured banter was authentic if he was telling the truth, and Solomon found no reason to think he wasn't. Then again, he was a mercenary groomed for the life since childhood, and he stood a lot to gain if the mission succeeded. Hasdai could intervene and influence the Caliph and that could lead to Jalal's manumission. An opportunity to attain the legal status of a freeman was a real possibility. Jalal must know this so why wouldn't they tell him who Solomon was before sending him on the assignment?

Too many questions. Stop already. Give it a rest, Solomon told himself.

"We need to get an early start in the morning," he said. "There's a lot of historical architecture I want to see."

"Are you sure about this lingering behind?"

Solomon felt the stab of disappointment. Jalal seemed ambitious and there was nothing inherently wrong with that trait. Unrestrained ambition, however, led directly to the political world where corruption ran rampant. The investigator still wasn't sure if his companion was looking out for the mission's best interests or for his own. In an honest moment, he realized he wasn't even sure about his own intentions.

Solomon knew he was being selfish and stubborn, but he'd learned to accept and live with these personal shortcomings over the years. The more he thought about it the more he felt inclined to trust himself. Mérida offered a world he desired to experience in more depth, an unanticipated gift evoking his poetic soul. He sensed a wonderful opportunity to enter more fully into the eternity of an ever changing world. He was determined to stay the morning and wasn't about to allow Jalal, with his ignorance or lack of curiosity, talk him out of this rare chance to explore this dimension of his life.

Chapter 18

It broke their hearts to set the two Galician stallions free before arriving in Mérida, but they couldn't risk selling them and having the new owners questioned by the Muslim authorities about the circumstances surrounding their possession of two mounts from an undeclared enemy's territory. Two horses showing no traces of Arabian bloodlines.

There was an additional reason behind the painful release. Lia's companion learned that walking pilgrims had priority over those who traveled by horseback. The man explained to Lia that proceeding on foot was necessary, a part of his plan to insure their safe journey home. He had planned carefully, knowing there was no room for error.

They entered the city separately. Lia piled her long red hair atop her head and hid it under the hood of a long pilgrim's cloak. She followed so close behind one band of pilgrims that it appeared she might be one of them.

The man rejoined her on the far side of the bridge and the couple trailed behind the pilgrims through the hustle and bustle of Mérida's busy streets until they arrived at one of the city's many shelters, all dedicated to followers of the Way of St. James. Lia and her companion left the street and followed the pilgrims into the refuge where they entered a large room with a clean, red-tiled floor. On one side of the room they saw a wooden table surrounded by eight chairs, three on each side and one on each end. Four additional chairs were stacked in a corner in sets of two. On the opposite side of the room there stood a dozen simple beds supplied with thin, cheap straw mattresses. Twelve cots arranged in three rows of four.

An old Mozarab couple, wrinkled and grey, worked at the table. The woman was placing small loaves of bread on wooden plates while the man filled ceramic cups with water he poured from a glass pitcher. The couple invited the pilgrims to partake of the simple repast and then they left by way of a hallway leading to the rear of the building.

Before sitting down to eat, the weary travelers realized they had two strangers in their midst. All eyes turned to examine them. The Galician woman asked to speak to the leader of the group and a tall, ascetic-looking man with long, scraggly hair stepped forward.

"I am brother Nathaniel," the man told her. "How may I be of service?"

Like most of the Andalusi pilgrims, hollow-cheeked brother Nathaniel was Mozarabic.

They spoke in Arabic.

As Lia shared her plight, the other pilgrims gathered around to listen to her story. She felt duty bound to speak the truth because it would be sacrilegious to travel with a band of devout Christians under a false pretext. She admitted to brother Nathaniel that she and her companion were fugitives from the Muslim authorities, but she was careful not to divulge too many of the details surrounding her flight. She asked if these devout folk would allow her and her companion to join them on the Via de Plata route to the north.

"We will have to consult on this matter," brother Nathaniel replied and he began to gather the pilgrims out of earshot so they might converse in private.

In addition to brother Nathaniel, Lia saw two couples among the group of pilgrims along with one other unattached man. While Lia and her companion waited for the decision, she explained to him what was happening in his native Galician tongue.

The pilgrims returned and brother Nathaniel stepped forward.

"You're asking us to place our lives in jeopardy," he began before Lia quickly interrupted him.

"We can follow close behind you and if you encounter any trouble we can step back and say we don't know you," she protested.

Brother Nathaniel held up a hand to stop her from continuing with her appeal

"It has already been agreed," he said. "We will be of service to you. What you've asked for is a simple act of Christian charity."

Lia exhaled.

Seeing the nodding heads of the other pilgrims, her companion understood the verdict. She wondered if the two women had swayed the decision in their favor. She decided it would be indiscreet of her to ask.

"Will you join us in prayer?" asked brother Nathaniel.

The couple could do no less. The six pilgrims, along with the two newcomers, spread out across the room leaving lots of space between themselves. They extended their arms out wide and each person took on the form of a human cross. Lia closed her eyes and intoned a prayer of thanks to her God.

LIA AND HER COMPANION had joined a small band of Mozarabic pilgrims who traveled along the Via de Plata. This name doesn't mean "the silver road," which one might suspect if familiar with the modern Spanish word for that precious metal and knowing of Mérida's role in Roman mining history. More likely, it originated from the Latin word "*platea*," meaning wide road. It's possible the name derives from the Arabic word "*al-balat*," which means cobbled road. Then again, the name could come from the Latin word "*Lapidata*," meaning stone road.

The origins of the name Via de Plata remain a bit of a linguistic mystery.

However, a road by any other name would still be this old road engineered by the Romans which was, and still remains, one of the major pilgrim routes in Iberia. It leads north from Seville to Mérida, continues on to Salamanca, and finds its terminus in Santiago de Compestela. The Via de Plata is the longest of the major pilgrim routes.

Lia and her companion were in good company.

Pilgrimages along this route, embarked upon by followers of "The Way of St. James," had begun from the time of the discovery of the remains of the Apostle. All the Galicians had to do was tag along with their new found pilgrim friends while duplicating a journey made successfully many times before over the course of more than a century.

Chapter 19

S olomon stood on the top step of a descending, semi-circular seating area at the apex of Mérida's ancient Roman Theater. His breathing was labored, a result of climbing up from ground level. Below him, twenty-eight rows of stone benches stretched one hundred yards wide to frame an area capable of seating an audience of six thousand onlookers.

Having grown up in Córdoba, with its superbly engineered arched bridge and massive city walls, he'd developed a familiarity with Roman architectural styles and building materials. Remains of ancient temples, mausoleums, and a smaller Roman theater, still scattered around the Andalusian capital, rounded out his knowledge.

Mérida's impressive Roman Theater dwarfed any site he'd previously encountered. Located adjacent to the city walls, at the at the edge of the old Roman city, nearby groves of fifty-foot tall cypress trees offered the only visual competition. This Roman theater was built in 16-15 CE by Consul Marcus Vipsanius Agrippa, son-in-law of Emperor Augustus, and modeled after the great theaters of Rome. Constructed using dry-stone methods, this remarkable structural achievement required the precise placement and interlocking of thousands of stone blocks.

After taking in an impressive view of the entire theater, Solomon walked down to the grandstand carrying a small pack with him. Poor, miserable Jalal dutifully followed as they walked down through all three zones of seating from the top tier, the five rows of the middle tier, and the lower tier's twenty-two rows. The bottom of the theater, where the wealthier social classes sat, had been excavated and gained its support from the slope of the land without any use of manmade supports.

They stopped just above the orchestra, an open space for the choir set in white and blue marble, and then Solomon crossed three wide marble steps where the movable seats for senators and the top officials attending the theater were once placed.

Looking up at the stage from below, they gained the most spectacular view of the theater property. Solomon guessed it to be about twenty feet wide, two hundred feet long, and fifty feet high. It stood framed by massive two-storied Corinthian columns whose bases and cornices were built of marble. The backdrop, adorned with sculptures in the spaces between the columns, contained three doors. A central door and two side doors gave actors ingress and egress to their scenes.

The aspiring poet found it easy to imagine plays once being staged here, but he didn't think there'd be any shows offered in the foreseeable future. Despite their appreciation of Greek science, philosophy, and medicine, the Muslims displayed little interest in the ancient world's dramas, either comedies or tragedies.

Solomon retraced his steps back across the orchestra, sat down on a bench in the theater's front row, and searched inside of his pack until he found what he was looking for. Tucked down into one corner were a small vial and a writing instrument. He took them out and placed them on the bench next to himself before extracting a small tablet, a leather-bound sheath filled with linen paper. Smiling quietly, he opened a container of pomegranate juice and dipped a reed pen gently into the liquid.

Enjoying the simple tools of his art, he began taking notes.

He didn't confine himself to a description of his physical surroundings: the monumental theater structure itself, the massive cypress trees on the hillsides beyond, or the puffy white clouds floating across a vivid blue sky. Solomon found his poetic nature just as receptive to inner impressions, how he felt about this world he was encountering and its emotional impact on his being. His aesthetic response later brought his attention back to the amphitheater as it rose up before him, an architectural and theatrical wonder. One attribute stood out above all others. The Roman presence as palpable, a lingering almost haunting influence. One couldn't escape either its physical or spiritual dimensions.

Before he had time to contemplate this effect further, Jalal once again voiced his reservations about the delay. The mercenary couldn't contain his feelings.

"You're going to sit writing poetry while she gets away?"

Solomon sensed the soldier's disdain and it rankled him. He didn't want to provoke his bodyguard, but the pressed-upon poet believed Jalal's attitude called for a little comeuppance.

"You know nothing about poetry," Solomon began. "You think poems are all about words scribbled on paper, but they are more than you imagine . . . so much more. Poetry captures the essence of emotional experience. An individual's intimations, feelings, thoughts, and sensations . . . a whole world of impressions . . . inside of ourselves and outside as well . . . given expression . . . or, perhaps hinted at using words and sounds . . . the longings and perceptions of the individual soul."

"I didn't know . . . "

"You're so ignorant, Jalal." Solomon interrupted. He supposed his irritation was quite evident, but he didn't care anymore. "You've probably never heard of the nomadic Bedouin warrior-poets and their archaic but elegant desert odes. Let me enlighten you my friend. Those desert warrior tribes held annual poetry competitions while congregating in Mecca. They didn't write their poems. They delivered them orally, sometimes singing them; and, the winning poem, embroidered on banners in gold thread, hung on display at an ancient shrine called "the House of God." Now called The Kaaba, it became the symbolic heart of Islam, the ancient stone building toward which Muslims pray, in the center of the Grand Mosque, in Mecca. Muslims circle the Kaaba seven times when making the mandatory once in a lifetime pilgrimage to Mecca. Hanging the winning banner at "the "House of God" tells us how vital poetry is to Arab culture. Warrior poets, the ancient Arabic language, and Islam cannot be separated."

"How do you know all this?" Jalal asked.

"We Jews aren't so different from our Muslim counterparts," Solomon confided. "For Islam, Arabic is a sacred language. For us, Hebrew is the same. Nothing less than the 'Word of God'" "That's why we respect and master their tongue as well as others."

"I didn't know . . . "

He's repeating himself again, thought the investigator.

"You call yourself a soldier, Jalal? You seem half a man compared to those desert dwelling warrior-poets who prized soulfulness just as much as physical prowess."

"I had no idea." Jalal confessed. "I'm sorry."

The mercenary turned and walked away, climbing the steps of the outdoor theater until he found a place to sit alone.

Solomon turned within himself while trying to calm down. He had been harsh on the soldier. Breathing deeply, he reflected upon his short-fused temper. He knew himself to be quick to anger and he often took offense at the slightest provocation. He never understood why. He hoped his saving grace was that he forgave others easily and didn't dwell on these flare-ups. They soon passed, allowing a more generous nature to reassert itself.

The poet returned to work, taking notes in a short-hand he'd later reconstruct, in Córdoba, when he possessed more time to reflect upon this earlier Roman world. He'd revise his impressions, shape them into finished poems, and commit this work to a better quality paper using a more permanent iron, oak-gall ink.

Solomon took his writing seriously.

He felt proud to be a part of a special group of young Andalusi Jewish poets taking Hebrew out of the synagogue and into the world as a viable language for celebrating the wonders of nature and the secular world.

Cousin Hasdai, as Nasi of Córdoba's Jewish community and Foreign Minister in the Caliphate political system, found himself in a unique position to encourage this remarkable development. In addition to lending his moral support to the effort, he became a patron of young poets who might have otherwise languished. As the movement's main patron, Solomon's distinguished older cousin almost single-handedly re-energized Judaism in Andalusia, enticing Jewish scholars and clergy from all over the world to make Córdoba a new, international center of the faith. He'd also fashioned a new Jewish calendar for Andalusi Jews, and he generously donated funds to Jewish communities around the world.

During the course of these reflections, Jalal returned.

Solomon noticed him remove small pieces of dry charcoal and paper from his own pack. Jalal sat down beside his disgruntled companion and began to sketch the outlines of the stage back-drop. The poet watched him begin with the marble columns.

His actions piqued Solomon's curiosity.

"What're you doing?"

"I became so intent on serving my assignment that I forget to serve myself."

"You're an artist?"

"I'm a scout. They send me to explore the terrain so observation and sketching are skills in my line of work. I can't afford to allow them to decline."

Solomon continued scribbling random lines of poetry and snippets of ideas he'd return to after assimilating this experience while Jalal deftly sketched the three dimensional theater structure into a reasonable replica on the flat surface of his paper, an image he might decide to render later with more accuracy.

Knowing their time limited, and desiring to visit other ancient sites, Solomon worked quickly. He had gained a co-conspirator and it wasn't long before they were on their way, retracing their steps out through the ground level seating area and back out to the road. They went to the Roman Amphitheater, an even larger venue than the adjacent theater.

At the height of its glory, the stadium seated fifteen thousand spectators. Chariot races were held in the arena along with gladiator combats with the highest priced seats placed dangerously close to the racing and bloodshed for optimal visceral effect.

Jalal was now taking an interest in their sightseeing, but Solomon was now having nagging doubts so they took only enough time to visit rooms once housing wild animals or gladiators waiting to go into battle:

"Can you picture yourself here as a gladiator?" he asked Jalal.

"I'd rather not."

"Then, let's move on . . . "

After visiting the Temple of Diana, Roman goddess of the moon and the hunt, they viewed the Roman Aqueduct. A sense of guilt began to gnaw at the investigator. Perhaps he'd not felt the urgency of his mission with the necessary ardor. Maybe Jalal had been correct to insist on focusing on their assignment. Now at odds with himself, Solomon sensed he needed to rededicate his efforts to the investigation. After all, the presence of the Galician woman in his world felt just as mysterious as the ancient Roman past.

Despite his misgivings, Solomon knew he'd been wise to spend extra time in Mérida, allowing a few random hours of bliss to counteract his apprehension at continuing on to the frontier zone. A partial day spent in pursuit of poetry and art, before trekking deeper into the center of a cultural backwater, couldn't hurt.

Taking leave of Mérida, like leaving any world rich and wonderful in its entrapments, is never easy. To venture from comfort into a realm of impending darkness demanded courage.

They had no choice.

"Go and find the Galician woman . . . " Hasdai implored. "Find her and bring her back to me so justice may be served."

And, Solomon had promised to do his best.

With renewed determination, they returned to the caravanserai, retrieved their belongings and recently purchased supplies, saddled the horses, packed the mule, and departed the former capital of the Roman province of Lusitania through Trajan's Arch, a forty-five foot high monumental gateway built to pay homage to the first Roman emperor born in the Iberian Peninsula.

Chapter 20

They weren't hard to identify. They wore loose cloaks protecting them from rain and cold, broad-rimmed all-weather hats, carried long walking staffs for support which doubled as weapons against thieves and wild animals, lugged attached calabashes used for drinking vessels and leather pouches carried on long belts, filled with bread and wine. Equipped with good shoes, they fingered rosary beads devoutly while intoning prayers. Packs strung by leather around their backs, or sacks tied with rope serving the same purpose, completed the pilgrim attire.

They traveled by twos and threes and in bands of a half dozen or more with an occasional brave, misguided soul enduring the journey in solitude. Some of them would fall prey to predatory animals as well eternally persistent human predators, thieves and murderers.

These pilgrims of the "Way of St. James" were more and more evident as Solomon and Jalal made their way north from Zamora. The two Andalusis found the pilgrims intriguing and realized that, given they'd seen none on the Camino Mozarabic, most of these spiritual seekers had begun their pilgrimages in Seville.

Black faces among them indicated some had journeyed all the way from Africa.

SOLOMON AND JALAL FOUND bands of these pilgrims walking by the side of the road along a route leading through oak and pine forests from Mérida to the town of Cáceres. They traveled on, encountering similar groups before arriving at the Alcantara Bridge and its strategic Citadel, the last vestige of Muslim power in the region. On the far side of yet another ageless Roman bridge, this one across the Tagus River, loomed the frontier zone.

Their first impression of the bridge: six immense arches, far fewer than on any bridge they'd come upon to date; and, it rested atop longer column supports than any structure they'd previously seen. It stood out in their minds as an impressive crossing over an unbelievably deep and dangerous river gorge. It was the end of May and water flowed downstream with an impressive velocity, but the height of the bridge provided a secure safeguard against flooding.

They passed a mysterious temple, on the river's left bank, before arriving at the bridge's southern entrance where they were greeted by two sentinels. Two additional watchmen stood poised on the far side of the bridge. After stating their business, one of the guards directed them to the Muslim Citadel, an imposing fortress situated on a nearby hillside.

Their hosts at the stronghold, lonely soldiers seeking camaraderie, naturally gravitated towards their professional counterpart, Jalal. These troops invited the travelers to join them for an evening meal in the mess hall where they were received by the post Commandant. Unlike his men, the clean-uniformed Berber officer was more inclined to pay attention to Solomon once he'd read Hasdai's letter of introduction. The investigator wondered if this light-skinned North African—whose features included a long aquiline nose, sandy colored hair and mustache, and squinty blue eyes—might've had ancestors who sailed across the Strait of Tariq from their North African homeland with the conquering Umayyad armies in 711.

Solomon wasn't so forward as to ask because Berbers were once considered second-class citizens by the Arab elite even though North

African regiments made up the bulk of the army. Arabs, who'd recently converted them to Islam, were a decided minority of the invaders but constituted a majority of the officers.

Berbers had been given the least desirable Iberian lands in return for their loyalty, settling mostly in poorer rural areas. Black-skinned Berbers fared worse than their light-complexioned counterparts whose blood mixed with Romans and Vandals. Resentment caused by unequal land distribution, coupled with discrimination, erupted into a Berber revolt in 740 CE. Umayyad troops from Damascus, in concert with local Arab led troops, crushed Berber uprisings in Andalusia and North Africa's Maghreb.

Although long term resentments were inevitable, much of the discrimination lessened with the emergence of Rahman's III's Caliphate. Loyalty and skill fueled the Caliph's army with little bigotry tolerated because of ethnic or religious backgrounds. Like other non-Arab Muslims, Berbers embraced the increased opportunities and served at the highest levels of the government's administrative and military bureaucracies.

Solomon chose not to reveal the nature of his mission, but the Foreign Minister's signet ring divulged his important connections in al-Zahra's power structure. The Commandant knew better than to pry. Court favor with this unusual young man ... obviously sent here on behalf of the Caliph . . . be charming . . . he might remember you upon his return to the Capital. A reassignment would be most welcomed. The investigator was guessing at his host's internal reactions to his presence, but he suspected he wasn't far off the mark.

Solomon even imagined the Berber debating with himself before his misgivings gave way an overwhelming curiosity and the officer requested a small favor of his guest.

"Would it be an imposition if I asked you to help me decipher a mystery or two?"

"I'd be happy to assist you," Solomon responded. "What's on your mind?"

"First, I must inquire . . . what I mean is . . . I'm hoping you read Latin."

"Yes, I possess the skill."

"It requires you to accompany me to the middle of the bridge and afterwards pay a visit to the temple."

"It's getting late."

"Shall we do it first thing in the morning?" the Berber asked. "It won't take long."

Jalal's attention drifted back and forth as he chattered with inquisitive soldiers while attempting to overhear his companion's conversation with the post's chief officer.

"What's the nature of these mysteries?" queried Solomon.

"I'll keep it a surprise."

Whet our appetites, Solomon thought. How clever of him to insure our cooperation in this manner. Out of the corner of his eye, at the farthest reaches of his peripheral vision, he found Jalal wincing. He probably thought they'd already spent too much time on all things Roman. The investigator was starting to agree with him and wanted to get on with the mission. However, acting rude to a high-ranking officer of the Caliph's army was not a wise course of action. His eyes focused back on the congenial Commandant as the Berber rose from the table.

"Until morning, gentlemen."

SOLOMON AND JALAL STOOD adjacent to the southern pier of the Roman bridge, studying six arches resting atop stone pillars. The distance below the arches down to the river appeared different for each, giving the bridge an asymmetrical appearance. They estimated the stones on the undersides of these arches to be at least one hundred and forty feet above the river's water mark and guessed the bridge's total height at close to two hundred feet.

They couldn't help but admire this great example of the civil engineer's art even though their thoughts gravitated towards the impending journey into the frontier zone.

"I hope he arrives soon," Jalal said.

"I must admit we are in total agreement," Solomon confessed.

"We call it 'Al Qantaret,'" boomed the voice of the Commandant as he approached them from behind.

"The Bridge . . . " repeated Jalal.

"Yes, 'The Bridge.' Because there is none other like it in the entire world. At least, that's what we choose to believe. Other than that, I call tell you nothing more about it. That's why I've asked you to join me this morning. Shall we proceed?"

"By all means," Solomon replied.

The Berber officer led them across the twenty foot wide roadway, a path heavy wagons and legions of Roman soldiers had passed over centuries earlier. He stopped before the triumphal arch, paused, and then walked over to stand in front of the bridge's right column. He pointed upwards to a marble plaque where an inscription, written in Latin, had been chiseled into the stonework.

"There is our first mystery," he said. "Can you interpret the words for me?"

Solomon clambered up on the side of the bride, steadied his balance, and looked another seven feet above his head to study the words etched into the plaque.

"The date of construction was between the years 105 and 106."

"It's more than eight centuries old," the Commandant calculated. "Praise be to Allah. It truly is 'The Bridge.'"

"To Caesar Imperator, son of divine Nerva, Nerva Traianus Germanicus Datius, Maximus Pontifex, Tribunitia Potestas for the 8th time, Imperium for the 5th time, Pater of the Patria." "The dates of construction and the inscription," the investigator began after translating the Latin into Arabic and paraphrasing the words . . . "indicate this marvelous structure is dedicated to the Roman Emperor Trajan."

Solomon jumped down off the parapet.

Surprised by his companion's agility, Jalal breathed a sigh of relief. The mercenary soldier had worried Solomon would lose his balance and go tumbling down into the river canyon. How would he explain that to his superiors? He found this ghastly scenario disturbing.

"Thank you so much," gushed the Berber. "Now, may we continue on to our next mystery?"

The sooner the better, thought the investigator.

The giddy Berber turned around and led them back across the bridge.

On the left bank stood a small votive temple, a rectangular building with an interior cell.

Built of granite, its exterior stone stairway led up to an entrance flanked by two Tuscan columns. Its gabled roof was also constructed from slabs of stone. At the entrance to the temple, below the roofline, a vertical recessed triangular space made of wood formed the center of a pediment, only it was missing the usual decoration. Beneath this, a marble plaque bore more inscriptions.

"The bridge and temple are built with granite blocks of equal size," Jalal observed.

Solomon and the Berber Commandant felt compelled to assess the veracity of this remark so they turned around to study the bridge.

The Commandant turned back to the mercenary and eyed him with new found admiration:

"I've been assigned to this Citadel for more than a year and never once had that fact occurred to me."

"He sketches," Solomon offered by way of explanation. "A skill he learned doing reconnaissance."

"And the inscription?" inquired the Berber.

Solomon walked up the six granite steps, taking him close enough to decipher the words below the temple's lintel.

"This tells us the architect is Gaius Julius Lacer. I believe this is his tomb. He dedicated this temple to the Roman gods and Emperors of Rome: Nerva, Trajan, Caesar Augustus, and Germanicus." The investigator paused to contemplate the remainder of the inscription, hoping to offer an interpretation in layman's terms. He repeated a sentence to himself: *Pontem perpetui mansurum in saecula mundi.*

"What does it mean?" the Commandant wanted to know.

Solomon was surprised by the acuity of the Berber's hearing.

"Gaius Lacer claims he leaves a bridge forever in the centuries of the world. In other words, he says this bridge will last forever. Will it last another thousand years?" he wondered aloud. "That remains to be seen."

"I see no reason why not," Jalal ventured.

"Nor do I," the Berber agreed.

The outpost's Commandant turned serious. He stared hard at Jalal while issuing a stern admonition:

"Proceed cautiously," he advised. "The frontier holds many dangers."

Jalal acknowledged the warning with a subdued smile.

"I hope I've solved your mysteries." Solomon said to the Berber.

"Yes, quite splendidly, and a good deed deserves reciprocation," the officer stated. "I'm going to assign an elite squad of my men to accompany you the first ten miles into the frontier. After that . . . I'm afraid you're on your own."

"Time for us to take you up on your offer," Solomon said. "In spite of your hospitality, for which we are grateful, we'll be leaving as soon as possible."

Jalal looked at Solomon with disbelief in his eyes. He hadn't foreseen this new sense of urgency. The soldier continued to stand transfixed as Solomon turned and walked back across the timeless bridge using long, fast strides.

At the far end of the bridge, Solomon turned and found the mercenary engaged with his army superior. He watched as the Berber shot his military inferior a quizzical look and all the Slav offered in return were raised eyebrows and a puzzled expression. The mercenary was promptly dismissed. Solomon waited as Jalal set out across the Alacantara Bridge to rejoin his suddenly impatient traveling companion.

Chapter 21

Their first day in the frontier zone brought nothing to be concerned about. They traveled along a route marked by human-sized milestones with numerals etched into rock surfaces, indicators left by the Romans who'd set them in place on their major roads to mark the distance between important towns and mining districts. A squad of eight cavalry accompanied them for a few hours before turning around to return to their Citadel on the Tagus.

They camped out in the open that night with few words passing between them.

Solomon wasn't sure about this next leg of the journey. They had left everything familiar about their world and he was beginning to worry about what might lie ahead. Anticipation tempered by an underlying fear. He wanted to move forward with the mission, but he understood this involved taking unavoidable risks.

He also sensed an unresolved tension between his escort and himself. Jalal had proven trustworthy, but the nascent investigator in Solomon still knew very little about the mercenary's background. The soldier might be looking for an opportunity to escape Andalusia altogether. While contemplating his hopes and fears, Solomon fell asleep on his bedroll.

The next day, shortly after noon, Jalal allowed him to take the lead while the soldier fell behind with the pack mule. A brief time later, Jalal rode up alongside Solomon in order to gain his attention.

"We're being followed."

"Are you sure?"

"I noticed them earlier this morning," the mercenary replied. "I count five."

"Are we in danger?"

"I don't think so. I quicken our pace, they increase theirs. I slow down and they do the same. They always maintain the same distance. They're well-trained. I think they're tracking us."

Solomon shared his worst fear: "Maybe they're waiting until we're deeper into the frontier before making a move."

"I hadn't thought of that," Jalal confessed and then he thought over the possibility. "It does make sense . . . dispose of us in some anonymous place far from the Caliphate . . . let the wild animals devour our carcasses . . . no trace of us . . . no investigation."

"Then, again," Solomon reminded him. "My cousin Hasdai has friends in León and they occupy high positions. Maybe these are soldiers sent to insure our safe passage to Galicia so we arrive safely in Santiago."

"I hope you're right, Solomon."

The frontier zone felt desolate and lonely.

The region had been almost completely depopulated in the wake of the Islamic invasion when the Christian residents of the region were transported north to León and to the mountains of Asturias. An occasional, unoccupied Muslim watchtower stood out against a deserted and uncultivated and barren landscape. The frontier zone had always been considered a place of danger, a locale to be avoided.

As the two men continued north towards Salamanca, Solomon couldn't resist looking back over his shoulder. He found the dark silhouettes still close enough to be seen. He counted quietly to himself. There were five trackers. He couldn't imagine Jalal having a chance in hell against that many men; and, he realized he wouldn't be much help if it came to a fight. He tried to suppress his fears, to act like he was still in control of his emotions. He didn't think of himself as a complete coward, but he'd never been forced to consider self-defense in a life and death situation.

Solomon felt a tight knot forming down in his stomach

Welcome to the frontier, he told himself.

This place felt different, ominous. The absence of any Muslim influence provided a sharp contrast and a less than reassuring feeling compared to their well-ordered existence in Córdoba. Were these intimations of the savage north? As much as he might resent Jalal, he began to realize he needed the man's expertise, strength, and training. Cousin Hasdai had chosen well.

Solomon would've been lost out in the frontier zone by himself.

Once again, he found the assignment grating on his nerves. He certainly hadn't asked to be summoned by his cousin, the Foreign Minister. He remembered being reluctant, at least at first. Still, he might have been guilty of giving in too easily, jumping at a chance to serve the Caliph to promote his own opportunity for financial success and occupational freedom.

Solomon knew his current predicament to be one of his own making.

Get on with it, he uttered under his breath. There's no sense looking back. Move on with the mission. It won't be long before you're in Santiago de Compostela and things aren't going to get easier. There'll be tougher challenges to face so prepare yourself inwardly and summon every ounce of courage you possess to see this through to the end.

"Are you feeling all right?" Jalal asked.

"I've never felt better," Solomon lied.

THEY REACHED SALAMANCA where they purchased supplies for the last leg of their journey. Celtic tribes lived in the area centuries before the arrival of the Romans. The town had been resettled by Christians, after the defeat of Rahman III's forces, a decade earlier at the Battle of Simancas. The same battle where the Caliph had been ambushed and forced to beat a hasty retreat, leaving behind his precious Quran. The same battle that had required Hasdai to spend seven months in the Christian capital of León to arrange for the return of a captured Muslim nobleman. Solomon and Jalal encountered another Roman bridge, another river crossing. This time the Tormes River.

They pushed on to the north. At Zamora, they crossed the Duero River. Their journey had required them to cross four of the peninsula's five major rivers. They left the frontier zone behind and entered what may be considered enemy territory.

Continuing on, they arrived at the ubiquitous fork in the road. Jalal halted their progress so he could take time to consult the map Hasdai had provided. He marveled at the amount of detail he found just as the investigator had been amazed by the specifics of the research notes.

As far as the map was concerned, Jalal didn't know Muslims had made dozens of forays into Galicia during the previous two centuries and the invaders also possessed the benefit of Latin texts outlining the Roman Empire's four centuries of rule over the Iberian Peninsula. These written accounts included maps of the main roadways and mining districts.

"There are two possibilities," he told Solomon.

The investigator turned his head from left to right to survey the two roads.

That much is obvious, he said to himself.

"The map indicates we should take the route leading west. Otherwise, we'll find ourselves in Astorga and dangerously close to Leon."

"My cousin is usually correct and we'd be foolish to think otherwise."

They rode a short distance along the west fork before the keeper of the map reined his horse to an abrupt stop. Jalal rubbed one hand along the bottom of his chin and his glazed expression revealed a mind lost in deep contemplation.

"Wait here," he suddenly shouted.

Solomon reined his mount to stop its forward progress while his escort rode up beside him with the mule and handed the Balearic pack animal's rope line over to him. He grasped it in one hand and watched as the mercenary turned his mare around and galloped back down the road while he, the bewildered traveling companion, sat waiting for an explanation.

Ten minutes passed before Jalal returned.

"Those five riders continued north," he informed Solomon.

"I bet they're heading back to León," the investigator ventured to guess. "They must think we'll be safe between here and Santiago de Compostela."

"What do you think?"

"What I think matters very little," Solomon replied. "I suppose it's an encouraging sign."

He handed the mule's guide rope back to his bodyguard, gave his horse a gentle kick in the flanks, and charged off down the road towards their ultimate destination.

The Slav rode out after him.

Jalal wondered why Solomon appeared to be in such a hurry. Why the sudden change of heart? He wondered if his companion wanted to put this whole ordeal behind him before he lost his courage. The disappointed mercenary was no longer enamored of the mission. He suspected he'd be better off in Córdoba where the opportunity to be assigned to troop movements was a real possibility.

For his part, Solomon entertained doubts they'd ever track down the Galician woman. And, what if they did. What difference could it possibly make? Umar was dead. The damage had already been done.

ANOTHER DIVIDE IN THE road presented itself at A Gudiña. Jalal checked the map for the desired route and then he shared the information that he had learned: "The Foreign Minister indicates we should take the north trail," he said. "It appears to be shorter than the southern route."

No need for discussion, so Solomon rode out ahead and set the pace as they followed a bucolic route through the remote Galician countryside. Magnificent mountains, rising up in the distance, would soon slow their progress.

Solomon had already reviewed Hasdai's well-documented notes.

Their trail led deeper into a land whose original inhabitants had been displaced by two successive waves of Celtic invasions, 900 and 600 years before the birth of Christ. After four centuries of Roman rule, the Suevi, a confederation of Germanic tribes living in lands invaded by the Huns, migrated across the Rhine and down into Iberia, where they formed a new kingdom. They were ousted, in turn, by the Visigoths. After the Muslim invasion, these Goths retreated to Asturias and Galicia to establish the only Christian stronghold left on the Iberian Peninsula.

The Andalusis were uneasy in this foreign territory, experiencing an unfamiliarity both cultural and geographic. The terrain proved difficult as they continued up into the mountains, but an undulating, green landscape provided them with an enjoyable visual compensation. Although conquerors had traipsed through these same mountains for some two thousand years, almost two millennium, the features of the topography had changed very little.

They skirted a deep river canyon and, soon after it, a steep descent brought them down into another tiny village. It was little more than a dozen farm houses so they didn't bother to stop. As they left the village and rode higher into the mountains the scenery and weather changed dramatically. Dense, low clouds enveloped them within a thick layer of moist, heavy air. A light drizzle penetrated the canopy forcing them to stop and unpack their rain jackets. They protected themselves from the elements inside water-proof, oiled sealskin outer garments.

The Galician forest offered a rich texture and interesting overlaps, and their adventure continued to unfold under this elaborate mesh of intertwining branches and twigs and leaves. No time for poetry now. Solomon would have to absorb these impressions and wring them out at a later time.

The grey swirling clouds lifted and provided delightful, stunning vistas as they emerged from the woods. They passed countless isolated hamlets, nameless villages where scattered farm houses, built with low stone walls and wooden doors and occasional windows, supported tall thatched roofs. Plumes of charcoal smoke spiraled into a grey sky, high above stone chimney tops, until the colors merged into an indistinct mass.

Despite the wet weather and the slippery path, Solomon refused to slacken their progress.

The sun came out again, in the early afternoon, but the Camino turned shady once more as they entered a cool, green, moist world where temperatures proved conducive to long stretches of travel without breaks. Solomon found himself in a contemplative mood so he slowed the pace. He soon began to realize he'd taken the presence of light for granted in sunny Andalusia. Shadowy Galicia was teaching him how the nature of light can prove elusive.

He pushed on, impressing Jalal with his determination and stamina.

They traveled through a long, flat valley where thin columns of blue smoke curled up out of house chimneys during the middle of the day, and homesteads were surrounded by gardens and fields, compost heaps, apple orchards, and tiny corrals. After passing a few more villages, they began a long climb up through low pines and heather until they reached a place called Albergueria.

Solomon decided to stop here to get a closer look at an unusual, arresting feature. Dotting the countryside were dozens of narrow, rectangular, gabled structures built from stone and wood. They resembled tiny one-room houses and were lying atop massive stone slab platforms resting three feet above the ground.

"What do you make of these?" Solomon asked Jalal.

"Maybe this is how they bury their dead," guessed the mercenary.

They took time to write and sketch descriptions of the unique configurations before starting off on a gentle ride down the other side of the mountain to an area much flatter, greener and more densely populated. They reached a village located on a large plain, nested at the foot of the mountains. Exhausted from the long, arduous ride, they made camp in a rock outcropping on the outskirts of the town, about a mile from the hamlet, in an attempt to remain anonymous.

Chapter 22

They left the mountains behind and spent the morning riding through farmland and pastures separated by stacked stone boundaries. Blond Galician cattle, a breed they'd never seen in Andalusia, grazed peacefully amidst the pervasive stone farmhouses, thatched roofs, garden plots, and smoking chimneys. The old Roman road turned pilgrims' path alternated between oak woodlands and open landscapes until they arrived in Xunqueira de Ambia.

Jalal stopped to look at the map.

"We'll be in Orense this afternoon," he announced.

"Which means we'll arrive in Santiago de Compostela, very soon." Solomon added.

The quiet isolation of the mountains became a thing of the past as hamlets merged into one another and they began to encounter more and more bands of pilgrims along the road. The trail meandered, taking them close to a river.

By early afternoon, Solomon spied yet another Roman bridge. It spanned the river a mile in the distance. "Looks like the Romans also settled in Ourense." He pointed ahead to a crossing supported by five arches.

Nearing the bridge, they found several small pools ringed with rocks and boulders, set back from the riverbank. Steam rose from the pools in spiraling updrafts of misty vapor. Jalal took the animals down to the river to give them water. He tested the temperature with his fingers and found it agreeably cool. Solomon dipped his hand into one of the ringed pools and discovered it contained hot, thermal waters. He joined his escort at the riverbank where they filled their goat-skin water bags.

"I think we've earned respite," suggested Solomon. "We'll camp here, near the river, and leave just after sunrise. We can pretend we're back in Córdoba bathing in the public baths."

They tethered the animals, slipped off their clothing, and eased themselves down between the boulders into hot water. The deeply penetrating heat soothed aching bones and released nervous tension. They barely noticed another fine example of arched bridge construction. The allure of Roman architecture and engineering had finally begun to wear thin.

"Did you know Berbers ruled Galicia at one time, Jalal?"

"No, I didn't know that."

"Amazing, isn't it? They left voluntarily about two hundred years ago because of a devastating drought. They returned all the way back to their original homes, in North Africa. These lands have been in Christian hands ever since."

Jalal eyed Solomon suspiciously.

"It's true. I'm not making this up."

Jalal didn't seem interested so the investigator changed the subject of their conversation so they might talk about his beloved Córdoba.

"I've missed the public baths," he admitted. "This feels so good."

"They make a soldier's life bearable."

"*Salus per aquam.*"

"What's that mean?" asked a curious Jalal.

"It means health from water. Roman soldiers always searched for hot mineral springs to relieve aches and pains after long marches and battles."

"Like I said. They make life bearable."

If nothing else, Solomon and Jalal shared this sentiment in common.

The hot waters and cool air lulled the two men into a contemplative state of mind, and another question occurred to the mercenary.

"What else do you miss about Córdoba, Solomon?"

"Just about everything."

"Too simplistic," Jalal protested. "What do you miss most of all?"

"I miss time spent with my poet friends, and surprisingly I miss my work."

"What kind of work are you engaged in?"

"I translate valuable texts," Solomon explained "I've been engaged in translating the work of the philosopher Aristotle from Arabic into Latin."

"Who's Aristotle?"

"He was a Greek philosopher and a teacher to Alexander the Great. Many consider him the world's first scientist. In my mind, his importance cannot be overestimated. He was the first and greatest teacher in everything. Shells, fish, plants, animals, man; there was nothing that didn't interest him. Observe the world using the senses. Before him, everything was attributed to the gods. I'm probably exaggerating because my love of nature and culture endears him to me. I know for certain his work would've been lost if not for the interest the Arabs in Baghdad took in preserving Greek texts."

A long silence ensued as they allowed the soothing heat to relax tired muscles.

"And you, Jalal, what do you miss most?"

"I miss my woman."

"What is it you miss about her?"

"I don't know you well enough to share my personal life with you," Jalal informed him.

The mercenary was painfully honest. Solomon groused about it, but he guessed it was an honorable trait. Did it mean he was trustworthy? This was difficult to know for sure. The investigator decided to change the subject once again and move the conversation to something that had been on his mind of late. He wanted to see how honest Jalal would be regarding his misgivings about the mission they'd been entrusted with.

"This whole situation makes little sense to me," Solomon confided as he began to share his frustrations. "I've been struggling to find some meaningful explanation, some real purpose in our circumstances. I don't understand the Foreign Minister's thinking. Why send us on a time consuming chase. How long have we been traveling?"

"Too long."

"Exactly what I was thinking."

"From a military and strategic perspective it makes perfect sense," Jalal told him. "If this Galician woman is an agent of the Christian north, we stand a good chance of finding her and uncovering important details about their plans. If this was a Fatimid attempt to create unrest from their perch in North Africa, which is the most likely scenario, then we're covering the Caliph's backside."

Solomon reconsidered.

The Fatimids did seem the most likely culprits. He thought of Ahmad and his journey from Córdoba to Tangier and probably beyond. Hiding his curls and traveling incognito he might've stumbled upon a Fatimid plot to overthrow Rahman III and seize complete control of the Islamic world given the disintegrating state of the Abbasid Empire, in Baghdad. Three different contenders vying for the right to rule Islam. It made sense to destroy the most viable enemy first.

Solomon wondered if Ahmad was traveling with an escort as powerful as Jalal. He hoped that was the case. He may have journeyed as part of an entourage. Ahmad hadn't shared the details of his mission. Neither had he. They hadn't had time. Had Ahmad discovered something to implicate the Fatimids? Was Umar's murder a political assassination?

This line of inquiry led the investigator into more speculation.

"What if this Galician woman didn't have anything to do with the murder?" he asked Jalal.

"Then maybe she's an important witness who knows something about the person or persons who did. Or, perhaps Umar was assassinated and this Galician woman was kidnapped and whisked away to North Africa where she was forced into a harem."

"The possibilities are endless," Solomon sighed. "We might as well continue with the mission until the outcome puts an end to our conjecture."

"If we find this Galician woman and bring her back to Andalusia, our mission will be deemed a success no matter who is responsible for Umar's demise." Jalal offered.

"I think you're right." Solomon agreed. "As much as I enjoy relaxing here, I think we'd better leave for Santiago first thing in the morning."

"Means we have time for a swim,"

The Slavic mercenary climbed up and over the boulders ringing the thermal pool and he ran for the riverbank, his naked backside visible for a few moments before he splashed his way into the river and made a diving leap out towards the middle of the stream.

Solomon laughed out loud.

Appreciating the audacity and spontaneity of the act, he decided to join his companion without taking time to calculate the extreme differences in water temperatures.

Solomon Levy was in for a shocking surprise.

SUNLIGHT, THE GREAT awakener, streamed down into the green Galician world as Solomon awoke the following morning feeling more relaxed than at any time since leaving Córdoba. He had fallen asleep to the gentle murmur of water, the river's ancient, regenerative song.

He looked around the camp and was surprised to discover himself alone.

Feeling warm under his blankets, he hesitated to crawl out from under them. Clouds of steam rose from nearby hot pools and wafted up into the surrounding colder air. The investigator gazed over at the dying embers of a fire that had served its purpose by warding off predatory wolves and bears. No sign of Jalal, but his tethered horse stood unsaddled next to the second mare and the mule. He's probably gone off to fulfill his natural functions. Solomon admitted to himself that he appreciated this consideration.

He didn't appreciate what happened next.

Three men entered the camp with swords drawn. Their leader stepped forward speaking a language and dialect the translator couldn't understand. The words and the structure of the tongue made no sense to his mind. Judging by the man's gestures and body language, it soon dawned on Solomon that despite the word barrier he'd found himself in a universal predicament.

These men desired to relieve him of his valuables.

He pulled a knife out from under his blanket as he rose up from his bedroll. Try to buy yourself some time, he told himself. Perhaps these men are Catholics who might understand a smattering of Latin.

"I'm traveling to an audience with the Bishop of Santiago de Compostela." he informed them in the Roman vernacular. "I won't disgrace his honor by fighting you."

The perplexed robbers laughed in his face.

Solomon took a deep breath and prepared himself for the worst.

Raising their swords overhead, the emboldened thieves took another step forward. Solomon knew he and Jalal would be rendered helpless if the animals and supplies were taken. Might as well be dead, he supposed, as he raised his knife and took a tentative step forward to meet his fate.

Time went still.

They all heard the roar, a harrowing, fierce animal like growl. This was no bear or wolf. This sounded like some otherworldly primal scream, an unnerving piercing noise. The thieves turned around to locate the intruder in their midst.

Jalal and his sudden appearance and threatening presence stunned everybody in the camp.

Solomon tightened his grip on the knife handle, ready to join in the fray. Jalal removed his sword from its sheath. A fine honed-blade glistened in the morning sunlight as he made a few slashing motions to warm himself up for the fight. He wielded the weapon with a remarkable expertise and dexterity. It became obvious the soldier had learned under the tutorship of a good master swordsman, but his wasn't a mere display of technical skill. A unique spontaneity and personal creativity were apparent in his movements and it became evident to the assailants that the bodyguard relished the impending altercation. Jalal's body seemed to expand with every stroke as he stood before the three robbers smiling confidently.

The leader of this thieving trio faltered and lost heart. Turning his back to the mercenary, he fled back into the woods from which he'd emerged with his two accomplices running swiftly after him.

Jalal didn't bother to give chase. He walked over to check on Solomon.

"Think they were sent after us?" Solomon wondered, breathing heavily while simultaneously uttering a sigh of relief.

"I doubt it," came the response. "Those cowards prey on the meek. The pilgrims probably make for easy pickings."

Solomon took a close look at the sword blade. It surprised him to discover no inscription had been etched into the metal. So much for clues revealing deeper aspects of Jalal's personality. Military issue, but still a fine piece of craftsmanship. Perhaps Jalal had left a favorite sword back in Córdoba, a prized treasure inscribed with a proverb or passage from the Quran. Why risk losing it on their mission. The mercenary's courage and willingness to do battle revealed more about his character than any inscription on a sword blade could offer.

"We should break camp immediately and get on the trail," Jalal advised.

And so they did.

THEY RODE THROUGH A dense forest of oak trees and bracken fern.

As the day turned grey and damp, a sense of melancholy oppressed them. Dreary, hard-going, and wearisome travel began to take its toll on their spirits. The pace slackened. Even the animals looked burdened. Solomon soon fell back into his old habit of assessing his escort as they rode silently along the trail, growing nearer their destination.

Did Jalal think he was superior with his obvious strength and physical prowess? That would be a bit ironic, thought Solomon. In the investigator's personal estimation the mercenary was intelligent and practical as well.

For his part, Jalal rode along while engaging in some sizing up of his own. *Solomon thinks his poetry and intellect make him better than others. The funny thing is he's also attuned to his natural surroundings and seems to possess an instinctive side. Although he tries to hide this part of himself, these traits have revealed themselves during course of our journey.*

Solomon experienced an eerie, disorienting sensation compelling him to share his foreboding. "This place feels spooky."

"Best not to talk about it," Jalal advised with sideways glance. "It only makes it harder for us to face our fears."

Ever the stoic soldier, thought Solomon.

They plodded on as a disquieting thought occurred to the investigator.

"Jalal, what if those five riders on their way to León included the Galician woman and her lover?"

"I had not considered that . . ."

"They might have arranged a rendezvous with three escorts." Solomon speculated. "Maybe they were agents of the King of Asturias sent to ferment chaos in Andalusia."

"To what end?"

"The Christians want to mount an offensive to overthrow the Caliphate and take over the entire Peninsula."

"Those riders looked professional," asserted Jalal.

"We'll find out soon enough."

THE SMALL BAND OF PILGRIMS paused at A Gudiña. Here, at the divide in the road, Lia's companion told her it was time for them to take leave of their devout friends. He explained to her why they should follow the southern route. He was almost certain their pursuers had chosen the northern trail since it was the shortest route to Santiago de Compostela, and they might be waiting in ambush for the couple. This stood to reason, thought Lia. Good thinking on his part. In her haste to return home as soon as possible, she'd never entertained this possibility.

A sense of gratitude began to overcome the Galicians.

They had grown fond of their fellow travelers, devout and humble pilgrims whose charity had enabled them to safely return to their homeland. And yet, as they found themselves closer to home and free from harm a feeling of elation began to set in.

Lia found her heart swelling in her breast.

The two Galicians hugged their comrades and wished them god speed on their journey to the Shrine of Saint James. As the band trekked off along the northern trail, brother Nathaniel and the others turned and waved goodbye.

Lia and her companion were now deep inside of Galicia which, along with its neighbor Asturias, constituted the only militant Christian provinces on the Iberian Peninsula.

Soon, they would be home.

It seemed to them the danger had passed.

Chapter 23

Solomon and Jalal entered Santiago de Compostela and found it wanting. A pre-Romanesque church dominated the center of the town while the nearby square of market stalls, exhibiting the region's available tools and foodstuffs, gave shelter to enclaves of pilgrims camping outside in the open. A few small inns, strategically placed down side streets, accommodated wayfarers with means. The town was rather small by Andalusi standards and it lacked paved roads and street lamps. Not a library, public bath, school, or hospital in sight.

"Welcome to the rest of Europe," quipped Solomon.

"Are all the cities this backward?"

"Worse. Many of them have garbage and raw sewage in the streets."

The Slav grimaced: "Where will we be sleeping?"

"Hopefully, the Bishop of Santiago will make arrangements for us."

They continued on to the church, past its tall wooden entrance door, and discovered a stone hitching-post on the far side of the church yard. The investigator assumed it was used for deliveries made to the church, but he wasn't sure. They dismounted and tethered the animals to an iron ring protruding up out of locally quarried stone. Solomon found what he was searching for in his saddle pack and he slung the satchel over his shoulder by its long strap.

"Wait for me, here," he instructed Jalal. "If I don't return in an a couple of hours come in and rescue me."

Both men laughed at this ridiculous scenario.

Solomon quickly went about his business and approached a gated entrance. Beyond the unlocked entryway lay a small garden where he found a young man with blond hair weeding a patch of earth with a long-handled hoe. His first look at the gardener was from the side and rear. A tall, lanky youth with the crown of his head shaved and left bare, creating a tonsure. But, he wasn't dressed in cleric's garb.

Solomon pushed the gate open and entered the church yard. He might only speak the local tongue, thought the translator. He looks like a peasant. Then again, four centuries of Roman occupation should've made the Latin tongue the *lingua franca* of the entire Iberian Peninsula.

He decided to take a chance.

"I'm looking for the Bishop's office," he called out in Latin.

The youthful gardener turned around. He had a rather solemn demeanor for one so young, and vague, expressionless blue eyes. He continued working the plot, taking time to collect his thoughts before answering.

Solomon wondered if he was intruding.

"You'll find the Bishop's headquarters around the corner of the garden," he replied in Latin, pointing back down the side yard a short distance. "Behind the church. You can't miss it. There's only one door."

"You speak very good Latin."

"I was once a priest," he answered

"Was once," Solomon repeated.

The man stopped working and leaned on the handle of his implement.

"I've been excommunicated."

The investigator offered a quizzical look.

"It happened a year ago, this past Easter, during the most sacred of our religious holidays," the young man began unabashedly. "The bishop caught me with a young girl. She came to Santiago with her older brother and sister. Just the three of them, From a farm out near the Finnesterre. We took a liking to each other. Me and the girl. I guess I should say young woman. Anyway, the brother caught on and the older sister as well. They informed the Bishop and he punished me. He can reverse the excommunication, but first he wants me to repent and so far I've refused. They keep me working in the garden because they'd starve to death if I didn't tend to their crops."

"I understand," Solomon commiserated, although he didn't comprehended much of what the young man had tried so hard to communicate.

"I don't think you do, outsider," challenged the former priest. "It wasn't unchaste desire motivating me. I didn't give in to a desire for a woman . . . as if any pretty face would do. No, we talked and laughed together and shared our hopes and fears. My only desire was . . . I should say is . . . for one special woman."

Solomon was beginning to feel uncomfortable. He wasn't used to strangers unburdening their souls in front of him. He tried to appear sympathetic.

"I'm going now," Solomon said. "Thank you for your help."

"You're from the south, aren't you?" the gardener asked. "I saw your horses when you entered town with the mule. I've never seen anything like them"

"Córdoba."

"Take me back with you," beseeched the young man. "There's nothing left for me here. I've been utterly disgraced."

"I'm sorry for your misfortune."

"Please, come back and see me after you talk to the Bishop," the young man pleaded. "Please, I'll wait for you right here."

Solomon was sure the ex-cleric would be waiting for him, but he wasn't keen on the idea of engaging in further conversation with him. He decided to remain noncommittal.

"We'll see . . ."

SOLOMON STOOD UPON the threshold of a recessed, rectangular opening. A single wooden door stood shut before him. He knocked on its surface half a dozen times and waited. No answer. He rapped again only this time more loudly. Again, he waited for a response. When the door opened a short, wiry woman with a dour expression greeted him.

"I'm here on urgent business," he told her. "I need to see the Bishop. "

"Please enter," she instructed.

The woman led Solomon inside to a large antechamber, a waiting room with a hard wooden bench and little else.

"Please tell the Bishop an emissary of the Foreign Minister of Andalusia is here to discuss a very important matter."

"Andalusia?" Her ancient eyes widened.

"Yes, Andalusia," he repeated so the woman could hear the correct pronunciation.

"Please, wait here."

She sauntered off, her feeble smile revealing a life of deep devotion.

Solomon did as he was told. He waited. And, he waited. And the wait lasted longer. He caught himself tapping his fingers nervously on the satchel's closed flap. The longer he waited, the more he found himself disliking the Bishop who had kept him waiting. Is he really so busy, Solomon wondered, or was he trying to send the courier a not so-subtle message.

The old woman appeared from out of nowhere and led Solomon to an open door. He'd been kept waiting for more than an hour before the Bishop of Santiago de Compostela finally initiated a meeting.

Now I know why they sent me, thought the translator. They wanted someone who spoke the Bishop's language. Maybe Hasdai didn't have too many options available. It was hard to know. Maybe his trust had increased after the success of that first assignment. Too many questions. Time to get on with his audience.

"You may enter," boomed a strident voice speaking in Latin.

The old woman ushered Solomon inside as the square-jawed Bishop of Santiago—looking overweight in his long, close-fitting, ankle length black cassock—bounded forward. He appeared light on his feet for such a bulky man.

"I'm Bishop Sisnand."

"Solomon Levy."

The Bishop extended his hand. His fourth finger, next to the little finger, was adorned with an outsized gold ring inlaid with a fiery red ruby. The gemstone's glow emitted light from some mysterious internal flame.

"Your ring is beautiful," observed Solomon.

He didn't kneel nor kiss the ring and this lack of ritual decorum wasn't lost on the Bishop.

"You're not Christian . . . "

"Jew . . . "

The Bishop frowned below bushy gray eyebrows.

"You are aware of the importance of this sacred site, are you not?" asked the Bishop.

"Vaguely," was the investigator's honest response. He realized his mistake and understood he was about to endure a history lesson. What might have been a promising beginning soon worsened as the overweight clergyman swallowed hard, his Adam's apple bobbing up and down.

"Our church is the burial-place of the Apostle Saint James who brought Christianity to Galicia and Asturias. He was beheaded, in Jerusalem, forty-four years after the death of Christ, but his remains were eventually returned here. Following Roman persecutions of Christians, his tomb was abandoned in the 3rd century. Can you imagine such a thing, abandoned? But . . . " the Bishop paused and a wide smile spread across his oversized mouth. "His tomb was rediscovered five centuries later by the hermit Pelagius who witnessed strange lights in the night sky that led him to this place. This miracle led to the construction of a chapel on this site. King Alfonso II, ruler of Asturias and Galicia, was the first pilgrim to visit the shrine he had personally financed. The chapel was replaced by Alfonso III of León who ordered the construction and consecration of this church. We are now becoming a major site for pilgrimage, and one day we will erect a monumental cathedral on this very spot."

The Bishop is amazingly long-winded, Solomon thought to himself. He had just learned a valuable lesson. One he wouldn't soon forget. It taught him to keep his lack of knowledge to himself while in the cleric's presence. It also occurred to him that the Bishop had this personal version of historical events memorized and he loved to parade it out for unsuspecting souls.

Solomon's benign expression couldn't hide his skepticism.

The shaggy-haired Bishop rose from his throne-like armchair and went over to stand before a sword and body armor. There was a wild gleam in his steely eyes as he licked his lips and picked up the long-bladed weapon with both hands. Sisnand raised the sword overhead, holding the pose for dramatic effect. He's either a good actor or he's totally mad, the investigator told himself.

Sisnand lowered the blade to the floor.

"You think relics and symbols are mere hocus pocus? Your hubris betrays you, Jew. Mark my words, we Catholics will rise up and drive the Muslims from your lands and St. James will lead the charge," bellowed the bombastic Warlord.

Solomon found himself nurturing an intense dislike for the man. Then, he remembered Sara. She seemed unpretentious and devout. Must be as many different types of Christians as there are Christians practicing their religion, no two are exactly the same; and, Muslims are no different, nor are Jews. But these thoughts on the relativity of worshipers didn't change how he felt about the Warlord.

The Bishop would've made it easy to dismiss all Christians as religious bigots, but Sara provided the counterpoint. She embodied what each of the major religions represented in their most essential teachings: practice love and humility and treat others the way you desire to be treated. So often preached; so often unpracticed. She personified what the investigator already knew. True religion begins in the heart and not in the mind.

There are good people to be found in all religions, Solomon reflected. And, those like this Bishop who are more interested in bending the precepts to attain their own ends. Teach love, but practice hate.

He sighed deeply as he stood waiting to see if Sisnand would continue his diatribe.

The Bishop, having taken no notice of him, returned the prized sword to its resting place and resumed his seat behind the massive desk. His library, unimpressive by Aldalusi standards, appeared to contain only tomes written in Latin. The investigator looked closely, but could find no Arabic, Hebrew, or Greek titles.

"You speak Latin," commented the Bishop.

"And Hebrew and Arabic . . . "

"Why in the world did the Caliph's Foreign Minister send a Jew into our Catholic stronghold of Galicia?"

"It's a long story . . . "

SOLOMON TOOK THE SATCHEL off his shoulder and rested it on the floor so he could open the flap to search for something. He found the letter of introduction, withdrew it, and stared down at a piece of cotton-fiber paper impressed with Bishop Racemundo's wax seal.

He handed the letter to the Bishop Sisnand.

"This explains a part of it . . . "

Sisnand broke the seal, opened the correspondence, and read quietly as another frown furrowed his brows and his mouth contorted into an unmistakable scowl. The Bishop of Santiago became preoccupied with something more than the text. The Warlord appeared as interested in the cotton paper as in the message written upon its surface. He fingered it and seemed to marvel at its very existence.

This really is a cultural backwater, Solomon thought to himself. This man has probably never seen cotton paper in his entire life. The Bishop's interest in the paper gave the investigator an opportunity to have a look around the room. The Bishop's sword, shield, and armor, obviously displayed for intimidation, left little doubt in his mind he was standing in the presence of a soldier. The dichotomy of a Bishop-Warlord wasn't lost on his once idealistic soul.

The library was likely a singular presence in Santiago de Compostela and that spoke volumes. Did they use their knowledge to control the less fortunate, he wondered. Were the Catholic clergy in Europe monopolizing learning as a basis for gaining power and control over their worshippers?

Solomon had hoped the contents of the diplomatic message would change the tone of the exchange, but they produced the opposite effect.

"Racemundo," fumed the Bishop. "That traitor."

The hostile remark took Solomon completely by surprise.

Despite the detailed briefing Hasdai had prepared for him there was nothing suggesting he'd encounter such deep enmity in Santiago. The Foreign Minister had arranged a truce with his friends in Leon, and the Asturians apparently kept Sisnand on a rather short leash. Given the Warlord's vehemence, the Andalusi wondered how long they could keep him in check.

"I have no respect for Catholics who work with Muslims," bristled the Bishop of Santiago. Solomon personally held no respect for Catholics who refused to work with Muslims. He also believed it his duty to defend the honor and integrity of Bishop Racemundo.

"The Bishop of Elvira is a respected member of the Caliph's diplomatic corps," he pointed out. "He represented the Caliphate as an envoy to Constantinople and the Byzantine Empire."

"I hold no regard for him or his ilk," repeated the Bishop.

Solomon thought of a venomous response but he refrained himself. Best to be cautious in the service of his cousin, the Foreign Minister. He settled for a different approach, more gracious and tactful.

"Didn't Christ say 'love your enemies?'" he asked the old Warlord."

This drew no response.

Solomon now understood Racemundo's letter of introduction would open no doors. He suspected reasoning with such a militant clergyman would be a waste of precious time. He ignored yet another frown while deftly turning the conversation back to the subject of the Bishop's earlier inquiries.

"Here's the other part of my story," Solomon began.

Then he waited patiently, allowing time for the Bishop to turn his attention to less contentious matters. "I'm here searching for a woman. We know she's from Galicia. I believe Lia is her name. She worked in Andalusia as an entertainer, a singer. That's all we know."

"Ah, yes, Lia." responded the Bishop with a smug look.

Solomon waited again while the Bishop considered his relationship to the woman in question and how much of the connection he desired to reveal to a foreigner.

"May I ask why you want to find this woman?"

"I'm not at liberty to explain. "

The Bishop smirked.

"We had reason to employ this woman," the Bishop admitted.

Probably so he could feast his eyes upon her on a daily basis. Solomon tried to quell his emotions and think like an investigator. This approach suggested to him that he follow his train of thought with another pointed question.

"Did you find her attractive your grace?"

"My concern was for her soul; but, yes she is quite a lovely young woman."

"Is? You've seen her recently?"

The Bishop's solemn smile was the only hint of a response.

"Unfortunately, we could only offer her a small room and her meals. She decided to seek employment elsewhere. I counseled young Lia not to make the journey south to Córdoba, not to enter a city of sin. She claimed she needed to earn a substantial sum of money to ensure the survival of her family's farm."

Solomon could barely hide his contempt.

"Do you know where I can find her?"

"I believe she lives on a farm somewhere between Santiago and the Finnesterre."

"Finnesterre? Isn't it Latin for end of the earth?"

"Yes, and make no mistake. It will be the end of the world for you."

Solomon's mouth fell open at the not so veiled threat.

"And, it will take you close to the Coast of Death," added the Bishop.

This sounded ominous, but the investigator didn't have time to seek elaboration.

"She lives with her family?"

"Her parents are dead, but I believe she has two siblings, a sister and a brother."

Solomon's original plan was to have the Bishop enlist the aid of local Latin-speaking clerics to help him locate the Galician woman's farm so it surprised him how forthcoming the Bishop was with information regarding the general location of the farm. Did he intend to make her a martyr and use this situation to drive a further wedge between the Christian North and Muslim Andalusia? Was the Galician woman a pawn in the Bishop's plan to initiate a Reconquest of the South?

"Anything else I should know?" Solomon asked.

"I can't think of a thing."

"Very well," he replied. "My escort and I need lodging and a bath."

"We have no room for you, and you should know that here in the north bathing is a luxury not a daily ritual."

The Bishop's reply, curt and dismissive, appeared to bring the conversation to an end. Solomon realized he'd receive no further help from the Warlord. The Bishop waved him out of his chambers, then stopped his progress just as he reached the doorway:

"I hope your stay in Galicia is a pleasant one," he shouted out.

The Bishop conveyed this sentiment in an unmistakably hostile tone, and Solomon had no doubt this so-called man of God fervently prayed his stay would be anything but pleasant.

Chapter 24

Solomon fumed as he left the Bishop's lair and retraced his steps to the side yard. He now realized the ring Hasdai had given to him held little sway in Galicia. The Bishop's ruby ruled this countryside. Seething inside, he rounded the corner and discovered the boyish looking gardener waiting for him.

A facetious comment entered his mind: "Just what I need."

The gardener eagerly approached, but Solomon chose to ignore him.

"Wait, please, I need to talk with you."

The investigator increased his pace and left through the gate. The agitated young man followed him out to the road where Jalal waited with their mounts. The bodyguard saw Solomon coming towards him and began unhitching the two horses and the mule.

"Doesn't look like we'll be spending the night as guests of the Bishop," Solomon informed him.

The ex-cleric interrupted before the mercenary had a chance to respond.

"You'll need a guide . . . someone you can trust . . . someone who speaks the local dialect," the young man blurted out.

"How do we know we can trust you?" asked Solomon. "The Bishop might be setting us up, and you just might be his spy."

The young man became silent, unbuttoned his shirt while turning his back to the Andalusis, and then he lowered the garment down from his shoulders until it gathered at the waist. Deep, raw wounds crisscrossed his backside. Solomon shuddered and looked over at Jalal to check his reaction. The stoic mask; the soldier had probably seen worse. The young man turned around and pulled up his shirt and said:

"The Bishop doesn't possess a lot of tolerance."

"What's your name?"

"I'm called Vitor."

"Meet us in front of the church before the morning mass, Vitor."

The ex-cleric accepted the offer with a slight nod and the barest hint of a smile.

AFTER FINDING LIVERY for the animals, Solomon and Jalal set out on foot carrying their valuables on their backs, in packs, like the pilgrims they'd encountered along the way. It was good to spend time at ground level after so much time in the saddle so they took time to peruse the diversity of foodstuffs and goods offered in the market stalls lining Santiago de Compostela's town plaza.

In the center of the square, pilgrims had created a lively make-shift camp. They should've appeared a ragged, tattered group, weary from long weeks of travel; but, there was a festive spirit among them as they shared a communal meal and swapped stories of pilgrimages. They looked joyous, beaming with beatific faces.

The church dominated the plaza from its vantage point across a dirt road. This vertical structure, the tallest building in the town, had been formed from block-units of stone mortared below a tile roof. Solomon noticed it lacked a bell tower. Although not measuring up to the aesthetic standards of Córdoba's Catholic churches, Solomon appreciated the builders' attention to detail. Their obvious pride of workmanship revealed itself in the church's rich external silhouette. He wondered about the appearance of its interior, but not enough to venture back across the road to satisfy his curiosity.

They continued to stroll through the plaza.

Down one length of the square sat tables displaying rye bread and honey; meats they recognized as hare and partridge, ham, and chicken; cold weather vegetables like cabbage, potatoes, and several root crops; and, an astounding variety of fresh seafood: octopus, oysters, lobster, cod, sea-bream, huge conger eels, pilchards, and lamprey.

Solomon didn't appreciate the sea's smelly invasion into his nostrils so they continued on through the market as it took a decided turn. Running off at a right angle they found tables stacked with goods catering to the pilgrim trade like leather sandals and waterproof cloaks. Rudimentary tools, all made of iron, were available in the market of Compostela: axes, mattocks, plough, billhooks, and sickles.

"What do you make of this place, Jalal?"

"Galicians don't appear to be an advanced people, but their land is abundant."

Leaving the square, they sauntered down a side street looking for a place to spend the night.

Knowing nothing of the town, they chose the first likely candidate because tiredness had overcome them. A sign announcing the name of a two-story lodging establishment, scripted in Galician, meant nothing to them. They had no idea the scalloped sea shell, painted on a banner hanging above the doorway, beckoned to rich pilgrims.

"You're definitely not one of the Silent Ones, Jalal, but it might be best if you remain mute in public. If Galicians overhear us speaking together in Arabic, it might not bode well."

Solomon made his way inside the lobby where an opening in the wall led next door into an adjoining small tavern. He took a peek inside A few men sat at tables scattered around the darkened room drinking from ceramic goblets and eating food from wooden bowls and plates.

The investigator resumed his business and approached the Innkeeper, a whiskered old man with drooping eyelids, sitting half-asleep behind a wooden counter. He hoped the proprietor understood some Latin. Merchants and tradesmen would have needed at least a little familiarity with the language to survive economically, he reasoned.

"I'm in need of a room for the night." Solomon pronounced the words slowly in Latin as he withdrew a gold dinar from his leather purse and placed it on the counter in front of the man.

The grey-bearded Innkeeper looked down at the gold coin and laughed out loud. He then looked Solomon over like he was some sort of curiosity.

"You got anything else?" the toothless Innkeeper asked in Latin. "Something you might want to trade?"

Good lord, Solomon thought to himself. These people use a barter economy. Better go back outside and see if we've got anything that might interest him.

"I'll be right back."

Outside, he searched through his saddlebags.

"Jalal, have we got something that might interest an Innkeeper?"

Jalal reached into his own saddlebags, searched around for a bit, and then produced two skeins of crimson silk: "We were saving these as a gift for the Bishop."

"You think it'll work?"

"No harm in trying," Jalal answered as he handed over the rolls of silk. "We don't need them now."

"I'll take one of them."

Solomon re-entered the Inn holding the skein at arm's length. The Innkeeper's eyes lit up as he rubbed his hands together in eager anticipation. The investigator laid the barter on the counter and the man's fingers quickly made their way over to fondle the soft silk.

"A night's lodging along with food and drink," he offered.

Solomon realized this wasn't a fair exchange, but he was in no mood to quibble after his disastrous meeting with the Bishop of Santiago. If his business took longer he could resort to offering the second skein for an additional night's lodging.

"Done . . . "

AFTER DINNER THEY WALKED. That meal began with a stew. They wondered what ingredients had gone into its preparation. Solomon guessed it to be a vegetable stock laden with cabbage leaves and small bits of lamb or goat meat. Jalal wouldn't even venture a guess and it became obvious the Caliph's personal military guard had been accustomed to richer fare. Half a loaf of rye bread, a Galician staple, helped alleviate their hunger.

They sampled the locals' favorite beverage, but the sour cider drink made their lips pucker. Two goblets of a local white wine erased that taste and rounded out their nourishment. No multi-course meals like they enjoyed back home in Córdoba or inside Mérida's caravanserais.

They strolled back to the town square as twilight snuck up on the day while night waited patiently in the wings for its opportunity to envelop weary travelers. The peddlers had already taken down their stalls and tables and returned to their homes. Pilgrims hunkered down for the evening, readying themselves for the cold Galician night. The church stood silent in the dusk, its locked doors offering no refuge to these transient souls, the open sky their only shelter. Solomon knew wealthier pilgrims were resting comfortably in rooms at the Inns or as guests at the nearby monastery.

They walked simply for the joy of movement.

So good to be down off the horses.

They turned around at the end of the plaza and began the walk back to their overpriced room at the Inn. They continued through the quietly devout town square and then back down a side street leading to their lodgings. They felt the languor of past efforts easing them into a sense of relaxation and quiet contemplation.

"I miss the amenities of Córdoba," Solomon said aloud.

The world had darkened as night set in and the absence of street lights made for little illumination. A misty fog settled down into the unpaved street and a dim glow, coming from the open doorway of a tavern two blocks away, served as their only beacon.

Solomon led the way as he continued to wax nostalgically about the comforts of life in the capital.

"I'm not sure I could survive in a place like this," he opinioned. "It appears deprived of any significant culture. It's more backward than I'd imagined."

This time the lack of a response caused him to stop walking for a moment. Jalal had dropped back a few steps, and Solomon soon heard the beginnings of a loud scuffle. What the hell is going on he wondered as alarm bells created a subliminal warning inside of him. He began to shake from fear. He turned around to get a closer look at the source of the disturbance when an unknown assailant thrust a hard punch upwards into his solar plexus.

The aggressor pushed him over and he fell to the ground, landing awkwardly on one shoulder. A stab of pain. He cried out as the attacker added a few hard kicks into his rib cage along with a final boot dug deep into his abdomen. He heard footsteps running away and a loud groan followed by more footsteps.

Solomon felt nauseated as the stew he'd eaten forced its way up into his esophagus where stomach acids burned the moist, pink tissue. The food lodged in his throat, chocking him and preventing him from catching his breath. He gasped for air. None was forthcoming. He struggled harder, desperate to inhale air into his lungs. His efforts proved futile.

Solomon began to panic.

He became dizzy and disoriented and his eyes widened with fear as he frantically shoved two fingers down his throat to dislodge the blockage. He regurgitated the stew and wine upon the roadway, the noxious mixture oozing back into his face. Solomon sucked in a deep breath before the world surrounding him vanished into the mist.

UPON REGAINING CONSCIOUSNESS, the first sounds Solomon heard were groans and cursing nearby. He recognized the sound of the voice and knew Jalal had also survived the attack. Looking back up the road, he found the battered mercenary crawling to his hands and knees before rising slowly, regaining his balance, and then making his way down the dark street to check on the investigator.

Solomon ran his tongue over his lower lip and tasted blood and salt. He experienced a burning in his esophagus. He was lucky to be alive given this circumstance. He glanced down at his hand and discovered the signet ring, wrapped snugly around his finger, exactly where it had been before the attack. That indicated to him the incident wasn't a robbery.

"I'm sorry," said Jalal. "This is my fault. I let my guard down. I didn't hear or see them coming until it was too late. They might have killed you."

Solomon had little doubt about who had orchestrated the attack

"They didn't want me dead. The Bishop wanted to send me a message. He doesn't like people poking around into his business."

"Are we through here?"

"Hell, no!"

"Are you sure, Solomon?" Jalal evinced real concern in his voice. "The next time it might not be a warning."

"I suppose you're right," Solomon agreed. "Still, I can't help but feel the old Warlord's hiding something. I'm convinced Lia's back here, in Galicia. If it comes down to protecting her, I'm not sure Sisnand will choose that option. He can't afford to risk a war with the Caliphate. Despite his braggadocio, he's not ready to initiate a Reconquest. At least not just yet. Rahman III would squash him like a bug."

"You called her Lia," declared Jalal. "Where did that sense of familiarity come from?"

Solomon thought about this for a moment, but he had no answer.

"I don't know . . . "

"You said the Bishop told you her whereabouts."

"I think he might be trying to use us in some kind of weird plot. I suspect he wants us to find Lia and take her back to Andalusia to stand trial. This will buy him time and help him create a martyr to attract others to his cause."

"What about the attack?"

"I think he wants us to go about our business as soon as possible. He's not comfortable with our presence in Santiago. The longer we stay in the town, the more we might find out about Sisnand and his motives and the people who are backing him."

"Now what?"

"Let's go get some sleep," Solomon said with a weary voice. "We have work to do in the morning."

SEVERAL HOURS LATER, as Solomon lay recuperating from his wounds, he began to experience a deep sense of homesickness. His thoughts returned to his beloved Córdoba as a series of images flashed before his mind's eye: he saw himself sitting at his desk writing a poem, and then he was browsing the merchant stalls in the souk, enjoying the public baths, and savoring a glass of wine with friends.

He looked across the room and found Jalal sleeping soundly.

His thoughts turned to Layla. Had he been stupid not to take her up on her generous offer. He wondered if she'd give him another opportunity and how he would respond if she did. In his imagination, he saw himself sitting next to her on the soft-cushioned sofa inside the living room with vermillion painted walls. He could almost feel the warmth of her breath and the pressure of her hips as they rubbed against his own..

Solomon was imagining kissing her soft lips when he fell into a desperately needed sleep. He awoke, at dawn's first light, and opened the room's only window to allow fresh air inside.

The last stars were fading in a pink and blue sky as the day broke, and a haunting, soulful melody echoed somewhere in the distance. The notes sounded alien, their source from some origin unknown. Our ears taste sounds just as our tongues taste flavors, he reflected. He'd never encountered these distinct resonances before. Another series of plaintive notes led him downstairs in search of the Innkeeper.

He stepped slowly down the dim, narrow stairway.

Candlelight and low voices emanated from the doorway leading into the tavern. An old man sat in the shadows behind the counter in the lobby.

"Where does that haunting music come from?" Solomon asked.

The Innkeeper, a thin old man with half-shut eyes and a soft grey beard, looked like he might be the brother of the afternoon attendant. They appeared so very much alike. The presumed brother looked up upon hearing the question put to him and he quickly regained his lucidity.

"I beg your pardon, Sir."

"That music . . . where is it coming from?"

"Bagpipes, Sir."

"Bagpipes?"

"It's a musical instrument, Sir. They make it from the skin of a small goat or sheep. The natural openings in the skin, for the animal's legs, are used to attach pipes."

Solomon felt perplexed. He couldn't visualize what a bagpipe might look like so he returned upstairs to his room where he contemplated the possibility it wasn't an honor to be sent north to search for the mysterious Galician woman.

Have they sent him into exile, he wondered. Maybe they hoped he wouldn't return, that he'd perish in the savage north. Perhaps this whole drama, murder and all, had been orchestrated by Rahman III to do away with an embarrassing, ungrateful scion. Maybe he was just a pawn in the game the same as Lia was a pawn in the Bishop's machinations.

Complete his mission or return empty-handed. Given the circumstances, neither choice offered a viable alternative. Solomon felt lonely and sad and he didn't know why. He closed his eyes and once again imagined the familiar sights and sounds of the Andalusian capital. He began to think he was beginning to understand the meaning of *morrina*, the homesickness inflicting one's soul Only his longing wasn't for this misty, melancholy land of the Gallegos. Solomon's heart yearned for his cherished golden city on the Guadalquivir, his own personal nostalgia.

A sense of unhappiness overcame Solomon.

So far from everything familiar. So far from home. What if he perished in the savage north and never returned home, never enjoyed Córdoba and all it had to offer, never smelled or touched or tasted that unique world again, or enjoyed its vibrant pulse coursing through his blood.

He remembered something Sara had told him and it began to make sense.

"Lia felt homesick. I think that is the key to this mystery," Sara had told him. "For Galicians the longing for home is a sickness."

Could this homesickness lead to a kind of mental pressure resulting in an act of passion? He thought about his own longings and found himself commiserating with the Galician woman. Maybe this wasn't such a thin motive. Perhaps a deep yearning could develop into a debilitating malady. More likely she was trying to earn some money before reuniting with someone dear to her and returning to far-off Galicia.

The music outside ended and the dawn gave way to silence as the mercenary continued to sleep and recover from the attack. Solomon closed the window and remembered the Nasi's instructions: "Find her and bring her back to me so that justice may be served."

Chapter 25

They emerged from a side street riding two mares and leading a mule. Solomon saw Vitor in front of the church pacing impatiently while throngs of pilgrims eagerly passed him by as they entered through the massive open door leading into Santiago de Compostela's singular house of worship. The ex-priest was scanning the town square, hoping to catch a glimpse of his potential benefactors.

His frown betrayed a sense of hopelessness. He hadn't caught sight of them and he was probably imagining he'd be abandoned and left to endure bitter memories of the strangers from Andalusia.

Solomon didn't call out to him.

It would've been useless. He was too far away and the church bells were tolling.

The investigator halted their progress at the churchyard they'd first entered a day earlier. He handed his reins to Jalal, dismounted, and walked down to the church. Vitor kept his gaze focused in the direction of the plaza so he didn't notice the approach. Solomon tapped him on the shoulder. The young man flinched and then he spun around.

Vitor exhaled a sigh of relief.

"I didn't think you'd come for me."

"You don't mind if I have a look inside first?"

Solomon walked on without waiting for an answer.

"It's alright for me to attend mass," Vitor called after him as he scurried to the door and crossed the threshold.

They stood against the back wall of the church, looking on as hundreds of travel weary pilgrims crowded together celebrating a morning mass. Standing at the altar, in Bishop's robes, Sisnand the Warlord conducted the mass in Latin. Solomon marveled at the dichotomy between the public face and the reality behind closed doors.

High above them, suspended on a long rope hanging from a ceiling beam of the church, a five-foot high silver vessel containing burning incense, swung back and forth above the worshippers spreading fragrant smoke into the air.

Solomon's eyes returned to the altar.

He knew in the past Catholic churches had served as safe deposit boxes for local treasures because previous Muslim forays into Galicia had raided many of the churches and discovered gold and silver and property deeds hidden behind the high altars and under the wooden floors.

He leaned back against the stone wall and observed the hundreds of pious pilgrims packed into the church. The ceremony meant nothing to him personally, but the sincerity of these men and women vouchsafed an unexpected epiphany upon his receptive, poetic soul.

Times would surely change and political and theological customs would come and go, but the deep desire for pilgrimage would remain an eternally present mystery beyond the dictates of any religious creed. This common thread united all religions in a tapestry destined to outlive the darkest night.

Solomon smiled inwardly as he moved away from the back wall of the church and retreated outside with Vitor close at his heels. He didn't feel like sharing his private revelation just yet so he made small talk about a subject he found intriguing.

"Last night I overheard some pilgrims in the square talking about the censer," Solomon said. "I wanted to see it for myself. I don't understand its purpose in the ritual."

"Its purpose is twofold," Vitor informed him. "To freshen the air defiled by masses of unwashed, pungent smelling pilgrims. The priests also believe the incense smoke protects them against many of the diseases the pilgrims might bring here."

"Can you ride a mule?"

"I grew up on a farm," replied the smiling ex-priest.

"We're going to take a chance on you," Solomon told him. "The Bishop is making our lives miserable, and the aid we expected from him hasn't been forthcoming."

"You won't regret your decision," insisted the young man.

"I'd better not," Solomon countered with a look of solemn determination.

SOLOMON FELT A TREMENDOUS sense of relief at departing Santiago de Compostela. The entire experience, from the uncooperative Bishop to the vicious nighttime attack, had left a bad taste in his mouth not to mention the lingering burning sensation in his throat. And, his shoulder still ached.

He kept his horse at a steady canter and Jalal followed his lead. Vitor had trouble keeping up on the mule and this forced a brief delay as they waited for him to catch up. The reunited trio decided it was time to give the animals a brief rest.

A random conversation led to a startling revelation. When Solomon informed the ex-priest he was searching for a Galician woman named Lia, a rare alignment of destinies divulged itself. He learned the Galician woman was the older sister of the object of Vitor's affections. This young woman, Sabela, had talked about their family farm many times in his presence. Although he didn't know its exact whereabouts, Vitor was certain he could find it by making inquiries in a nearby town she had mentioned.

This seeming coincidence made it feel like their finding Lia was somehow meant to be although they had no idea how or why this amazing turn of events might be stitched into the fabric of their destinies. Solomon felt like he was experiencing a scenario that had been waiting for him, one that he had unconsciously intended. A rare confluence of fates bringing together mysterious unseen forces.

They headed towards the village of Cee, riding through green countryside as a light drizzle began to fall. Anticipating the almost daily occurrence of inclement weather, the Andalusis were already wearing their sealskin raincoats. They continued on the western trail passing pilgrims who had taken shelter under the canopy of trees growing on both sides of the road. It was a strange sight, thought Solomon. Pilgrims traveling to the Finnesterre and the end of the known world after they'd fulfilled the requirements of their pilgrimage by paying homage to St.James the Apostle, in Santiago de Compostela.

The narrow road was waymarked throughout with milestone markers.

The rising and falling terrain provided shade as it passed through oak forests along paths that were little more than old walled lanes and woodland tracks. The route provided them with a glimpse of authentic rural Galicia: small churches, wayside crosses, plumes of smoke spiraling up from stone farmhouses, and the ubiquitous Roman bridge at every river crossing.

A couple of hours later, when they stopped for lunch, two overweight pilgrims trudging along the trail jostled Solomon's memory so he asked Vitor about the desire of some pilgrims to extend their pilgrimage.

"They're going to the ocean to find scallop seashells. By possessing a scallop shell, a pilgrim proves he or she has finished the pilgrimage and seen the end of the world at Finnesterre," enthused Vitor. "The shell also serves a practical purpose since it can be used for gathering water to drink or as a makeshift bowl for eating. And, it's become an important metaphor. The grooves in the shell, which come together at a single point, represent the various routes pilgrims travel until they arrive at a single destination."

Solomon shared the gist of the conversation with Arabic-speaking Jalal.

The mercenary's eyes lit up as he offered an animated response.

The investigator felt the information important enough to translate for Vitor. "Jalal says the scallop shell is an important symbol for Islam as well. The pearl inside the shell is Allah's gift to the world, the Quran."

They broke out the food.

After devouring their lunch, they resumed their journey.

They found themselves far from Santiago, in a verdant land of rolling hills, where scattered farmhouses and inconsequential villages marked their progress. Solomon recognized more of the narrow, raised wooden structures perched on pillars raised above foundations of stone or earthen berms. Crosses stood mounted on both ends of the roofs below which a small door had been added. He had been struck by their absence in Santiago de Compostela.

"What are those structures, Vitor?" Solomon asked as he pointed out one in the distance. "We thought they might be a way to bury the dead, but we didn't see any in Santiago."

"They're called *horreos*," Vitor chuckled. "They're used to store grain, to get it up off the ground and protect it from the elements and from vermin. Which explains why you see them in the countryside in close proximity to a farmhouse."

Solomon shared the news with Jalal and the two men enjoyed a good laugh even though it came at their own expense.

A strong wind blew in from the ocean. It carried with it a hint of salt spray and this suggested to Solomon that he was growing closer to the Coast of Death and the Finisterre. Soon they would be traveling close to the end of the world.

THEY STOPPED OUTSIDE of the harbor town of Cee in the late afternoon. Solomon sent Vitor into the village to buy supplies and, more importantly, to inquire about the location of the farmhouse. He and Jalal remained behind so as not to draw undue attention to themselves.

The ex-monk made the rounds of a small fishing village that supported itself by the bounty of the sea and staples supplied by a few shops catering to pilgrims' needs. After a few unsuccessful attempts, he found a local butcher who remembered the family. He'd bought pigs from them in the past. He provided the information they required, but only after Vitor convinced him that his intention was to be reunited with the family's youngest daughter. His description of the family allayed the merchant's doubts, evoking a familiarity that made his request seem natural.

Once they knew the whereabouts of the farmhouse, Solomon decided to take advantage of the longer hours of June daylight to join in with pilgrims headed for Cape Finesterre. The end of the earth was less than five miles away and the farmhouse not much further. They were all tired and he reasoned their encounter with the Galician woman could wait until morning.

The investigator still wasn't sure about the extent of Bishop's Sisnand's threat. If the old Warlord wanted the Andalusis to find the Galician woman and return her to Córdoba so that he might turn her into a martyr to rally his troops for a Reconquest of the South, his attack had done the trick. Solomon now believed the attack had been meant to hasten them on their way.

But there was no way he was going to come this far and not see the end of the earth. He shared this sentiment with Jalal, but sensed a stiff resistance. He wondered if Jalal possessed a sustained feeling of compassion for anybody, including himself. He was always on duty. Solomon knew he'd never return to the savage north. Never have another opportunity to see what the end of the earth was all about. How could he pass up this opportunity? Less than half a day could hardly make a difference, he rationalized. Especially since they'd be getting started for the farm so late in the day.

Lighten up, soldier.

Let's have a little fun for God's sake.

Was this another manifestation, like the extra time spent in Mérida, of his rebellious nature? Was there a part of him that secretly desired not to find the Galician woman? Or, maybe he was just born with a curious mind. He didn't know the answer, but he harbored no doubts about what he wanted.

"We're going to the Finnisterre."

It sounded like an order.

It was meant to.

THREE MEN STOOD ALONG the top of a promontory looking out towards a mighty spur of adjoining granite jutting out from the Galician mainland into the sea. This natural headland led their vision out into the vastness of a timeless ocean in the extreme northwesterly quarter of the Iberian Peninsula. A cold mist, brought in from the sea by the western winds, refreshed them as they stared out at the water.

They remained spellbound, listening to the sound of the waves crashing on the rocks below.

They were a long way from anywhere, close to the wild heart of nature, standing in a place where the world seemed to stop and the earth and heaven and the sky and sea met in an almost mystical embrace, suggesting an ageless melding of natural elements.

"I suppose we have to go out to the end of the cape, to the actual end of the earth, to satisfy you?" Jalal asked with a certain bitterness in his voice.

"No," Solomon answered. "This will be fine. The end of the earth is beyond the horizon, beyond what we now see with our eyes."

"What do they call this ocean?" Jalal wanted to know.

"They call it *Mare Tenebrosu*, and that translates to the dark sea," Solomon replied. He translated the Arabic response into Latin and Vitor agreed with his interpretation. The investigator wondered what might exist beyond that dark, unfathomable sea.

They had arrived at this place of contemplation by following pilgrims along yet another Roman road, a trail hugging the cliffs and coves of the coast until it took them up a steep and sinuous stone path where they guided the horses and sure-footed mule past slippery moss covered boulders.

Vitor had joined Jalal in complaining about Solomon's decision to embark upon the arduous climb to the top of the mountain, but a change overcame him when they reached the summit with its breathtaking view of the sea and with offshore islands so close he imagined he could reach out and touch them. They were witnessing nature at her most sublime, an experience difficult to duplicate during the course of normal daily life.

The world of man was represented on the mountaintop as well so they returned from their reveries and followed a trio of pilgrims to a spot where a dozen low stone walls lay in ruins, circular and oblong configurations with narrow entrance thresholds. These weren't vestiges from the Romans, but the foundations of ancient huts, constructed of wood or mud and long since consumed by the elements.

Vitor assumed the role of guide:

"The Romans arrived here about a thousand years ago, but the people who built these structures lived here a thousand years earlier."

"The original Galicians," Solomon responded.

"Exactly. We call them the *cultura castrexa*," the ex-cleric continued, "and their dwellings are known locally as *castros*, from the Latin *castrum*, which means castle. It is said these people worshipped the sun. It's also been said there are mysterious beings hoarding treasure under these abandoned hill-forts. They are called Mouros."

"Do you believe it?"

"Galicians are more superstitious than religious."

"But, you were a clergyman."

"I am a Galician."

They led the animals across an entryway into one of the abandoned *castros*.

Small groups of pilgrims had taken shelter in nearby dwellings—little more than stone walled enclosures—and had started small fires. Despite an abundance of twigs and branches on the mountain top, some of the pilgrims were taking articles of clothing and tossing them into the flames."

"I don't understand why they're doing something so irrational," Solomon confessed. "It's cold up here and there's plenty of wood nearby."

"There's a tradition," Vitor explained, "When you reach the end of the world you must burn your past. The pilgrim's quest is to be reborn in spirit. A second tradition is to witness the setting sun here at the end of the earth. "

The investigator wanted to learn more about these pilgrims and their longings.

"What motivates the men and women to undertake this journey, Vitor?"

"Having never embarked upon a pilgrimage myself, I can only offer my personal thoughts on the matter. I believe the arduous travel replicates the trials and tribulations of an apostle or saint's life. The pilgrimage brings the traveler a deeper understanding of the spiritual strengths of the individual they venerate, thus helping them find these same virtues and resources within themselves."

Solomon contemplated the ex-priest's response.

"Thank you for your insight."

"Wait, there's more to it than that," insisted Vitor. "The pilgrimage also serves as a kind of penance. A successful visit to the shrine absolves the pilgrim of past transgressions and sins. They're staking a claim for a brighter future and it begins with the completion of the journey."

HOURS LATER, THEY JOINED with pilgrims at the edge of the mountain as the sky transformed itself into a blazing fire and the Galician sun sank down into the dark and endless sea.

"The Romans believed the world ended here," Vitor began. "This is where they came to watch the sun being swallowed up by the sea at night. This is where the sun died at dusk. Before that, a sanctuary existed on this site where Galicians worshipped the deity Berobreus, lord of the Otherworld and beyond."

Solomon watched the last traces of sunlight fade from the day. He left his companions knowing he'd created an enduring memory, returning alone down the path towards their enclosure guided by the light of a dozen campfires. They had trusted the pilgrims would respect their property and not disturb the animals and their confidence had been rewarded. As he passed by a nearby pilgrim's camp, its small fire flaming brightly and casting shadows into a twilight world, Solomon surprised himself by committing an act both spontaneous and uncharacteristic.

Feeling compelled, he walked into the pilgrim's *castro* where he removed his sealskin rain-coat and held it over the fire. The onlookers became entranced as they watched him drop the valuable jacket down into the flames. Smoke emerged from under the sides of the garment and then it erupted into a blaze of light. The fire crackled and sparks flew out in all directions, but the brief pyrotechnics unnerved the pilgrims less than the unforeseen act they'd witnessed.

Solomon wondered if he was dreaming; the uncharacteristic act. The unexpected feeling of elation.

"Guess I won't be needing it," he told the amazed pilgrims.

He turned to leave and found Jalal and Vitor standing outside the enclosure staring at him in disbelief. He wasn't sure what to tell them so he grinned and rejoined his uncomprehending friends as they returned to their temporary shelter and settled down with the animals for the long night ahead.

That night, a heavy mist rolled in from the sea.

It brought a wet, cold drizzle that chilled them to the bone.

Chapter 26

L ess than half a day's ride and blessed sunshine. The farmhouse lay in a sheltered crease between verdant hills. It was set back into the hillside, a two-storied stone structure with a slate roof. Its doors stood almost next to each other, framed by granite rocks with wooden lintels. One of the two doors was a pair of doubles.

There was a large window to one side of the single door and a smaller, higher opening to the left side of the other. This was simplicity exemplified. Not a single window on the second story. A stone fireplace. The ever present grey spiraling smoke of rural Galicia so familiar to the investigator. He'd already seen it many times before.

Solomon found himself standing at the edge of a woods studying a clearing below, perhaps a tenth of a mile in the distance. No hint of anything unusual about the farmhouse. Nothing to reveal it might be the abode of a murderess. He wasn't even sure if Vitor had led them to the correct farmhouse or if the ex-priest had really intended to guide them to his girlfriend's sister's home.

This is complicated, he thought.

And, then he saw her.

She sat upon a milking stool looking earthy and sensuous as morning sunlight dappled down through the trees surrounding the farm. She gently squeezed swollen pink teats on a dairy cow's bloated udder. White liquid splashed down into a round wooden bucket.

She fit the description Sara had given him.

Her vivid red mane, pulled back from her forehead, framed an oval jawline.

Her smile suggested contentment.

Solomon could feel his heart pounding wildly in his chest; time to make his move. He hurried down towards the farm leaving Jalal and Vitor behind with the animals. As he drew closer, the woman heard his approach and it startled her. She looked up apprehensively and turned to find him marching towards her.

Determination, written all over his face, translated itself to her emotional core with the force and swiftness of a lightning bolt. She rose, quite deliberately, and then she sprinted for the farmhouse door.

Solomon ran after her, cutting off the only avenue of escape.

"Wait!" he commanded in Arabic.

She ignored him and continued running and then she began screaming for help.

He caught up with her, grabbed her around the waist, and held on tightly. The woman spat in his face as she struggled to escape his grasp. He shifted his grip and grabbed her by the wrists. She screamed again.

Solomon was resolute. He ignored her screams and pushed the left sleeve of her blouse up past her forearm. Blemish free milky white skin, smooth and flawless, with no sign of a purple birthmark. Its absence sent a shock through his mind.

He'd miscalculated.

"Who are you?"

The young woman's green eyes opened wide with fear before she fainted, falling backwards into Solomon's outstretched arms. Her dead weight dropped him to his knees and he felt wet grass soaking through his pant legs.

He heard the door of the farmhouse swing open and looked up as a giant of a man bounded out into the farmyard.

Searching with his eyes, the man found the woman lying in Solomon's arms. The snarling behemoth became enraged and sprinted madly towards them. The man's fierce eyes bore down upon him as the threat of violence drew closer. Your knife, Solomon, grab your knife he told himself. He heard shouting behind him, but he didn't have time to turn around. Solomon assumed it was his companions. As he reached down for the knife, he knew it was too late.

The farmer raised an enormous fist, but a hard kick delivered right into the man's groin doubled him over putting an abrupt end to his aggression. The man yelled out in pain as he tumbled headlong to the earth. The tip of Jalal's sword rested against the man's jugular vein before either the assailant or the investigator understood what had happened.

The well-trained Slav kept his prisoner at bay, applying light pressure to the man's neck. Vitor stood beside them, bent over with hands gripping knees, gasping for air. Solomon released his grasp on the unconscious woman and scrambled to his feet. He gave the mercenary escort an appreciative glance before something else caught his eye.

She stood in the open doorway, no longer an apparition, staring out into the farmyard like a dream taking on flesh. She resembled the young woman Solomon had held in his arms only she appeared older and more composed. The investigator began to understand his confusion. The two women were sisters. Even from a distance, the short-sleeve peasant blouse left the birthmark on her arm exposed. A splatter of purple. Isn't this what Sara had told him?

"Are you Lia?" he shouted in Arabic.

A wide-eyed expression revealed her understanding of the language; and, a slight nod of the head confirmed what he already surmised. He watched tears well up in the woman's melancholy eyes and trickle down her cheeks.

Solomon Levy had found the Galician woman.

THE ANIMALS WERE SHELTERED inside the farmhouse. The double doors led into this enclosure, an interior barn with a hard packed earthen floor and a chicken coop in one corner. There were no stalls for the two horses and the mule, but they would be safe from the elements and any marauding predators. The ceiling consisted of a series of wooden planks set across sturdy beams. It served as the floor of the second story.

Through a set of interior doors and also inside the farmhouse, Jalal guarded the two prisoners whose wrists were bound with rope. Lia and a man Solomon had learned was her younger brother, Roi. Vitor had dispelled the investigator's earlier notion that the man traveling with the Galician woman was her lover. The investigator took a long look at Roi, a broad-shouldered man who dressed himself in a woolen shirt and woolen pants tucked into knee high boots. He was probably used to being in command of every situation given his size. Now the tables were turned as Jalal had him reduced to the status of being a prisoner in his own home.

Meanwhile, the ex-cleric spent his time trying to console Lia's sister, speaking with her in their native Galician tongue. He'd already convinced Solomon that it wasn't necessary to bind his inamorata, taking full responsibility for the outcome.

Solomon wanted to be alone with his primary suspect.

Desiring to talk to her without interruptions, he took Lia back outside and led her over to the farm's rustic granary which he now understood was not an above ground burial site. He stopped below the stone foundation and turned to her. She stood face to face with him, gazing at him as she waited for the questioning to begin.

Solomon looked into luminous green eyes.

Lia didn't look afraid and he discerned a fiercely independent nature. On one of her fingers, he found the ring made of jet lignite. The oblong black stone, mounted in a gold setting, looked well-worn and natural on the second finger of Lia's right hand. He observed no telltale trace of lighter skin on any of the other fingers, but he couldn't rule out the possibility she'd worn another ring.

He removed a leather pouch from his coat pocket, loosened the drawstring, and extracted something from inside. "Please," he implored, as he took her hand and tried to slide the gold ring on one of her fingers with no success. She watched him carefully as he struggled to fit it on her other fingers to no avail. His attempts brought them into close physical proximity, so close he could smell her blouse and the skin beneath. He searched for an accurate word to describe her scent and settled for herbaceous.

"Have you seen this ring before?" he asked, choosing to conduct his inquiry in Arabic although he suspected she might speak Latin as well as Galician.

Their eyes met again, his probing for an honest answer.

"Never," she replied without hesitation.

Solomon believed she'd spoken the truth.

He returned the ring to safe keeping, but there was something else inside the pouch. He took it out and once again she watched him closely. He unfolded a quadrant of paper.

"However, this does belong to you," Solomon insisted as he removed a strand of hair from its wrapping. He held it up so she could examine its length and color. He then placed it next to her own and compared the color and texture to its luxuriant source. She drew away from him, but her eyes held his gaze.

"You can see for yourself."

Solomon was attracted by her voice, a warm, engaging tone with a rhythm pleasantly altered by a slight but somewhat evident Galician accent. If this is her speaking voice, her singing voice must sound divine. She transported her audiences to another dimension. Isn't that what Sara had told him before his mind came up with that terrible pun he hadn't dared to share with her.

"I spoke with your roommate, Sara."

Lia's expressive eyes registered surprise.

"You spoke with Sara," she repeated as her voice softened.

"It was part of my preliminary investigation," he told her. "She's concerned about your welfare. She believes you returned to Galicia because you were homesick."

"I miss Sara so much," she sighed.

Solomon felt like he was beginning to lose the thread of his inquiry. As much as he appreciated Lia's sentiment, it was time to get down to business. He needed answers that had thus far eluded him. Only then could he decide how to proceed, whether it would be necessary to take her back with him to Andalusia so as Hasdai had phrased it "justice might be served."

"You spent time alone with Umar at his apartment."

"I've never denied it." she said defiantly.

"I'm not your enemy," he asserted. "Not even your accuser. I simply need to discover the truth about Umar's death."

"Umar's dead?"

Solomon saw a look of horror in her eyes as they widened in response to the unintended revelation.

"You didn't know he was dead?"

Lia didn't answer. Her expression turned grave as she reflected upon the news. She retreated inside of herself, withdrawing her emotions to some hidden interior place. The investigator felt confused by her answers so he decided to press on.

"You admit spending time with Umar."

She refused to answer.

Solomon realized he had unintentionally opened a deep wound. As he stood in the shadows of the barn, her eyes pierced straight through him: his ignorance, his stupidity, and his arrogance. He felt naked, exposed in a way no clothing could conceal.

"Do you enjoy this type of work," she asked.

"What?"

"I asked if preying upon the vulnerable gives you satisfaction."

You can hardly consider your brother vulnerable, he thought to himself. She had turned the tables on Solomon. He'd gone from being the interviewer to the one being questioned. What was she hoping to accomplish, he wondered.

"I'm a professional translator," Solomon answered. "I was sent to Galicia to find you because I understand Latin. I derive little pleasure from this assignment, but the future of the Caliphate may be at risk."

"Because of me?"

"Possibly, but I can help you."

"No, you cannot."

There was a long, uncomfortable silence. Solomon waited, but his sincere and generous offer had been refused. He couldn't think of anything more to say. He sensed their conversation was finished and she'd answer no more of his questions, but he found himself respecting her resolute individuality. Only now, the investigator felt helpless, unable to press ahead with his inquiries.

Grey clouds filled the sky and raindrops began to sprinkle down on them. Preoccupied with her own thoughts, Lia didn't seem to notice. Maybe she just didn't care. She didn't look up at him. Her downcast eyes found a place of refuge on the earth below.

Solomon wanted so badly to help this Galician woman, but he wasn't sure what to do or what to say. He tugged gently on the rope fastened around her wrists and then he took her cupped hands into his own and led her back inside the farmhouse.

Chapter 27

A light rain continued to fall as the musty smell of wet earth wafted in through the open door of a stone farmhouse divided at ground level into two rooms. The spacious main area housed a kitchen and eating space. An aromatic fire burned in the hearth at the far end of this room. The second room, partitioned with a stacked and mortared grey granite wall, contained a closed doorway leading into the barn.

There was a wooden stairway and Solomon guessed it led upstairs to sleeping quarters.

A clean, slate floor worn down from decades of use, and a ceiling above their heads mimicking the barn's, provided unpretentious living. Within these walls, the three outsiders found the simple oneness of things ordered. Cooking implements hung down from a rack suspended off an open wooden beam. A long, roughhewn rectangular table, surrounded by half a dozen chairs, had yet to be set. Ceramic goblets and plates were stacked neatly on a rustic-looking pinewood sideboard, plank cut, knots and all.

The three inhabitants sat at the table, the man at one end and the sisters side by side, while Jalal kept his eyes trained on them. Solomon stood with the excommunicated priest as they warmed themselves by a fire which not only heated this dwelling, but also ensured a different type of sustenance. Hanging over low flames, an iron kettle released a steamy, savory aroma into the farmhouse.

The fire seemed deficient to Solomon as its heat only extended out a few feet into the room at best. A couple of lit candles notwithstanding, the farmhouse felt dark and cold and dreary. And this was the end of May. He could only wonder what it would be like during the winter months. No wonder these people suffered from melancholia. The investigator found himself aching for the warmth of the Andalusian sun.

There they were, six bewildered souls huddled together like a bunch of lost lambs, nobody knowing what to do or what to say. Sabela broke the hex when she rose from the table and went to the fire. She carried a ladle and pushed her way in between Solomon and Vitor to taste a soup.

Lia soon joined her, nudging the men aside as the two women reclaimed their birthright.

Sabela offered her sister a sip, holding the ladle steady as her bound sibling slurped some soup between her lips. Lia whispered something into her sister's ear before the two of them returned to the table.

The day wore on as did the rain. The captors and their prisoners spent what felt like an eternity fending off the discomfort and monotony of a long and uneventful afternoon. Vitor stood and abruptly motioned for Solomon to join him. The investigator wondered what might be on the young man's mind. He followed the ex-priest, climbing the stairs until he reached the second story where he found Vitor waiting for him on the landing. There was a door on either side and he followed the ex-priest into one of the rooms.

The bedroom contained a single bed with a blanket covering a straw mattress. On top of an old dresser a blue ceramic pitcher lay inside a matching wash basin. Solomon felt certain Roi slept inside this monastic cell. Not even a window. The room felt danker than the room below them. Simple and spare, it wasn't all that different than the bedrooms Lia and Sara had slept in back in Córdoba. Solomon looked around the room but found no sign of the entertainer's costume. He hadn't expected to. He'd have to search the bedroom across the hallway. He wondered if it would ever turn up.

Vitor leaned in close and the former cleric spoke in a voice barely above a whisper.

"I had a hard time explaining to Sabala why I'm here with two foreigners, two apparently hostile foreigners. I think she's accepted my account of how this transpired. She's more embarrassed than anything, ashamed for not putting up a fight when you grabbed her. Galician woman are strong and proud. Lia would've likely given you quite a battle. Sabela, however, is a sensitive soul. Which is why I fell in love with her."

"This is why you brought me up here?" Solomon interrupted.

"I'm sorry, I digressed. It's Lia. She refuses to answer any more of your questions in Arabic. She says she won't listen to one word you speak. I tried to talk sense, but she won't listen to reason. It wasn't easy, but I've convinced her to respond to your inquiries in our native Galician, with me acting as interpreter."

"A rather convoluted arrangement."

"The best I could do," insisted Vitor. "The only reason she trusts me is that she knows her sister's welfare is my first concern."

"Lia is certainly bent on defending her autonomy," Solomon observed, changing the subject as well as the tone of their conversation. "Leaving Galicia to work as a singer, in Córdoba, took real courage. She must really love this farm"

"Sabela told me they were in danger of losing their land. This farm has been in the family for generations, but they were threatened with eviction because they couldn't afford to pay the annual taxes and lease. This land is owned by the church in Santiago de Compotela. Bishop Sisnand has vowed to exercise his rights of emphyteusis. The church confiscated many properties like this under the pretext of continuing Roman law after the Emperor's legions were ousted from Galicia."

"The Warlord never mentioned any of this to me."

"They've resisted invading tribes, the Visigoths, and even Berbers," continued Vitor. "After the Muslim invasion, Gallegas were taken to serve as concubines in the harems of the south. Now, they go willingly. Poor farm girls trying to help their families or seeking a better life for themselves in the city, perhaps a life of luxury. Lia didn't want to walk that path. She knew her voice would gain her employment. She didn't plan to stay in Andalusia forever."

The decision to bring Vitor with them had provided an unanticipated dividend. His relationship with the younger sister gave the investigator a window into their world. Solomon decided he'd have to risk trusting in the veracity of the interpretations he offered in spite of the ex-cleric's infatuation with the younger sister.

"I appreciate your translating for us, but I'll need more than a verbal interpretation," the investigator told Vitor. "I need you to listen carefully to Lia and Roi's inflections, to see if you can discern what parts of their answers might be true or if they might be attempting to mislead me."

"I'll do my best."

"There's something else, Vitor," Solomon continued. " I'd like you to glean some information for me, but I need for you and Sabela to keep it to yourselves."

"I'm listening."

"I want to know how much it would take to buy this farm outright from Bishop Sisnand."

"Oh, and Vitor ... please tell Jalal I'd like for him to bring Roi up here. I need to ask him some questions. I'll need you to return with them so you can translate for me."

"Of course," replied the compliant Galician.

SOLOMON STOOD TOE-TO-toe with the Galician woman's younger brother. He didn't know if any of his questions would elicit a response, but Vitor stood nearby ready to assist him. The investigator observed the farmer closely, hoping his emotions or body language might offer a clue when he delivered his answers.

"Ask him what he knows about the murder of Umar abd-Rahman and what role he played in his sister's escape."

Vitor translated from the Latin while Solomon waited patiently for an answer. He sensed the brother would be uncooperative and perhaps resist answering altogether. The language barrier didn't make it easier.

Roi unleashed a torrent of words the investigator found unintelligible. The brother was surprisingly animated and he didn't appear to be holding anything back as Vitor's eyes grew wide. The words streamed forward as his story unfolded. When he'd finished, Roi gestured to the ex-cleric to share his revelation with Solomon.

Vitor reflected for a moment and then began.

"Roi said he went to Córdoba to try to convince Lia to return to Galicia. He followed her to the evening's performance and waited outside, hoping to surprise her. He saw her leave with a man, an Arab, and he shadowed them to the apartment. Someone ran down the street just as he approached. That person was hooded and unrecognizable. When he entered the apartment to find his sister, Umar was dead and Lia lay unconscious at the foot of the bed."

Vitor paused to collect his thoughts.

"Go on . . . " encouraged Solomon.

"Roi says he carried Lia to safety and then devised an escape plan. He was aided by two older men, Latin speaking Christians who had agreed to watch the two horses he had brought with him from Galicia. Roi approached them inside a church, in a Christian neighborhood in Córdoba, after witnessing his sister leave following a mass."

He brought two horses with him, the investigator mused. One for his sister and one for himself. He probably believed he could talk her into returning home to the farm, never imagining they'd be using them to make their escape from Andalusia.

"Ask him how they eluded us."

Vitor asked and then both he and Solomon watched as a broad smile widened the corners of Roi's mouth. The answer came almost as a whisper and Vitor leaned in to hear the words before translating: "They used the horses as a ruse and then followed you to Mérida. They set the horses free and then fell in with a group of pilgrims."

Solomon detected no falseness in the story or in the man delivering the accounts.

The good-natured farmer looked pleased with himself, proud of his considerable accomplishment. He'd outwitted representatives of the mightiest kingdom in Europe. Although Solomon found this unlikely scenario giving him an occasion to smile, he was also beginning to realize how vulnerable the situation had become. At that moment, Solomon realized he should return to Andalusia as soon as possible.

TWILIGHT ARRIVED AND more candles were lit to ward off the impending darkness. A flurry of activity in the kitchen resulted in six table settings. A steamy soup was ladled into wooden bowls and brought to the long table. The small family, and their three uninvited guests, sat on opposite sides. Sabela passed out seashells to scoop up the soup. Hands were untied and everyone began to eat soup in painful silence. Jalal unsheathed his sword and rested it against the bench. He appeared poised to strike at a moment's notice, ruining the already strained ambience.

The two Andalusis emptied their bowls and asked Vitor to arrange for a second helping. As they were being served, Solomon decided small talk was preferable to an uneasy truce and sullen faces.

"This soup is very nourishing," he said loud enough for all to hear.

Vitor shared his comment with the Galicians.

They responded with dour expressions and a stonewalled silence. The ex-priest didn't enjoy being caught in this emotional standoff. Solomon was sure Vitor felt grateful that he'd helped him leave

Santiago, but he sensed the cleric was conflicted because he also didn't want to risk antagonizing the older sister and brother of the woman of his dreams.

The investigator appreciated his attempt to remain neutral.

"It's called *Caldo gallego*," Vitor began. "It's a broth made from turnips, cabbage, and white beans. Sometimes they add other greens. Whatever's available at the time. When they're lucky, they have a bit of meat to add to the soup."

Despite his initial skepticism, Solomon found himself growing to like these Galicians. What they lacked in cultural refinement found compensation in an abiding connection to their land. Something far deeper and more precious than book learning. He respected this living relationship to nature and the earth, but he found his appreciation also left him conflicted. A part of him wanted to pretend he'd never found the Galician woman, to enlist Jalal in a secret conspiracy of silence; but, he could never forsake his responsibility and his mission. He could never turn his back on his people and his own land.

As they cleared the table, Solomon observed Vitor and Sabela speaking to each other in hushed tones. Lingering stares and warmhearted smiles revealed an obvious affection and in a paranoid moment the investigator wondered if they might be hatching an escape plot. He decided it was time to take control of the situation, save his doubts and questions for another time.

"We don't want to hurt anybody," Solomon insisted, raising his voice. "If you all cooperate, we won't have to take any extreme measures."

Roi looked to Lia. A look of perplexity filled his broad face. Brother and sister exchanged looks. Solomon wasn't sure what the nonverbal message might be. Did they possess a secret code? He couldn't read their faces so their emotions remained locked in mystery. He hoped they wouldn't attempt to flee. He didn't want to act on his threat. He didn't want the mission to end in tragedy.

"Tell them what I said, Vitor," Solomon instructed. "Make sure they understand the consequences of any attempt to escape."

When the ex-priest had finished, everyone understood the gravity of the situation.

"We're leaving in the morning," explained the investigator as he stood and walked to the head of the table. "Lia and Roi will be returning with us to Córdoba as our prisoners. Sabela is free to remain behind, or to join us if she wishes. You may also join us, Vitor. And, don't bother translating. I know Lia hears what I say. She can explain to her brother."

Solomon searched her eyes as Roi absorbed the information from his older sister.

"I've changed my mind," announced Vitor as he folded his hands and placed them on the table. "I'm staying behind to help with the farm and to offer Sabela my protection. We knew this betrayal was coming. I told Sabela as much when you were interrogating Lia outside."

"Don't you think interrogation is a rather harsh way of describing my asking questions?"

Vitor ignored him. "The thought of traveling to Andalusia scares Sabela to death. When the family stayed in Santiago de Compostela, during Eastertime, they heard rumors spread by the Bishop and his followers about the evils of the south."

"So, you've discussed this?"

"I told you," Vitor reminded him. "When you were outside questioning Lia."

"I see . . . "

"Is it so difficult to see where my loyalties lie?" Vitor wondered aloud. "We'll remain here. Somebody has to take care of the farm until they return."

"What do Lia and Roi think about this?"

Solomon looked down the table but his eyes met with impassive expressions.

"As I told you, Galician women are very independent. Sabela is free to decide for herself in these matters."

Solomon began to feel impatient, disturbed by Vitor's sudden defiance. He suspected the youth was attempting to redeem himself for cooperating with strangers who now threatened the well-being of this Galician family's existence. He wondered if the ex-priest had thought through the implications of his actions.

"What if her sister and brother can't return?"

"She didn't do it," Vitor insisted with a new found passion in his voice. "You can't possibly believe Lia is a murderess?"

"I have my doubts, but I'm charged with taking her back to Andalusia for a fair but thorough inquiry," Solomon said, making his intentions clear. "Time we all try to get some sleep."

The ex-cleric bit his lip and held his tongue. The women left the table with a flickering candle and retired upstairs to their bedroom. Roi's wrists were rebound with rope before he was marched upstairs by Jalal. Vitor followed with Solomon trailing behind.

FOUR MEN AND A SINGLE bed, Roi's bed. But all was not lost. The Andalusi's had the forethought to bring their bedrolls upstairs and Sabela had produced a couple of blankets for her inamorata. Before taking the first watch, Jalal asked Solomon to join him in the hallway so he could share his doubts.

"Do you believe this woman and man are brother and sister?"

"I suppose I do," the investigator replied. "Vitor would have told us if they weren't."

"Are you sure? What if the man is an imposter? How do we know Vitor isn't siding with these Galicians to plot against us? I'm just saying maybe you shouldn't be so trusting, Solomon. I know you like them, but don't get attached."

"To be honest, I'm tempted not to take them back with us," Solomon admitted.

"Are you serious?"

"I don't believe she murdered Umar, and I certainly don't imagine Lia is part of a plot to reconquer Andalusia. She's all about saving her family's farm and I've learned the Bishop has designs on it. If we take her back to Andalusia we're giving Sisnand a wonderful chance to cheat the family out of this land and also give him an opportunity to champion Lia as a martyr for his cause. Don't think the old Warlord won't make use of her in this capacity during her absence. For a while I doubted it, but now I'm not so sure. We'll be doing him a big favor. He suspected we'd find her with or without Vitor's help. He's been counting on it."

"Listen to me, Solomon," the mercenary pleaded. "We've got to take them back and deliver them to the Foreign Minister. We're expected to uphold our mission without questioning the wisdom behind it. If they don't return with us that makes us traitors and we both know the penalty we face if the truth ever came to light."

Spoken like a true soldier.

"I'll think about what you've told me, Jalal."

As soon as he said it, Solomon dismissed these thoughts from his mind.

Jalal carried his bedroll out to the landing where he set up for the first watch. This way he could keep an eye on both bedrooms. He didn't trust the women any more than he trusted Roi or Vitor. He wasn't even sure he trusted Solomon anymore.

Solomon lay covered up on the wood plank floor waiting for sleep to come.

He thought about Lia and how she could have created a comfortable life for herself in Córdoba. But her family and the farm they had toiled so hard to preserve and the land itself—cold, misty, melancholy Galicia—meant more to her than her own well-being.

"Find her and bring her back so that justice may be served." We found her cousin Hasdai. And we found her brother or maybe he's her lover. We don't know for sure. We'll bring them both back. We'll bring the Galician woman all the way back to al-Zahra even though we don't know if she's guilty. In truth, we believe she is innocent of the crime. Will you give her a fair trial. You've promised as much, Mr. Foreign Minister.

God help us if we don't.

We'll lose our souls in the bargain.

Chapter 28

Two restless mares and a Balearic mule stood packed. Everybody gathered outside the farmhouse, Sabela uttering tearful goodbyes to an older sister and brother whose hands were once again bound with rope. Solomon hated this aspect of his mission. At the same time, he believed the precautions were necessary. He didn't understand the Galician banter, but it was natural for him to assume Lia was giving final instructions to Sabela and Vitor because the ex-priest nodded his approval whenever she spoke.

The investigator took his mercenary escort with him as they led the animals a safe distance away, close enough to take quick action if necessary, but far enough away to allow privacy. Lia and Roi appeared resigned to their fate so Solomon didn't believe they would attempt to escape.

The cold, grey morning found him feeling oppressed by the absence of sunlight and once again yearning for the warmth of the Andalusian sun. He could only imagine what the winters must be like. The Finnesterre might have been a preview. His reveries were cut short by his companion.

"I'm not sure we'll exit Santiago in one piece," Jalal said, voicing his misgivings.

"We're not traveling in that direction."

"What?"

"The Foreign Minister has arranged for a ship to meet us down the coast at the harbor town of Fistera," Solomon informed the surprised soldier. "From there we'll sail to Lisbon, Cádiz, up the Guadalquivir to Seville, and then home to Córdoba. This route offers a safer journey and will take less time. We'll sort out this mystery when we get back. I fear there are no answers for us here."

"Why didn't the Foreign Minister send us here by ship in the first place?"

"I believe he thought we might overtake them on the road."

Solomon sensed Jalal's hurt feelings, knowing him well enough by now to understand his bitter disappointment at not hearing of the plan in advance.

"I would've told you about the galley, but I've been so preoccupied it slipped my mind."

Solomon feared his excuse rang hollow.

"What about the horses and the mule?" Jalal asked, taking the snub in stride.

"The galley is a horse transport so we can take them with us."

"Good, I'm growing rather fond of the mule."

"Time we depart," Solomon said.

The two men returned to the others and the investigator asked Vitor to relay instructions to Roi. After they'd helped the stout, wrist-bound farmer mount the mule, Solomon assisted Lia up behind her brother. The mares would bear the burden of what little supplies they had left.

As the foursome rode away from the farmhouse, Solomon turned around for one final look. Sabela and Vitor had retreated inside. Smoke spiraled up from the chimney while chickens scratched for food in the farmyard and the dairy cow waited to be milked. The investigator knew he'd never set foot on this land again. A part of him experienced sadness. Another part was glad to be returning to Córdoba and the world he loved.

Turning back around, he caught a glimpse of the Galician woman.

Her fortitude had deserted her and Solomon found tears streaming down the sides of her face. His heart ached with compassion. Although he had succeeded in his mission, he had strong misgivings and a deep apprehension about the possible consequences of returning Lia and Roi to al-Zahra.

"Find her and bring her back so that justice may be served."

Solomon almost wished he hadn't.

THEY RODE SOUTH THROUGH a forest hugging the coastline of an inland sea, a bay reaching all the way north to the harbor town of Cee. Ten miles to the west, separated by a rugged peninsula, lay the *Mare Tenebrosu*," the dark sea," The sky overhead was laden with grey clouds but no rain fell upon them. Solomon longed for sunlight.

"How did the Foreign Minister calculate our timing?" asked an inquisitive Jalal.

"I'm not sure," Solomon answered. "I imagine the galley has been waiting for us for days, if not weeks."

They reconnected with the road from Santiago de Compestela, the one leading to the Finnesterre, the end of the earth. They had journeyed there, experienced its magic, and now they were going home. The investigator allowed Jalal to take the lead while he brought up the rear behind the two somber looking Galicians.

Jalal kept a brisk pace, pleased at knowing they had succeeded in their mission despite all his misgivings about Solomon and the way the investigator had approached their challenge, the constant delays, and his seeming reluctance to return their prisoners to al-Zahra. He had a sneaking suspicion his efforts would be recognized if not rewarded at the highest levels.

Finister, much like the town of Cee, harbored a fishing village that also lived upon the revenue generated by pilgrims making their way south in search of the end of the earth and its cherished seashells. Solomon searched the town for the appointed meeting place. It wasn't long before they found themselves outside a tavern with yet another seashell banner waving in the afternoon breeze. Solomon left Jalal outside to guard the two Galicians sitting with their hands bound with rope.

Inside he found the Captain of the transport, a barrel-chested Arab with a thick grey beard. He sat at a table playing cards with a few of his crew. He turned when he saw Solomon and his face brightened upon seeing Hasdai's signet ring. He suggested to his men that they might want to leave him and go regale themselves with more drink. They understood his subtle command and left the table to their Captain and the newcomer. Solomon sat down across the table from the Captain.

"Have you been waiting long?"

"That's of little consequence," replied the Captain. "I'm under strict orders."

"How shall we proceed?" Solomon asked, submitting to the mariner's judgement.

"We'll stay the night and leave first thing in the morning," the captain announced. "You'll meet us at a sandy beach just north of here where my men can put down our ramp so you can load your animals. How many do you have?"

"Three," replied Solomon failing to mention one of them was a mule. "What about our prisoners?"

"They'll be safe with me."

"I'm sure they will be," agreed Solomon.

Everybody's working for the Caliphate and everybody's working for themselves, thought the investigator. The captain probably thinks there'll be significant remuneration for himself if he delivers us successfully to the docks in Córdoba. Didn't he think something similar about his own prospects at the very beginnings of the mission. Only now he didn't care so much about himself and his hopes for reward. He kept having this gnawing doubt he might not be doing the right thing in returning Lia and Roi to face justice in al-Zahra. He wondered if perhaps he should have left them behind.

SOLOMON'S ROUTE WOULD take him south along the coast to Lisbon where they would disembark to spend the night and resupply the galley. The city had surrendered to an Umayyad army without a fight in 718, and the strategic port now gave Rahman III control of the coastal Atlantic waters.

From Lisbon the investigator's nautical journey would take him to Cádiz, the oldest city in Europe. Founded by the Phoenicians in 1100 BCE, the port was an important commercial center trading in Baltic amber, British tin, and Spanish silver. After that they would sail up the Guadalquiver to Seville and then home to to the freshwater port of Córdoba.

Solomon and Jalal stood waiting in anticipation, with their horses and the mule, on a stretch of sandy beach. Out in the waters of a calm bay the horse transport maneuvered into place and began to approach the shore. A door thirty feet long was lowered from the back of the vessel into shallow water and the two men smiled at one another. They were going home. The two men guided the horses out into the water and made their way towards the ramp.

"Let's get a running start," shouted Jalal as he sprinted off with his horse and the mule trailing behind him.

They ran the animals up the ramp to where sailors were waiting to take the reins. Both men, shoes and pants soaked by sea water, were breathing heavily from the exertion. Jalal's face widened into a smile. Soon both men stood on deck laughing out of sheer exuberance. There was a time when they doubted this precious moment would become a reality. Now they realized they were actually going home to Córdoba.

After Solomon had regained his breath, he turned to find his Galician prisoners sitting on deck with their hands and feet tied with ropes and guarded by one of the sailors. The Captain ordered the ramp to be hauled back on board and gave the order for his oarsmen to prepare for departure.

"How soon will we be home?"

The barrel-chested Captain smiled: "That depends upon three things. We'll need to get some wind in our sails, we have to avoid sea monsters, and the Captain can't get drunk." The old seadog waited for the full effect of what he'd told them to sink in. When Solomon's eyes widened in disbelief he sprang his trap.

"Hah! Hah!" bellowed the Captain. "You believed me? I was just playing with you. I only drink when I'm on land with the *terra firma* solidly underneath my feet"

"You tricked us," laughed Jalal. "And to think that I almost believed you."

The Captain gave the order and the oarsmen began a rhythmic motion, rowing the ship away from the shoreline, out towards the open sea. Solomon could only think about one thing. The bearded seafarer hadn't yet elaborated upon the need to avoid sea monsters. Was that also said in jest? He had heard stories of sea monsters as a child. At such an impressionable age his imagination had run wild. Now he found some of those frightening images floating before his mind's eye as his memory dredged them up from some forgotten, buried past.

Chapter 29

It seemed to Solomon that little had changed in al-Zahra during the time he had been away. The army still patrolled the streets, troop movements were evident everywhere, and the Tangerine still guarded the door outside the Foreign Minister's Office. Surprising, the investigator now felt a degree of confidence inside the corridors of power.

"You've done well, Solomon," praised Hasdai. "I felt confident you would succeed in finding the Galician woman. You have a gift."

Solomon was relieved to be back in Córdoba, but he knew only half of his mission was completed. He'd found and brought back the elusive Galician woman, but he wasn't convinced she had murdered Umar. He still had a lot of questions about the circumstances surrounding the crime, but few answers.

"I feel like I haven't yet finished my assignment."

"What do you mean?"

"I found Lia, but I'm not sure she murdered Umar."

"You're serious?" asked the weary looking older cousin.

"Quite. I need to interview all the suspects again." Solomon walked to the far window with its view of the old city. Hasdai quietly joined him and draped an arm around his shoulder in a gesture of affection: "What can I do to help?"

"I believe the Imam could convince Umar's widow and his brother to cooperate more fully in our investigation," Solomon told him. "Perhaps the Caliph could set up a meeting for me with the spiritual leader outside the Great Mosque."

"I'll try to arrange it," Hasdai promised as he removed his arm.

Solomon turned and went across the room to the chess set. The rock crystal and red marble figures had been organized for a new match.

"Looks like the Caliph won that last contest."

The Foreign Minister followed him over to the table as his mouth rearranged itself into a sly grin.

"On the contrary. I observed the move I prevented you from making, and I decided to make use of the strategy it suggested. That turned the tide and I managed to turn an apparent defeat into a resounding victory. The Caliph is anxiously awaiting our rematch."

Solomon could only muster a weak smile before making a beeline for the chair opposite the Foreign Minister's desk where he plopped down and exhaled a weary sigh. Hasdai followed his lead, pulling out his own chair and sitting down to continue the meeting.

"What about the Galician woman's brother? Don't you think he might have murdered Umar to protect his sister?"

"He certainly possess the strength to accost Umar single-handedly, but I don't picture Roi as a murderer. Then again, I could be mistaken. I'll need someone to translate Galician for me when I question him. I had a good translator in Galicia, a young priest who had been excommunicated by the Bishop of Santiago," Solomon declared. "It was probably a blessing for him. I don't think Vitor is cut out to be a clergyman."

"You seem to have grown very close to these Galicians."

"It's complicated," Solomon replied. "Maybe you can arrange for one of the Caliph's Galician concubines to translate for me?"

"Yes, of course," Hasdai reassured him. "By the way, Ahmad has returned from Tangier. It doesn't appear there was any Fatimid involvement in an assassination attempt. Zanata intelligence predicts they'll attempt to use the navy as their chief weapon. They already control Mediterranean shipping lanes and believe they can undermine our economy to the point of creating massive discontent here in Andalusia."

Solomon simply didn't understand why sects practicing the same religion had such a difficult time finding common ground. If the Jews, Muslims, and Christians of Córdoba could co-exist somewhat peacefully surely different Muslim branches were capable of overcoming the destructive effects of factionalism to create peace among themselves.

The Foreign Minister asked a question that still bothered him.

"Are you sure it wasn't the woman or her brother?"

"I know that would make life easier for us all. I also know the Caliph's jailers have methods of making prisoners confess to crimes they never committed. I hope it doesn't come to that."

"Believe me, Solomon. The Galicians will receive fair treatment at their respective detention centers. You have my word."

"There is another suspect, but I don't feel comfortable revealing the identify of an individual of whom I'm not yet certain," Solomon volunteered. "At any rate, I won't need help with that one. Oh, and one last thing. I need to interview an expert on Muslim inheritance laws. I'm thinking perhaps a professor of law at the University of Córdoba."

"Anything else I can do to help?"

"I'm not sure yet . . . "

SOLOMON WAITED OUTSIDE the main entrance to Córdoba's Great Mosque. He arrived early, giving him an opportunity to study the architectural marvel. His eyes were drawn to an elaborately decorated wooden door surrounded by intricate tile mosaics. The door was one of nine, all similar in appearance, all leading into the interior of the Mosque. Arches in a variety of styles, sizes, and designs, had been used as both structural and decorative elements in the façade. Solomon found the attention to detail interesting without being overwhelming.

He turned his gaze to the minaret, source of so many calls to prayer. Rahman III was in the process of replacing the two centuries old minaret with a new one containing two staircases built for the separate ascent and descent of the turret. On its summit, the architect proposed placing three decorative apples, two of gold and one of silver, with lilies of six petals. The new minaret would be four-faced, with arched windows resting upon columns made of jasper.

Residents of the city had been apprised of the plan.

The site of this Great Mosque had a history. It had sustained a Roman temple dedicated to the god Janus and a Catholic Christian church dedicated by the Visigoths to Saint Vincent. After the Islamic conquest, the building was divided between Muslims and Christians. On this site Rahman I chose to raise his Great Mosque. He generously offered to buy the church and the plot. He could've taken it by force. Under terms of the transfer, Christians were permitted to rebuild a ruined church formerly dedicated to three deeply revered Catholic martyrs.

Solomon directed his attention elsewhere.

Perfume sellers had set up booths on the perimeter of the square. Vendors offering more malodorous goods were consigned to an area further away so their wares wouldn't deter the devout and diminish attendance at prayer services. The square at the Mosque's main entrance had taken on an elevated importance because the Supervisor of Markets plied his trade in the square and important funeral rites were conducted here.

The investigator wouldn't be allowed inside. Entering the Great Mosque was a privilege rarely accorded non-Muslims. Non-believers

were left to imagine the splendors inside. Occasionally visiting
dignitaries were allowed a glimpse into the hallowed space, but that
was a rare event.

Still, Hasdai had worked his magic.

The Caliph had interceded with the Imam on behalf of the
younger cousin. The meeting arranged by Hasdai and the Caliph
was timed so it wouldn't be interrupted by the noon call to prayer.
Solomon waited patiently and soon the door to the main entrance
opened.

A BEARDED HOLY MAN dressed in the traditional *Abayah*, a
high-collared white coat, stepped outside into the early morning
shadows along the Mosque's western wall. His head was covered with
a short rounded skullcap, also white, called a *tagiya*. The Imam's
face glowed like polished alabaster. Illuminated from within, his eyes
seemed to be infused with the light of wisdom and understanding.
Solomon experienced a sense of peace and well-being in his presence.

"I'm sorry to inconvenience you," Solomon apologized.

"It is not an inconvenience to serve my people, the Caliphate,
and most of all, Allah."

He sounds like a Muslim version of cousin Hasdai, Solomon
thought as he endured the uncomfortable twinge of a guilty
conscience while owning up to his own selfish nature.

"I wish I could allow you inside our Mosque so you could
experience the majesty a divine and infinite intelligence can inspire."

"I understand that won't be possible," sympathized the
investigator.

"How may I be of help to you, my son?"

Solomon felt ill at ease for the first time in the Imam's presence.
He didn't know how to address the religious leader. Should he call

this man Your Grace or Your Eminence? He decided to dispense with titles altogether and simply state his business.

"I need your help," Solomon told him. "I'm encountering difficulties in my investigation into the murder of Umar abd-Rahman."

"There's something you should understand," the Imam informed him. "Umar was a troubled man. He had not yet embraced the Prophet Muhammad. He had turned his back on Allah. I'm not sure how I can be of service to you given these circumstances?"

"Please, I need for you to speak with the family. Talk to his wife Nuzha, and his brother Hasan. Enlist their cooperation," continued the investigator. "Ask them to be more forthcoming when I interview them again."

The Imam reflected for a moment.

"I would be happy to do so, young man. I'll meet with them on Friday after worship. Not at the same time of course. The women pray separately. However, they both come to this Mosque to pray. If I could invite you inside, you might understand why they choose to make the journey from al-Zahra."

"I appreciate your assistance, Sir."

"They told me I would be meeting with Solomon Levy."

"I am he."

"Aren't you the man who recovered the lost manuscript?" the spry old man asked as he stroked his wispy white beard.

"How do you know about that?"

"The Caliph keeps few secrets from me," replied the Iman. "He believes I can be trusted in all matters."

"I'm sure you can."

"The Caliphate is in your debt, my son."

This meeting had been going well, Solomon thought. He was amazed at the mention of the manuscript and even more surprised by the positive response of the Iman.

"You approve of my rescuing a botanical encyclopedia?"

"Of course I do. Religion and science can co-exist in peace. The Prophet Muhammad instructs us to 'seek knowledge from cradle to grave.'" The Imam's liberality took Solomon by surprise. "Andalusis should be grateful to you since we are all a manifestation of the magnificent and generous nature of our boundless creator, Allah."

The more Solomon thought about this the more it made sense. He understood the Quran to be neither myopic nor exclusive. It made provisions for approved religious minorities called *dhimmis*, protected peoples also known as "People of the Book," Jews and Christians with a revealed scripture recognized by Mohammad himself as divinely inspired.

Three books—the Torah, the Bible, and the Quran—and their emphasis on man's spiritual nature had elevated the desert tribes, inspiring them to rise above degradation and brutality. The essence of all three books was love God with your entire heart and being and love your neighbor as yourself. We all have trouble with that last part Solomon realized upon reflection. He included himself among the challenged.

Though the Imam spoke using superlatives the investigator found himself liking him nonetheless. He wasn't physically imposing and his was a face of cross-hatched wrinkles, but the brown eyes were perpetually smiling. He exuded character and Solomon wondered if he were a bit of a spiritual anomaly.

A small crowd began to gather around the charismatic Imam, but a hand waving gesture quickly dispersed them.

"You do the famous King Solomon proud," the Imam said, complementing the investigator.

"I often wish I possessed a fraction of his wisdom."

"The Quran explicitly states "No compulsion is there in religion," but we have many willing converts. Both Christians and Jews. Have you ever considered Islam?"

Solomon was well aware of the curve of conversion and how the Ibero-Roman population had steadily, over more than two centuries, converted to Islam for a variety of reasons, not the least of which was relief from taxation and economic constraints. Others accepted Islam simply because they believed it offered a superior, healthier way of life. The new Iberian converts and their descendants, along with the Muwallads, now outnumbered their Arab and Berber brethren in Andalusia.

Solomon, however, didn't embrace any particular creed.

"Jews and Christians are "People of the Book", but I'm also interested in the Book of Nature," he told the Imam.

"Are you a nonbeliever?"

"I'm not sure what I am," he confessed. "I have faith, but I also possess doubts. A bit confusing. I wonder how I'll ever know if I'm making spiritual progress?"

The Imam remained silent for a moment and then a wide, benevolent smile spread across his serene face: "If you're happy, Solomon Levy. If you're happy and doing harm to no one, then you're making spiritual progress."

"I really must be going, Sir."

"May Allah guide your steps," came the Imam's blessing.

It may be too late, Solomon thought to himself.

Chapter 30

Solomon entered through the unlocked, wooden gate. *She'll never change. Why would anybody want her to change?* He had missed Layla. He didn't realize how much until the journey north. Maybe it was time he accepted her generous offers. He took a deep breath as he walked across the shaded, green courtyard. He found red geraniums flowering. New blooms in the terra cotta pots. The front door was still painted a bright indigo.

Solomon rapped four times in succession. She had remembered their secret code last time, but he had been gone so long. The door swung open and he anticipated a warm greeting, expecting her to welcome his visit like she had in the past.

Layla looked taken aback.

"Surprised?" Solomon asked with a grin on his face.

"I wasn't expecting anyone."

"Aren't you going to invite me inside?"

"I'm sorry," Layla demurred. "I can't."

"What."

Solomon sensed a change in the courtesan, and he quickly understood an important element in their relationship had also changed while he was away. He had no idea what the cause might be. Had he done something to antagonize or embarrass her? Had he refused her advances one too many times?

"Layla, what's going on here?"

"I'm sorry, darling," she said, gazing up into his eyes. "I've met somebody special."

"I thought I was special."

Layla took his hand and pressed it gently.

"You are, Solomon," she reassured him. "You always will be."

He pleaded with his eyes.

"Wait for me in the courtyard," she said. "I'll return shortly."

SOLOMON WAITED QUIETLY. He sat on a bench in the courtyard garden surrounded by potted plants and listened to the plashing of water in the corner fountain all the while suspecting his own indecisiveness had created this turn of events. In the distance, he heard the noontime call to prayer invoking a time for meditation.

Layla returned a short time later and sat down next to him.

She didn't move in closer.

"I need help," he told her while trying to rise above his personal disappointment. "You've always been my confidant, and I've always relied on your judgment."

"I don't quite understand."

"I'm interviewing each of my suspects one more time, but they all have plausible motives. I need to ferret out the truth. You're the most emotionally intelligent person I know, Layla. What should I be looking for?"

It took some time before she offered her advice. Feeling vulnerable, Solomon wondered if she had decided not to help him. He was about to stand and leave when she began.

"Study their eyes. They'll reveal more than anything they might tell you. Watch how their bodies respond to your questions. Do they appear at ease or on edge? Remember, a good liar can trick your mind. Trust your heart to know if they're telling you the truth.

Finally," she continued, "Consider your own motives. If your own heart is confused it can trick you into making an error in judgement."

Solomon felt relieved. Layla had offered her best advice and proven herself a trusted ally. So what if she had met somebody new. She deserved to be happy. Now they could be friends with no ulterior motives, none on his part and none on hers.

"You'll always be my friend, Solomon," she told him.

"I swear you can read my mind."

ENJOYING THE WARMTH of an early summer morning, Solomon crossed the quadrangle of his alma mater, the University of Córdoba. Although Hasdai had been born into a wealthy family in Jaen, fifty-five miles to the east, he too had attended school in the Capital, only this was half a dozen years before his younger cousin had sought to further his education.

Solomon continued on his way. The weather on this day was nothing like far away, misty Galicia. Thank God for that. The dry heat welcomed him back home. While he strolled across the campus, he looked back affectionately on his student years and his language studies and dating young women. Nothing serious had developed from these liaisons and he now found himself between relationships.

Layla had become one in a series of missteps.

The investigator passed the current crop of undergraduates and marveled at their youth. Had it been that long? Some things hadn't changed. The international complexion of the student body being one of them. They arrived in Córdoba from every corner of the world. Both the students and the faculty.

Solomon found the building and the office he was seeking.

He knocked on a windowless door and it soon opened.

Invited to enter, he seated himself inside a tiny, book-lined cloister across from an enormous man dressed in flowing white robes. The law professor's hefty frame dominated the cramped space. His shaved head and curly black beard were typical of a Muslim Andalusi male. After the usual formalities had been dispensed with, Solomon commenced the arranged meeting with an honest admission of ignorance.

"I understand nothing about the Islamic laws of inheritance," he began. "Perhaps you can enlighten me."

"Islamic law is a vast subject," stated the erudite professor as his squinty eyes opened wide. "Maybe we should confine ourselves to your interest in Umar abd Rahman and the application of Muslim inheritance laws in this specific instance."

Solomon began to realize the man was more intelligent than he looked as the professor placed his beefy hands on the desk and folded them.

"Let's begin with the basic facts. Umar had one legal wife even though by law he is . . . was allowed four. He kept half a dozen concubines. The law allows as many concubines as a man can afford to care for and Umar certainly possessed great wealth. A rather odd household, but it's been said the Caliph's nephew . . . " the professor paused, tilting his head to one side as he searched for words to communicate his thoughts.

"Liked to sleep around," Solomon offered, completing the other man's thoughts.

"Thank you. Yes, liked to sleep around," repeated the professor. "Now we can establish that Umar has many children, but only one designated heir. There's also his widow and a full brother. I believe both his parents are deceased."

"This is also what I've been told," the investigator confirmed.

"There are assorted uncles and aunts as well as a paternal half-brother and sister, now residing in Egypt, along with a gaggle of nephews and nieces."

"It sounds so complicated," Solomon ventured to point out. "And this is just one small family. Most Muslim families are larger from what I observe in Córdoba."

"And complicated it might well be, except . . . the son blocks all but his mother from receiving a share. And, the shares are all prescribed by Muslim law. There is no . . . " there came a slight pause before the professor lifted his index finger to indicate he had found the correct nomenclature " . . . dickering. There is no dickering. The Law is specific when it comes to the fractions or percentages of the shares. That applies all the way down the line. No pun intended. You know, the lineage . . . those lining up to claim a share."

The professor opened a drawer, withdrew a piece of cotton fiber paper, and laid it flat on the desktop. He picked up a reed pen and dipped the sharpened tip into a reservoir of ink and then he began to scribble something as beads of perspiration formed on his forehead.

"Are you reporting the details of our meeting to the Caliph?"

The professor ceased writing and looked up with a smile.

"No need to worry Solomon ben Levy." laughed the rotund professor. "I'm writing out the exact shares due to each heir. You may then take this information with you to aid you in your inquiries. In this particular case, the division is simple. The widow receives twelve and one half percent while the son inherits the bulk of the estate, eighty-seven and one half percent to be exact. It works out to one-eighth and seven-eighths in fractions."

The loquacious professor finished writing down the details of the inheritance and passed over the information.

"It's clear Umar's intention was for his son to inherit the lion's share of his estate. That young boy will need some protection. Predators abound, even in Córdoba and al-Zahra. How old did you say he was?"

"I didn't." Solomon responded. "I believe the boy is ten years old."

The investigator's focus changed for a moment. Again, the idea of suicide came into his mind. Maybe for all his swagger, Umar secretly loathed himself but felt incapable of reversing his downward spiral into life's dark side. Maybe he wanted to protect his son from this depravity and dissolution. Insure a brighter future for the one person in the world he loved most. Solomon quickly dismissed the idea as naive on his part. Remembering the angle of the dagger served to reinforce his skepticism.

The law professor rose from his chair, the pull of gravity slowing his ascent.

"Will that be all, Solomon ben Levy?" he wondered. "I really must get out for some air. This office is stifling during the summer months, even this early in the season."

Solomon stood and graciously bowed to his host.

"May Allah be with you," invoked the professor.

"And you as well," the investigator replied. "Thank you for your assistance. You have proven helpful to our investigation."

"Perhaps you could forward a good word to the Foreign Minister?"

"Consider it done."

Without uttering another word, the smiling professor rushed out of the room. He waited for Solomon to exit behind him before locking the door to his little sanctuary and rushing down the hallway towards the nearest exit.

Chapter 31

Solomon came well-prepared for his second round of questioning. He began on al-Zahra's uppermost terrace where the view across the valley to Córdoba remained breathtaking. During his absence, the pollinated white blossoms of the almond trees had transformed themselves into multitudes of green kernels. By the end of summer they'd be ripe for harvesting.

Outside the palatial estate once belonging to Umar abd Rahman, a single eunuch stood guard. The investigator recognized him from his first visit to the compound. He was the tallest of the two original sentinels and his personal escort into the interior of the villa. The soldier wore the same required military uniform and stood like a statue, not moving a muscle.

The guard suddenly came to life as Solomon stepped down from a familiar two-wheeled cart. Once again, Hasdai had arranged for the old teamster to act as his driver. The towering eunuch, possessing a memory undiluted by time, motioned for the investigator to follow him down the marble walkway. The luxuriant green foliage had yellowed, a result of constant exposure to the burning rays of the Andalusian sun.

They stepped through an arched entryway into the dreamlike reception area and Solomon found himself appreciating the light and airy interior, an expansive sense of space lacking inside his own tiny home. He began recollecting the arched portals, remembered how they led deeper into the compound's guarded apartments. His escort disappeared through one of them leaving him free to marvel at the domicile's majestic antechamber.

Soothing aquamarine walls and brilliant gold lettering greeted him. How could he have forgotten the stylish calligraphy? He realized how preoccupied he had been, how the journey north had added new experiences to his life while subtracting memories of past occurrences. Does it all balance out in the end, he wondered. Comforting sounds floated in the background. The warm-hearted laughter of women and children, coming to him from distant rooms, reached his ears and it brought a warm glow to his face.

Then he saw them.

The two women walking towards him were smiling radiantly and laughing out loud. They appeared quite at ease. They came unveiled. Their exquisite silk robes also suggested the period of mourning had come to an end. He observed them closely as they approached. They wore make-up and there was more, something intangible, an invisible nuance. They exuded a hint of perfume. It smelled musky like the essence of patchouli oil.

Nuzha stepped forward to greet him:

"Solomon ben Levy," she announced. "So good to see you"

"Really?"

"I owe you an apology," Umar's widow admitted. "I treated you rudely when we last met. Please forgive me."

"We were all under a lot of pressure."

"That's no excuse for my shameful behavior."

"I do need to ask you more questions."

"Let's sit down," Nuzha suggested, inviting the investigator to join her on a long marble bench lined with silk-covered pillows. Set back against a wall, it had been designed for the comfort of visitors and guests asked to wait in the reception area. The second woman joined them, sitting beside the widow. Solomon remembered that she was a concubine and not a wife. Umar only had one wife. That could be important, he reminded himself.

Remembering Layla's advice, he turned and looked directly at Umar's widow.

She possessed skin as smooth as the finest porcelain. He found her delicate nose and full lips decidedly sensuous. The fiery intensity of her eyes had been replaced by a softness Solomon found most welcoming. Long, luxuriant black hair cascaded down along the sides of her neck.

"Did you find Umar's murderer?"

He focused on her eyes.

"I need to find out more about your relationship with Hasan," he began, ignoring her question.

"Hasan adores me," Nuzha confided.

"And you?"

"Hasan is given to flights of fancy," she giggled. "We're friends and nothing more."

The concubine nudged closer to join in the conversation. "Everyone can see that Hasan loves his horses," the concubine quipped. "There lies Hasan's one true love."

The two women shared a hearty laugh at Hasan's expense. This led Solomon to believe that Nuzha spoke the truth. She didn't look tense. Quite the contrary, she appeared relaxed and cooperative. The line of questioning didn't faze her. This is the women he had remembered from official functions: charming, witty, and refined. Solomon was glad she had returned to her natural self and he sensed this provided a unique opportunity to brooch a delicate question.

"Do you think Hasan capable . . . "

"Of murdering Umar to marry me?" she interrupted. "I don't think so. No, many times in the past I have made it clear to Hasan that I haven't the slightest interest in his attentions."

He'd have to take this matter up with Hasan in person. No need to press Nuzha further on the subject. His inquiries might not even prove relevant to Umar's murder. Hasan might be innocent of the crime. It was time to ask about another subject, one that might have a more direct bearing on the case.

"Muslim law entitles you to a share of your late husband's inheritance."

Deciding it was time to enlighten him, Nuzha changed the subject.

"You must realize that in our culture it is the woman who receives the dowry, not the man." He had been taken by surprise. She read it in his eyes. "My dowry was extremely lucrative, extravagant by most standards. My husband had many shortcomings, but Umar was a good provider and a loving father."

Her portion of the inheritance was no longer the issue, but the son and his share might provide the skeleton key for unlocking this mystery.

"You told me the inheritance of Umar's wealth is up to the Caliph," Solomon began. "Not quite true, is it? According to Islamic law . . . "

"I did not lie to you, Solomon ben Levy," she began, interrupting him again. "To drink alcohol is forbidden by the Quran, but Muslims are only human as you've no doubt witnessed. The ruling on wine drinking has been extended by jurists who at first allowed only the drinking of honey wine. Now a great deal of wine is consumed in Andalusia. Men desire to wear silk, again forbidden. So they have threads woven into cotton garments attempting to circumvent the religious law. I will repeat what I told you before. No matter what the law claims, the Caliph has the final say in all matters under heaven and earth. This is the reality of our existence."

Seeking an opportunity to study the two women's facial responses simultaneously, the investigator stood and turned to face them.

"However, we both know the Caliph is a devout Muslim. If nothing else, he wants to appear devout. I imagine he won't intervene in the distribution of Umar's estate. Based on my information, your son will inherit most of his father's wealth."

"And well he should," Nuzha replied as she gazed directly into his eyes. "If you remember, I also told you that despite Umar's faults he was a good father. He loved his son. Loved him so much that he made sure Ali was his sole designated heir."

The concubine remained impassive.

"You must also realize the son blocks the full brother, in this instance Hasan, from receiving any share," Solomon responded. "It was only a matter of time before Ali would inherit his rightful share. Umar couldn't live forever."

"You're right, of course," she replied.

He sensed another gesture of conciliation rather than a deeply held belief. Perhaps she had wanted her son's inheritance to happen sooner rather than later. Perhaps Nuzha had lost all patience with Umar given his many affairs. Solomon reached into his pocket and withdrew something shiny.

"Have you seen this ring before?"

Nuzha took the gold ring and held it between her thumb and forefinger. She regarded it carefully and took her time before answering.

"No, I don't believe I have," she replied, before handing the ring back.

"And, you?"

He showed the ring to the concubine.

"No . . ."

While he gauged their responses, the widow embarked upon a new theme.

"Every mother wants what's best for her son . . . or, her daughter. Do you think my being a murderess is what's best for Ali?" she asked, her voice rising an octave.

Solomon decided the time had come to end the interview. Nuzha, gracious and cooperative, had displayed none of her former vitriol. More questioning might feel like harassment. He pocketed the ring.

"I'm sorry I've had to ask these questions," he apologized. "You've been extremely cooperative. Time I have a talk with Hasan."

The two women stood to say goodbye.

"Don't bother going to Hasan's apartment," advised the concubine "You're more likely to find him at his stables."

"They're located a mile east of the Caliph's stables," added Nuzha. "Umar purchased the land in exchange for his brother's management of the business. Their business arrangement was probably a better marriage than our own."

The widow's radiant smile gave proof she had let go of the past.

The Imam has certainly worked some magic, thought Solomon. He wondered if the questioning would go as smoothly when he interviewed Hasan.

SOLOMON FOUND PEAR-shaped Hasan leaning on a fence post while a small cadre of workers went about the business of grooming, feeding, and exercising two dozen or more Andalusian horses. This operation paled in comparison to the Caliph's immense stables which employed hundreds of laborers to care for thousands of horses. Those thousands created tons of pungent horse manure which the investigator knew wouldn't go to waste. Once dried, the

Empire's agronomists applied it to every conceivable candidate: flowers, vegetables, root crops, berries, and all acid loving plants.

The investigator sniffed the air. The tang of Hasan's stables had remained in proportion to the size of the enterprise although it still exuded the distinct odor of equine feed and its aftermath. The moment the horse breeder spotted him approaching a scowl contorted his face.

Umar's brother turned back to his horses.

Hasan ignored him.

"You're the younger brother?" Solomon guessed.

"What of it?" challenged Hasan, answering his question abruptly with one of his own.

"Umar found incredible success in the world."

Hasan seemed ill at ease. Taking his arms from the fence post, he shifted his weight from foot to foot. Gravity, not just the laws of physics, but the gravitas of the situation, began to anchor Hasan to the ground.

"I'm not ambitious, if that's what you're getting at."

Those bulging eyes and that doughy face. No wonder Nuzha had resisted his advances. "A member of the royal family isn't ambitious?"

"There's nothing wrong with ambition. I possess my fair share, but I take exception to obsessive ambition. The kind that led to my brother's downfall."

"Umar's ambition was unrestrained?"

"You saw his apartment, you have been to his estate, and surely you've delved into his background." Hasan began, stating the obvious. "You and your cousin are not stupid."

He's done some probing of his own, thought the investigator.

"Tell me more about your horses and the business agreement with Umar?"

"A lucrative business. We sell our brood stock directly to the Caliph. Umar made the arrangement. In return for that, and for his supplying capital to launch the enterprise, I agreed to manage the day-to-day operations."

Hasan waved an arm in the direction of the exercise track where two experienced riders took powerful black mounts through a variety of gaits: walks, trots, and canters. They did everything except gallop the horses.

"Look at those two stallions. Aren't they the most beautiful creatures in Allah's entire creation?"

Solomon looked out to the track. He couldn't help but admire the strongly built, compact yet elegant black stallions with their long, thick manes and tails.

"Having spent the better part of the month on the back of an intelligent Andalusian mare, I agree whole-heartedly," he answered, attempting to erase the tension between them.

"You brought the Galician woman back to al-Zahra." Hasan stated. This wasn't a question. The horse breeder made the assertion and then looked to Solomon, awaiting his response.

So much for erasing tension.

"How did you find out?"

"Surely you must realize I'm well connected," grinned Hasan. "I hope she ends up with her head rolling on the ground."

What a despicable little man. He stinks in more ways than one. The scent of Garlic oozes from his pores making him even less endearing. Avoid a confrontation. Stay focused on the investigation. Solomon took a couple of steps backwards, putting some distance between himself and Hasan.

"Tell me about your relationship with Umar's wife."

"You mean his widow," corrected Hasan. "My brother treated Nuzha despicably."

"You didn't answer my question," challenged the investigator with a bit of rancor in his voice. He was growing tired of getting deceptive responses. Apparently, the Imam's magic had produced little effect upon Umar's brother.

"I asked you about your relationship."

"I'm in love with Nuzha," Hasan admitted. "Is that what you want to hear?"

"Everybody knows that. What I want to hear is . . . "

"Listen, Levy . . . I didn't kill my brother."

"I hope you can prove it."

One by one, Solomon was turning the tables on his suspects. Stonewalled and despised by them for the investigation he had agreed to conduct, he'd finally gained the upper hand. He wasn't yet certain who the murderer might be, but it was only a matter of time before he discovered the truth.

"What happens to your business now that Umar is dead?"

"If Nuzha doesn't want her son to purchase his father's share of the business, I have a long list of interested investors. But you must understand," Hasan insisted, "The business aspect is secondary for me. Just an excuse to spend my time around these beautiful animals. I swear as Allah is my witness, I would never subject them to sinful behavior."

"Yet you took your brother as a partner."

"I had hoped Umar might spend more time out here with me and the horses, that he might be led away from the life he desired to lead."

"Did Umar know how you feel about Nuzha?"

Hasan swallowed hard and turned his eyes away from Solomon. This wasn't encouraging.

"I tried to be discreet. After all, she is . . . was my brother's wife."

Hasan leaned his back against the fence and considered his response. It took some time for him to articulate his feelings.

"Umar didn't deserve Nuzha. I realized that from the beginning, but I had no say in the matter. Otherwise, I would have attempted to prevent the union. No doubt, you've talked with her. I have nothing to hide."

Solomon peeked at the breeder's hands. Like his brother, and most men in Andalusia, all his fingers were bejeweled. The lavish adornment left no doubt the gold ring in his possession didn't belong to Hasan. There wasn't room for another ring and none of his fingers revealed the telltale sign of lighter skin.

Solomon took the ring from his pocket.

"Have you ever seen this ring?"

"I don't remember it," Hasan answered. "Should I?"

"I'm not sure."

The investigator had exhausted his questioning and this led to a moment of reflection. Hasan had no reason to kill his brother for money. The son's share rules over the brother and blocks Hasan from any inheritance. Umar's death doesn't impact the business. Hasan has investors lining up to get a share of the Caliph's largess. Still, he might have done it out of jealousy and a desire to have Nuzha for himself. Maybe he thought he could overcome her resistances. Marrying the widow was a devious way to gain direct access to the untold riches of the son.

"I have no further questions at this time," Solomon said.

Having left the door open for future encounters, he took a final look at the stables. Out beyond the railings, two magnificent black stallions continued to please their trainers. As he turned to leave, Solomon couldn't help but notice the frown forming on the face of Umar's equine obsessed sibling.

"I didn't kill my brother."

"We'll see about that."

Chapter 32

They sat together, side by side, inside a bleak prison waiting room. One of the two men, Bishop Racemundo, had the look of an Old Testament patriarch. A tall, bearded and imposing figure, he grasped a crosier in one hand, a curved wooden pastoral staff. Solomon wondered if it were merely a prop, but he didn't dare ask because it might also double as a potent weapon. A piece of linen cloth, attached to the staff just below the crook, served as a handkerchief.

Bishop Racemundo wore a hooded black cloak.

A gold, pectoral cross hung down from the Bishop's neck on a long chain and an impressive circlet of gold, a ruby set directly into its center, surrounded the fourth finger of his right hand. Solomon's thoughts immediately turned to Bishop Sisnand and his remarkable ruby. He didn't find the memory of the old Warlord comforting.

"I think you have an affinity with Saint Anthony," chuckled Bishop Racemundo.

"What do you mean?"

"Saint Anthony is the patron saint of seekers of lost articles."

"Lia isn't exactly an article."

"I'm sure the saint made an exception in your case," the Bishop insisted good-naturedly. "He probably widened the definition for you, but I was actually thinking of the lost manuscript."

The investigator swallowed hard.

"How did you find out about that?"

"The Caliph is very forthcoming with his inner circle. He thinks we can be trusted. When the theft of the manuscript occurred your cousin Hasdai was floating the idea of sending me back to Constantinople to meet with representatives of the Byzantine Emperor. I was going to request the services of a Greek-speaking Byzantine monk, a man named Nicholas, to help us translate *De Materia Medica*. The mission is still under consideration."

There was a degree of transparency at the highest levels of state that Solomon had never imagined possible in his society. The Caliph's trust was evidently based upon a wide reaching mutual respect among his inner circle. While this translator-turned-investigator sat in amazement pondering the inclusiveness of Rahman III's governance, the door to the dreary little office swung open.

A woman walked into the reception room followed by a prison official. Solomon guessed the man to be the institution's superintendent. Bishop Racemundo leaned into his staff as he stood to welcome this odd couple. Andalusia's highest ranking Catholic cleric then extended his hand in greeting, first to the woman and then to the man. Solomon followed his lead as they were introduced to one of the Caliph's many Galician concubines. Noela, a honey-colored blonde who arrived elegantly dressed in a floor length red silk tunic with matching red shoes, appeared curvaceous despite her ample figure.

"Shall we go visit the prisoners," asked the warden.

Detainees is more appropriate, Solomon thought.

"By all means," replied the Bishop. "First, however, I would like to speak with Noela."

The unlikely quartet remained in the dismal reception area another ten minutes while Racemundo and Solomon conversed with the concubine.

―――――❦―――――

THEY FOLLOWED THE OFFICIAL down a long hallway filled with oppressive, dank air until they arrived at the entrance of a guarded cell. Bishop Racemundo gestured towards the door. The obliging warden opened the heavy, clanking metal barrier and our trio entered a spacious cell at what had euphemistically been called a detention center.

At first glance, the private room didn't look deficient for a prison environment. It contained substantial amenities: a comfortable bed, an oversized dresser, a metal wash basin with assorted towels and wash cloths, and a chamber pot. Solomon spied a single barred window, opened to provide fresh air.

A plate emptied of food sat on the floor near the doorway.

Roi stood as the visitors entered his temporary chambers. The robust Gallego didn't appear injured or underfed. These were good signs, an indication Hasdai had wielded his considerable influence on behalf of the suspects. The mute foreigner seemed surprised by the visit as he waited quietly for someone to speak.

Noela spoke first. Fluent in both Galician and Arabic, she had rehearsed her questions earlier with the Bishop and Solomon. Listening intently, Roi found it impossible to take his eyes off the concubine as she asked her questions. She relayed his answers in Arabic.

"He says he's been treated well, and he confesses to killing Umar."

"What!" shrieked Solomon. "He's changed his story. When I questioned him, at his farm in Galicia, he told me he had gone to Umar's apartment to find his sister. Said he saw someone leaving as he approached. They were hooded and unrecognizable. He said when he entered the apartment looking for his sister, Umar was already dead and he found Lia lying unconscious at the foot of the bed."

Noela turned her gaze to the tall, black-robed Bishop.

"I suspect he's lying to protect his sister. Tell him I consider it a sin to lie to us even if he holds his sister's best interests at heart. Noela, tell him God will forgive his sister, but will show him no mercy for premeditated lying to a representative of God."

Noela delivered the message in the softest voice imaginable.

The brawny farmer listened quietly to her soothing tone and ruminated for a moment. To the surprise of all present, he sat down on the bed and buried his head in his hands and then he began to rock back-and-forth like a child. The compassionate concubine took his hands into her own and held them gently. Roi glanced up into her blue eyes. As tears began to fill his own, he whispered something to Noela. She continued holding his hands while turning back to the Bishop to offer her translation.

"You were correct," she told him. "He lied to protect his sister."

Bishop Racemundo knelt on the stone floor, took rosary beads from the pocket of his cloak, and began to pray out loud: "Hail Mary, full of Grace . . . " he began.

Out of reverence for the clergyman, everyone knelt on the cold, stone floor.

THEY WALKED WITH NOELA along another damp, claustrophobic hallway, following the prison official until he came to an abrupt stop in front of one of the numerous cells. The man unlocked a huge padlock which secured an iron bar across the heavy door. He removed the barrier and the foursome entered the room.

Everyone's heart skipped a beat.

Solomon swallowed hard when he caught his first glimpse of Lia.

It had only been a couple of days since they'd arrived back in al-Zahra, but the Galician woman's physical condition already appeared to be deteriorating rapidly. She had lost weight and appeared listless and unfocused. A plate of food—couscous, cheese, and a variety of fruit and raw vegetables—sat atop her dresser. It had been left untouched. Solomon found her vacant stare even more unnerving. He saw that her captors had tried to take good care of her, but Lia apparently hadn't made any attempts to take care of herself.

"She won't eat or speak," ventured the official. "She survives on liquids alone."

"Have we broken her spirit?" Solomon wondered aloud.

"You misunderstand what's going on here," responded the Bishop. "A hunger strike is a courageous act of freedom and self-worth. An act motivated by strength not weakness. She's protesting her return to Andalusia in the only way possible under the circumstances."

Bishop Racemundo and Noela went to her bedside.

Rendered speechless, Solomon found refuge in one corner of the cell. He couldn't help but wonder if he had made a huge mistake. Maybe he should've left the brother and sister at the farmhouse. Umar was already dead and there was no bringing him back to life. He suddenly felt guilty and speculated that he might be the cause of a second death, this time from self-induced starvation. Would she take it that far? Was she exhibiting her vulnerability or her strength? Perhaps the Bishop is mistaken.

Noela leaned in close and whispered something into Lia's ear. A knowing smile formed on the Galician woman's lips.

The Caliph's concubine continued to chat, but only the two women understood the meaning of the words. The Bishop and Solomon remained outsiders to the one-sided conversation. They witnessed Lia's eyes communicate something back to Noela, a message beyond words. Noela took the prisoner's hands into her own and held them tenderly while offering one final consolation. The elegant concubine addressed her powerless escorts.

"There is nothing you can do to make her talk to you."

"What made her smile?" Solomon inquired of the concubine.

"I told Lia that her brother is safe and well."

"What do you suggest we do?" asked Racemundo.

"I've begged her to regain her health," Noela replied. "I think she'll begin to eat again, but I can't be sure. She seems to like me. I told her I'll return to visit her and bring more news of Roi. This may give her some hope for the future. Perhaps they'll be reunited."

Solomon went over to the bed and stood silently above the former songstress. He struggled to find words to convey his deeper feelings. He summoned up a weak smile and uttered something in Arabic. He wasn't sure she would listen to him or even cared about what he was trying to communicate to her.

Lia looked up into his eyes.

Her weak smile gave him a glimmer of hope that she would eventually come around.

"What did you say to her?" Noela wanted to know.

"I can't tell you."

"We should leave now," insisted Bishop Racemundo.

Chapter 33

Solomon stood at Sara's doorstep oppressed by a guilty conscience. His stomach had tightened into knots, but the reluctance to share news of transpiring events was outweighed by his desire to see her once again. He glanced back across the street and registered the absence of the two Muslim spies who were hanging out in a shaded doorway the first time he'd visited this eastern suburb. Blue paint, still peeling off the weathered door, lay in tiny flakes at his feet.

Solomon knocked and hoped he'd find her at home. When the door opened, the attractive young woman he remembered so fondly peered up at him with a smile.

"Solomon," she said, with surprise in her voice. "Please, come inside."

She'd recalled his name and her invitation sounded far different from the hesitant attitude of their initial meeting. He had changed since then. Why would he doubt that she hadn't also changed during the time he'd spent away. He took a moment to study her dark hair, olive-skinned complexion, and ample lips. His opinion of her physical attributes had not changed. She could pass for a Jewess or an Arab woman.

Sara allowed Solomon into her home and closed the front door for privacy.

"Come, sit down."

She led him over to the once forbidden sofa and tucked herself down into one corner while he, not wanting to appear too eager, sat himself down on the opposite end. She turned and faced him, but made no attempt to move closer to the center of the couch.

"You brought Lia back to al-Zahra," she began. She squirmed on the couch; he sensed her discomfort. "Everybody in Córdoba has heard of it."

There was so much he wanted to tell her. In Hebrew, Sarah is a feminine name and means Princess. Biblically, the name was originally Sarai, wife of Abraham. When that Sara gave birth to her son Isaac, at the age of ninety, she laughed and cried at the ridiculousness of her plight. Sarai figured prominently in the mythology of the "People of the Book".

Solomon knew this Sara valued her independence, but he suspected she viewed the world from a naive perspective. Sara means pure or excellent in Arabic, but she was probably already aware of this so he kept this piece of information to himself.

This wasn't why he came to see her.

"I saw Lia this morning," he told her. "She won't eat or speak."

"I'm worried, Solomon," she admitted. "What's going to happen to her?"

"Hard to say, Sara," he answered.

In the exchange of given names, a relationship began to blossom.

"Trust me," Solomon said. "If I could I'd take you to see Lia, I surely would."

She seemed to have developed a confidence in him and he found this surprising. She offered a hard won smile and the investigator returned the compliment. He gazed across the sofa for a closer look at her and caught a glimpse of the flesh beneath her white linen tunic.

"What's going to happen now?" she asked.

"I'm going to gather all my suspects together in one room and force the issue."

"Do you know who murdered Umar?"

"I have my suspicions," he admitted. "But I'm just guessing."

"Who do you think did it?"

"I can't share that."

"So why did you come to see me, Solomon?"

"I just wanted very badly to see you again," he admitted. "It's that simple."

"You're a Jew and I'm a Christian," she replied. "It isn't simple at all."

Sara stood and beckoned towards the door.

Solomon followed her slowly to the threshold. He deliberately took his time and then paused before leaving. They stood facing one another, lost in the moment. Sara brushed her fingers against his forearm as they lingered at the doorway. Her gesture felt like an intimation of a possible future intimacy.

"Be careful, Solomon."

He sensed a sentiment sincere and deep. He wanted to take her in his arms, but he feared this impulsive act might frighten her. He realized that he wanted to see her again once the investigation had come to a close.

Go home, Solomon told himself.

Go home and try to gain some understanding.

LYING ON HIS BED, SOLOMON felt the pain of deep discouragement. To have traveled all that way and endured all those hardships and mishaps and still be no closer to the truth of what had happened that night in Umar's apartment left him feeling empty inside. He wanted to ruminate about his plan of attack, but his mind wandered, seemingly disinterested in particulars.

Every individual in Andalusia was capable of committing an act of passion, murdering another human being in the rage of fervor or fear, he reflected. He realized his solidarity with these unfortunates because he understood only too well that he was also capable of such an act under the most trying of circumstances.

The five suspects that he would bring together, along with cousin Hasdai and himself, were three Andalusis and two Galicians. The majority representing a relatively harmonious society and two from a militant Catholic stronghold.

Returning to his homeland, a culture where three different religions found willing adherents, led him to further reflection. Despite his naturalistic bent and preference for humanist poetry, he believed each faith had something to offer. None was perfect, yet they all shared one essential truth. Love thy neighbor as thyself.

Doing unto others remained a challenge beyond measure. Most understood the various scriptures, few put the sentiments into practice. While the Umar's of the world thrived, many of the devout in Andalusia merely survived.

Solomon knew practitioners of all three religions had endured eras of violence and brutality directed against them, their religions inspiring attempts to create a more humane approach to daily affairs. That's why his encounter with a Christian Bishop who, was also a Warlord, felt so alien to him, an affront to his soul. The man embodied the antithesis of any true religious sentiment.

But there was much more to the Andalusian soul than religion. A growing scientific impulse had taken hold on the Iberian Peninsula. Advances in medicine, astronomy, mathematics, botany, and a slew of other sciences were creating a dynamic earth-centered worldview that co-existed peacefully with the faith based. In Solomon's mind the science of his times offered a means for gaining an awareness and deeper understanding of the outer world. Andalusian art, to his way of thinking, led to a deeper acknowledgement and expression of an eternally present inner world of images, and metaphors, and symbols.

Then it hit him.

He realized his inclination to philosophize about these matters had been leading him astray. The time had come to dwell on particulars and direct observations. Theorizing doesn't work, the nascent investigator thought. Take away ideas, preconceived notions, and what's left. That strand of hair and the mysterious gold ring; these two minor miracles of the material world would lead him to the truth. Solomon was certain of this. Think, he implored himself. Think hard.

How do these two pieces of evidence point to Umar's killer?

Chapter 34

Five murder suspects sat in chairs arranged along a horizontal line inside the Foreign Minister's office. Solomon reasoned it would be easier to interrogate and intimidate the quintet if they faced forward, making it difficult for them to see or react to each other's responses. From left to right sat Ahmad, Nuzha, Roi, Hasan, and Lia.

The Tangerine stood guard behind them, scimitar at the ready. Noela stood quietly in the background prepared to translate the proceedings from Arabic into Galician when Solomon questioned Roi.

"What you see and hear inside these chambers remains in this room," began the Foreign Minister. "There will be no exceptions. It may well be a matter of life and death, including your own."

That was the investigator's cue.

Solomon stepped forward to address the gathering.

"What do we know?" he asked, indulging in a bit of conjecture. "We know Umar abd Rahman was stabbed to death with a knife, a murder weapon inscribed with Celtic symbols. This type of dagger is available in numerous marketplaces in Córdoba and al-Zahra."

Hasdai added a thought of his own.

"We also know Umar chose to limit himself to a single wife and a half-dozen concubines. A rather small harem for a man of his wealth and status," interjected the Foreign Minister. "This suggests he preferred his dalliances with young, unattached women unacquainted with his eccentricities."

Solomon took over from his older cousin.

"The only hard evidence we have are a gold ring and a single strand of red hair."

Ahmad rose abruptly from his seat.

"Why am I here?" he demanded.

Ahmad's outburst attracted everyone's attention. Moving swiftly, the Tangerine came up behind the handsome suspect and applied downward pressure on one of the Arab's shoulders with his huge widespread hand. The frightened Ahmad looked up into menacing eyes and a threatening sneer and this hastened his descent back down into the security of his chair. The dark-skinned mercenary removed his curved sword and held it up as a warning to the other suspects.

"I'm sorry, Solomon," Ahmad apologized. "I panicked. I meant you no harm."

"Your question is a good one, Ahmad," Solomon responded. "However, I think you can provide the answer to it. I have to admit, it took me a while to make the connection between you and Umar."

Ahmad's eyes widened. He looked bewildered.

"What are you talking about?"

Eight pair of eyes bore down upon the investigator.

They waited for his explanation.

"I did a little sleuthing, Ahmad, and I discovered you were a frequent visitor to Umar's hilltop estate. Then, it struck me. Your nervousness when I encountered you in the corridor, after we had been given our respective assignments, seemed unusual for somebody who had trained themselves to appear unflappable if the occasion called for it. I sensed then that it wasn't just the journey to Tangier weighing on your mind, but I dismissed this. I was too preoccupied thinking about my own mission."

Solomon walked over and stood before Ahmad.

"The lack of rings on your fingers, another of your peculiarities, like wearing your hair long, jolted my memory. I had forgotten what

I had observed on that occasion, a little detail easily dismissed because it might be considered trivial. The telltale circle of lighter skin on one of your fingers. This indicated you had worn a ring at one time."

The sheepish Arab looked down at his finger.

"It was you who ransacked my apartment searching for your ring."

"I only did it to protect myself," Ahmad protested. "If I was identified as the owner of the ring it would cast suspicion upon me."

Solomon took something from his pocket and bent over his suspect.

"Please hold out your left hand."

Ahmad glanced back at the Tangerine standing behind him and then quickly turned to comply with the request. The investigator quietly slipped the gold ring on Ahmad's fourth finger. The other suspects, each with a different viewpoint of the proceedings, attempted to glimpse the results of the encounter taking place at the far end of the horizontal row of seats.

"The ancients believed that a vein ran directly from the fourth finger on the left hand to the heart," Solomon elaborated, indulging in an eccentricity of his own. "Because of this hand-heart connection, they chose the descriptive name *vena amoris* for this particular vein. Latin for the vein of love."

Ahmad blushed, an unconscious reaction beyond his control.

"This is your ring, is it not?"

"Yes, the ring is mine," Ahmad conceded. "But I didn't kill Umar."

"However, you and Umar did have a relationship?"

"Yes," the Arab admitted.. "We were close friends . . . "

"You're not telling us the full truth, Ahmad."

"All right, we were lovers . . . "

Solomon allowed the ring to remain on the finger of its rightful owner.

Meanwhile, Hasdai had walked down to join him, hoping to study Ahmad's emotional reactions now that the secret love affair had been disclosed. The Tangerine lingered behind the suspect, an ever threatening presence.

"Umar came to me asking for help with his son. Ali was having difficulties with his studies and his father employed me to tutor him. I witnessed Umar's tenderness towards his son and became attracted to him. I found excuses to increase the time I spent tutoring the boy so I could be near Umar. We began seeing each other. Umar and myself. One thing led to another. It just happened."

Everyone in the room except Roi listened to the confession with rapt attention.

"You have to understand," Ahmad continued, "Umar slept with men and women. At least he did before we became serious. He gave me this ring as a pledge of his devotion and loyalty to our relationship. He didn't care about his wife or his concubines. Outside of his son, I think I'm the only person Umar ever truly loved."

"Let me guess," Solomon interrupted. "The Galician woman Lia came into the picture and messed up your plans. Umar was smitten with her beauty. She represented a challenge he couldn't resist and a threat to your future."

"Stop!" shouted Ahmad.

"You went to see Umar and you fought over Lia," the investigator insisted, pressing on with his speculation. "At some point you became so infuriated that you removed the ring from your finger and threw it at Umar in a rage of anger."

"I may have done what you're saying, but I didn't kill Umar," protested the deflated suspect.

"No, you didn't."

SOLOMON LEFT AHMAD and circled behind the line of suspects, buying himself time to collect his thoughts. He walked around the Tangerine, came to the end of the row of chairs, and turned the corner. He decided to pass by the next suspect so he could stop in front of Roi. The powerful Galician farmer sat mute, staring into callused hands clasped together tightly in his lap. Roi took notice of his presence and looked up to engage the investigator eye to eye.

"Let's skip Nuzha for the time being," Solomon began. "I'd rather concentrate on our least likely suspect. This may seem odd given that Roi is the one person physically capable of overpowering Umar."

Hasdai soon joined his cousin.

"Noela, please help us," the Foreign Minister requested. "We need for you to translate Solomon's words into the Galician's native language."

"As for Roi, I admire his courage," the investigator declared. "He journeyed to Andalusia not knowing a word of Arabic. He came south with the sole purpose of convincing his older sister to return to the family farm. His rather untimely arrival at Umar's apartment coincided with the night in question. These things sometimes happen."

Solomon paused, allowing Noela time to share his thoughts with Roi.

"At first, I thought the man dear to Lia was her lover," he continued. "This was a mistake on my part. The man dear to Lia is her younger brother. Roi had followed his sister to Umar's apartment. When someone came running out, he ventured inside where he discovered Umar gasping for breath. By then it was too late."

"That doesn't explain how they managed to escape to Galicia," Hasdai pointed out.

"I couldn't grasp that myself," Solomon confessed.

"Well?"

"They tricked us by packing their horses' saddlebags with heavy stones and sending them down a side trail knowing that we probably wouldn't follow. My escort believed two heavy men were riding those mounts. Roi and Lia waited for us to pass, and then disguised as pilgrims they followed behind us all the way to Galicia until our paths parted ways."

Noela shared the story with Roi.

"What they couldn't imagine," Solomon continued . . . "is that Bishop Sisnand of Santiago had no interest in their well-being. They believed he would protect their whereabouts and keep the location of their farm a secret, but he had his own plans for their farm. He wanted to evict them so he could dole out the property as a reward to his followers. The Warlord saw an opportunity to further his cause against the Caliphate and to consolidate his hatred of Muslims so he revealed the general location of the farm to me in hopes that we'd find it, along with our missing murder suspect, and bring her back to Andalusia."

"Is he that vile?" wondered the Foreign Minister.

"Oh, yes, cousin. They are merely pawns in his dream of Reconquest."

Solomon waited for his words to be translated before offering additional thoughts regarding the farmer's innocence or guilt.

"Roi admitted to killing Umar, but a guilty conscience got the better of him. We now understand he was only attempting to take the blame for his sister. What amazes me is that he believed his own sister capable of such an act."

The Caliph's concubine translated the words into Roi's native tongue. The Galician lowered his eyes from the investigator's gaze. For all his physical strength, his emotional stamina weakened. Muttering something inaudible to himself, he buried his head in his hands. Noela gently stroked the big man's back and then returned to her station nearby.

"However, I do not believe Roi is our murderer. He may be fierce when it comes to protecting his family," Solomon asserted with conviction. "Little else provokes him. Deep inside I sense a gentle giant."

The investigator retreated back down the line and stood before Umar's widow.

"Time we consider Nuzha."

Solomon saw her dark eyes searching his face, wondering what he intended to say.

"Muslim laws of inheritance provide a widow only a tiny portion of the total inheritance; but, Nuzha had easy access to the entire fortune through her son. Either way, she's a wealthy woman. She also possesses her marriage dowry which is rumored to be the size of a king's ransom."

Uncomfortable at having her family finances subjected to public scrutiny, Nuzha pulled the folds of a smooth silk tunic tightly around her bosom before letting out a deep sigh to release her tension.

"We have to consider that she may have grown impatient with Umar because of his many liaisons although she had probably grown used to the situation. As much as Nuzha may have detested Umar, I believe she loved her son far too much to deprive him of his father, a man who actually treated the boy in a kind and gentle manner. "

"Thank you," said the widow, knowing she had just been exonerated.

Solomon positioned himself in front of Hasan, relishing the opportunity to engage Umar's belligerent brother on neutral grounds. This wasn't the dead man's love nest, and it wasn't Hasan's beloved stables. The spacious office of the Foreign Minister deprived Hasan of a certain advantage he had previously held over the investigator.

"Hasan also possessed strong motives. Under Muslim law his business venture with Umar, those beautiful Andalusian horses he adores, will remain in his hands. He's admitted investors are lining up for a piece of the action so continued funding for the operation is practically assured."

Beads of sweat formed on the Arab's forehead.

"No, it was jealousy that stoked his fires, unrequited passion for his brother's wife. Fratricide is as old as Cain and Abel and has continued unabated down through the ages."

"You have no proof that I killed my brother," Hasan blurted out. "You're bluffing."

"Am I?" Solomon asked. "All of al-Zahra and Córdoba are aware that you are in love with your brother's wife."

Hasan spat on the ground directly at Solomon's feet. The Tangerine quickly moved to intercede, but the investigator held a hand up to stop his forward progress.

"Don't worry. I can handle this," Solomon declared. Tangerine lowered his scimitar. "The new wealth you might generate with your business will make you an ideal suitor for Umar's widow. Marrying Nuzha would also give you a rather devious entry to her son's untold riches."

"You can't prove a thing," Hasan sneered.

"However much I detest you, Hasan, you're correct. I have no proof you killed your brother. As much as you're infatuated with your brother's widow, Nuzha has made it clear to you on many occasions that she doesn't desire your attentions. Why would she?"

Hasan's face reddened and his beady eyes bulged in their sockets, but he endured the insults without offering a challenge. Solomon approached closer. He bent down on one knee and grasped a piece of the Arab's floor length tunic in his hand to wipe a splat of saliva off his shoe.

"I suppose you think I should apologize," Hasan grunted.

Solomon ignored the comment and trained his eyes on Lia.

SOLOMON WALKED OVER and stood in front of the woman from Galicia. He bent down, placed hands on thighs, and stared directly into her eyes. It was time to confront his worst fears which meant it was time to share his deepest suspicions with the others present inside of the room.

"There's something you all may be forgetting. Although each of you may have had personal reasons for disliking Umar and his aberrant behavior, nobody hated him enough to commit an act of premeditated murder; and, we discovered that political enemies of the Caliphate didn't perpetuate this crime. As it turns out, this was simply a crime of passion, evil and destructive perhaps, as the drive to aggression usually is, but at least understandable given the circumstances." The investigator resumed standing. "This leads us to one final suspect, a woman I literally traveled to the end of the earth to find and was beaten for my troubles. A woman whom I refused to believe in my heart was capable of murder."

The woman from the North looked up at Solomon with tears in her eyes. She looked stronger now, at least physically. Perhaps she had been eating since he last saw her.

"Tell us why, Lia," he coaxed her. "How did it happen?"

His eyes bore into hers.

Everyone in the room sensed the change in Solomon's demeanor, but even a resolute voice couldn't hide his feelings of keen disappointment. He tried hard not to overreact, to find compassion in his heart.

"I didn't want to believe it, Lia. I was so hoping you were innocent. Naive and unsuspecting, you actually thought you could tame a man like Umar with your voice. A voice like an angel, but you were dealing with a devil."

Tears streamed down Lia's cheeks and wet her clothing.

"Why don't you tell us about it."

"You're right, Solomon," she began as she spoke to him in Arabic. "I went to Umar's apartment hoping to sing for him and to explain to him my personal circumstances. I had hoped that he would help me. Reward me with enough gold to return to my family and rescue our farm from Bishop Sisnand. I missed my homeland so terribly."

Solomon shot a quick glance at Noela.

Raised eyebrows and a slight angling of the head informed him that not all Gallegas experienced the same nostalgia. But, he remembered Galicia and his personal experience of that deep and authentic longing of the soul. Solomon's attention was interrupted when Lia rose from her seat, standing upright where everyone could see her if they turned their heads.

She began to share the details of her ordeal.

"Umar laughed at me. He told me he had already heard me sing and this was not what he was interested in. He came at me and tried to take me in his arms, but I pushed him away. All he did was sneer. It was a mean and vicious look he gave me. He came at me once more. This time he tore open the top of my blouse. I slapped him hard in the face."

Lia's breathing became rapid and shallow. She ceased her narrative, hoping to catch a few breaths of air and regain some composure. Everyone saw how reliving the events of that horrendous night had made her attempt futile. A torrent of words gushed forth.

"Umar's face turned sullen and angry. This time he hit me hard with a clenched fist and I fell backwards unto the bed. Before I knew what was happening, he had jumped on top of me knocking the air out of my lungs with the weight of his body. I was terrified, afraid for my life. In desperation I yelled out to him. I told him I would comply with his wishes, do anything he wanted. When he heard my words, he relaxed for a moment."

Lia began acting out the final scene of her nightmare as she thrust an imaginary dagger into the air and then continued with her harrowing story "That's when I pulled my dagger out from my boot and stabbed him in the side. He pushed himself up off me with fire in his eyes and he clenched his fist again. I panicked. I was afraid he was going to kill me so I thrust my knife deep into his heart. I rolled out from under him and pushed him over and got to my feet and looked down at him lying in the center of his bed with blood dripping on his tunic."

Lia lowered her arm to her side.

"Is that when you left the apartment?"

Yes, I ran," cried the Galician woman. "I pulled my cloak up over my head and I ran madly. I didn't know if Umar was alive or dead. I only knew that my days in Andalusia had come to an end."

Although he didn't understand the words she had spoken, Roi sprang to his feet at the sight of his sister baring her soul in front of a room full of strangers. Noela rushed over to prevent an altercation while the Tangerine held the farmer at bay with his blade.

The investigator generously completed the scenario for the other suspects.

"Roi followed you and revealed himself. It was he that came up with an escape plan that would take you both safely back to Galicia."

"He had no right to hit me and force himself on me," Lia insisted. "I was acting in self-defense."

"I think we've heard enough." said the Foreign Minister. "I remind you, nothing you've heard or seen leaves this room."

Nuzha rose from her chair and went to console the woman who had slain her husband.

"I believe her," Nuzha admitted, directing her gaze at Solomon and then turning to Hasdai. "This woman speaks the truth. She had no other recourse."

With tears in her eyes, Lia turned to Umar's widow.

"I'm so sorry."

Nuzha wrapped her arms around the Galician woman and drew her close, offering the foreigner much needed solace.

"You are all free to go," Hasdai announced. " All except for you, Lia. You will be returned to your quarters to await the Caliph's decision."

"What's going to happen to my sister?" Roi shouted.

Noela came over to translate the Foreign Minster's response.

"Now, go," commanded Hasdai.

The four suspects and the interpreter left as Hasdai gestured to the Tangerine. The guard took Lia gently by the arm and escorted her from the office.

"Thank you, Yusuf," the Foreign Minister called to the mercenary before turning to his investigator. "Solomon, I would like you to remain behind. I need to speak with you."

The door shut leaving the two men alone inside the voluminous office.

Chapter 35

Solomon spoke before Hasdai had an opportunity to utter a single word. He had already decided that he would make a simple request although he knew his intentions might be misconstrued. It was a chance he would have to take to salvage his sense of justice.

"I have a favor to ask of you."

"That favor is?"

"Leniency," he implored. "Please, cousin, convince the Caliph it would be in his best interests to spare Lia's life, to simply banish her from Andalusia."

"Is it in his best interests?"

"I believe so."

Hasdai sighed deeply: "I'll do what I can."

"Thank you, cousin."

"Did we really need this charade?" asked the Foreign Minister. "Bringing them all together like that."

"I believe it was necessary. I was trusting in my instincts. Not one of the suspects stood to benefit from Umar's death. Nuzha didn't care enough to bother about her husband. And as much as Hasan lusts after Nuzha, he loves his horses more. As for Roi, the apparent lack of a major struggle convinced me it was somebody whom Umar was at least somewhat familiar with. I couldn't conceive of Ahmad killing his lover in a moment of intense anger so the ring became irrelevant. The only evidence left was the strand of hair and it pointed to our

Galician Woman. Lia's self-punishment in detention reinforced what I came to suspect. In the end, I believed it could only have been Lia. I couldn't prove it so I needed to get her to confess. "

What if she had stonewalled us and refused to admit to her crime?"

"I hoped I had read her heart correctly."

"You were a little harsh on Hasan."

"He has a grandiose sense of his own self-importance," Solomon explained. "Men like Hasan are a curse to the world no matter what their religion or ethnicity might be."

"The Caliph will be relieved to learn this was a crime of passion. He'll be reassured to know that the empire isn't facing an imminent attack by one of his many enemies."

"At least, not yet."

"I'm going to confide in you, and this stays between you and I. Rahman III is also gratified he won't have to execute his own nephew. Umar was a thug and that option had been under consideration for a long time. This Galician woman has inadvertently helped the Caliph dispose of an ungrateful scion to the royal lineage."

"Then a royal pardon and banishment are only fair."

"I'll send word to you when the Caliph has made his ruling."

Solomon realized he had been dismissed. He crossed the room, but paused at the threshold.

"I said some things before leaving for Galicia, and I feel I owe you an apology. I actually learned some things on my journey to the North."

"About the nature of the world?"

"Yes, I learned many things about the world, but about my own nature as well. I tend to be selfish and to think of my own needs first."

"I think you're selling yourself short, Solomon. I think you learned something deeper. Something much more important."

"What might that be?"

"You've had a glimpse into the nature of real knowledge. To love the light but not know of the darkness is naive. To love the light even when you've experienced the darkness is wisdom. I believe this holds true even in personal matters"

"I'll have to think about that?"

"This isn't something to intellectualize, cousin. It's a lesson you must learn to carry in your heart. The Caliph's gratitude is boundless," Hasdai continued as he adeptly changed the subject. "You're going to reap the benefits of his largess. I imagine you'll have the opportunity to give up translating and devote yourself full time to your poetry. I suspect you'll enjoy being independently wealthy."

Somehow, it didn't seem all that important.

"I would like to be with Lia and Roi when they depart on their journey back to their homeland. I feel I owe them one final goodbye."

"Of course, Solomon," Hasdai replied. "You've already assumed the Caliph will grant my request for leniency?"

"He always does."

TWO MASSIVE TRIANGULAR sails with broad, vertical red and white stripes of stitched linen, the same color scheme used for the horseshoe shaped arches inside Córdoba's Great Mosque, rose above the galley's planked and framed hull. Two oar banks were divided by the deck, with the first oar bank situated below while the second oar bank was positioned above deck. One hundred and twenty rowers were arranged, sixty on each side of the vessel, with twenty-five oarsmen beneath and thirty-five above the deck on each side.

Coptics, the Christian and indigenous people of Egypt and the direct descendants of the ancient Egyptians, provided the bulk of the crew for this Muslim vessel, as they did for the entire fleet of Andalusia. No other mariners sailed the seas with such expertise.

Standing on the deck of the hundred foot long galley, Lia and Roi leaned over the railing to wave a final goodbye to a disheartened couple imitating their gesture from onshore. That couple, Solomon and Sara, stood on one of the numerous wharves lining the Guadalquivir River, south of the old capital.

Solomon had asked Lia's roommate to accompany him so that they could both offer moral support at the departure of the Galicians. They both understood that banishment from Andalusia was a blessing for Lia and Roi. On this occasion, they spoke of themselves and of their hopes and fears and they entered into the dream talk of bodies and minds engaged with one another.

They had said their goodbyes sometime earlier.

Sara had watched as Roi grasped Solomon's forearms in his beefy hands as a way of thanking this old adversary for arranging safe passage for himself and his sister. The behemoth followed this exchange with a tight bear hug. Saddened by the knowledge that, in all likelihood they would never see one another again, Sara and Lia had embraced with tears in their eyes.

They changed partners.

Solomon gazed one last time into sea-green orbs that drew him down into the depths of Lia's soul. The Galician woman surprised him with a kiss on the cheek while her younger brother released Sara from a tight squeeze with barely enough time for her to catch her breath.

This poignant scene had given way to practicality as the Captain of the Caliph's personal galley sniffed the winds and beckoned the Galicians on board. The morning had remained calm, but overhead billowy clouds were moving rapidly so the mariner expected the winds to gain strength as the day wore on.

The Captain wasn't the only sailor predisposed to act in accordance with the weather. Along the docks of the river, the crews of cargo carriers and horse-transport vessels unfurled their sails and made ready to embark upon the rippling waters flowing south to the freshwater seaport of Seville.

Caliph Rahman III had honored his Foreign Minister's request, made on Solomon's behalf, agreeing to banish the Galicians from Andalusia for the remainder of their lives. He had also arranged to make his galley available for the return trip to their homeland. In what at first appeared an extraordinary gesture of goodwill, there existed important political considerations. There remained a sullen, yet dangerous faction of Arab cronies still devoted to Umar; and, rival Fatimids always searched for opportunities to create unrest among the populace. A Christian woman killing Muslim Umar, even though it was an act of self-defense, might not sit well with many.

The galley, also called a runner, would take the Galicians far away from Andalusia and as quickly as possible. From Seville, they would sail the normally safe route: Cádiz, Lisbon, and Vigo. Once on shore, Lia and Roi would be left on their own. They were well-equipped thanks to generous funds offered unexpectedly by an anonymous benefactor. They had taken turns wondering who the donor might be. Bishop Racemundo, the Foreign Minister, or perhaps the Caliph himself.

Back onboard, oarsmen put their muscles to the task and the galley floated away from its moorings. The experienced Captain maneuvered the vessel out upon the Guadalquivir, changed his course to due south, and the vessel began gliding along with the downstream current. The Galicians soon disappeared from sight leaving Solomon alone with Sara.

"IT WAS GOOD OF YOU to help them," Sara told Solomon.

"How did you guess it was me?"

"You're not the only one who possesses the gift of inner sight."

Solomon felt a laugh erupt from his belly. Of course, she also experienced inner sight. Maybe they both understood things without knowing how they knew them. Perhaps everybody possessed the gift. He wasn't sure. There were still aspects of life he couldn't fathom.

"I've never known a Jew, Solomon," Sara admitted.

"You don't really know me," he said, before he caught himself wishing he hadn't spoken the words. He knew right away that it was a mistake. He hoped she wasn't offended by his comment and hadn't misinterpreted his words. But it was too late. He could see that she was embarrassed as her face reddened in response.

"I'm so, so sorry," she stammered.

"No, don't be. I'm the one who should be sorry. I didn't mean to sound patronizing," he apologized. "It's just that I'm a bit of a mystery even to myself."

Sara thought about this for a moment.

"I know that feeling all too well," she commiserated.

"Shall we go?"

They walked quietly and soon Sara took his hand into her own. He felt a surge of energy as the warmth from her hand infused his entire body. He knew that she felt the mysterious, upwelling current in her being as well.

Sara looked at him with a sense of wonder in her eyes, but found him looking straight ahead. She had to share her impression with him, let him know that the experience had spoken to her on a deeper level.

"I've never experienced anything like that before," she confided.

"Neither have I."

They stopped and faced each other.

Solomon hesitated for a moment. Don't be a fool, he admonished himself. Don't wait. This chance may never come again. Risking embarrassment, he took Sara in his arms. Surprised by a moment of shared magnetism, they found themselves sliding deeper into relationship. Biologically deep like water and air, an attraction dwelling somewhere down inside of their bodies, beyond the conscious mind and its intentions where lies a wisdom as profound as bones and blood and marrow. Sara's willingness and her warmth and her enthusiasm made Solomon feel like what he had done was the most natural thing in the world.

"Will I ever see you again," asked Sara.

"I hope so."

"Soon?"

"Soon?" Solomon repeated. He took a moment to consider the question. "You will if my cousin the Foreign Minister doesn't give me a new assignment."

Sara brushed her fingers against his forearm.

She does that a lot, he observed, remembering the times he had already spent in her presence. Solomon could wait no longer. Overcome by desire, he drew Sara closer. Feeling no resistance he kissed her pliant lips ever so softly. He hoped that this moment would never end.

"What now?" she asked with an innocence in her voice.

"I'm not sure," he replied.

They were entering unchartered waters. Sure, Christians and Jews got along on the deceptive surface of life, as did their Muslim counterparts. But Sara and Solomon both knew that their developing relationship would be frowned upon by some in their own communities. Solomon was ready to disregard the social implications. This woman enchanted him, and she made his world a sweeter place.

They quietly withdrew from the warmth of their embrace.

They walked on, linked hand in hand.

In the early morning light, Solomon Levy experienced a deepening sense of contentment. Despite all he had recently endured, he'd attained a calm acceptance of his fate and a willingness to face the future whatever it might portend.

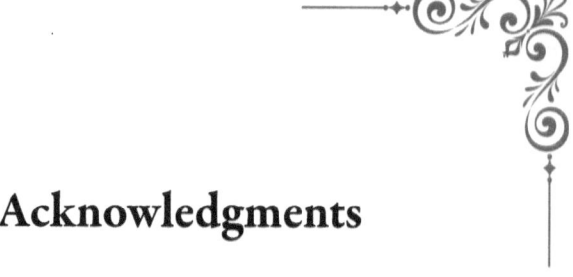

Acknowledgments

I owe a debt of gratitude to María Rosa Menocal who introduced me to the world of Islamic Spain in her stimulating book *The Ornament of the World: How Muslims, Jews, and Christians created a Culture of Tolerance in 10th Century Spain*. It was in the pages of this fascinating account that I first encountered the amazing Hasdai ibn Shaprut.

I'm grateful to the following readers who reviewed portions of early drafts of the manuscript: Aaron Kaiserman, Kim Aiken, Kevin Sparrow, and Cassidy Colwell. I especially want to thank Visnja Murgic, Besty Natter, and Bibiana Jiménez Ramírez who critiqued the entire novel.

In Mexico, I'm indebted to editors Alejandro Grattan-Dominguez and Judy King for an opportunity to pursue and succeed at a lifelong dream. Judy published a dozen and a half articles in her ezine, *Living at Lake Chapala*. Alex published seven Cover Stories in *El Ojo del Lago*, Mexico's most widely read English-language magazine (print and online editions.).

Invitation to Readers

THANK YOU FOR READING this novel. If you enjoyed the story, please consider leaving a review on your favorite book seller's website. This is the most generous act you can make to help a first-time author find new readers.

Reviews are hard to come and give credibility to the book. They are greatly appreciated. If you aren't interested in posting a review, please consider leaving a rating. Thank you, again.

William Mesusan

The Andalusian Trilogy

THE ANDALUSIAN TRILOGY brings to life the exotic world of 10th century Islamic Spain during a little known time in history when Muslims, Jews, and Christians created a harmonious society based upon religious tolerance and enlightened self-interest.

THE BONE RELIC

One of Islam's most sacred relics, the arm bone of the prophet Muhammad, is stolen from the Great Mosque of Córdoba, calling into question the legitimacy of the Umayyad Caliphate and threatening the future of 10th century Europe's most enlightened culture. Solomon's search for the holy relic requires a perilous journey from romantic Córdoba to the Andalusian ports of Seville and Cádiz (Europe's oldest city) and leads him into a murky world where desire and need drive the intense competition for stolen relics.

Don't miss out!

Visit the website below and you can sign up to receive emails whenever William Mesusan publishes a new book. There's no charge and no obligation.

https://books2read.com/r/B-A-YWML-GKKIB

BOOKS 2 READ

Connecting independent readers to independent writers.